NEVER

Me

Kate Stewart

Dedication

For my Diamond in the Sand. Thank you.

Prologue

I WAS A THIEF of men … a whore.

Not the conventional type that got paid for sex. I was the girl you talked about in your sad inner circle. The girl you shielded your boyfriend from as you cleverly covered him with your body when I came near.

I was a threat to you. I dressed like sex. I knew how to get the attention of any wandering eye. I saw how hard you tried to keep his eyes from me. But they were … on me, filled with longing and curiosity. Keeping him safe in your grasp was smart. I would happily sleep with him if given the chance. It's not that I wanted to out of spite to hurt you. Half of you would not ever know my motive or catch on. It's that I needed to do it. I needed to see that want in his eyes—the kind of lust and need you only see in a man's eyes the first time they had you. It was perfection. It was lust. It had nothing to do with love. It was animalistic and I made sure they brought their A-game.

Every.

Single.

Time.

It would never be better than the first time. No, I didn't have daddy issues. I loved my father, though he was no saint himself. He showed me the ropes. I took my best cues from him, though he was unaware. It was simple. I loved sex and I loved men. It wasn't an addiction. It wasn't a hobby. I wanted what wasn't mine. No, I wanted to borrow what wasn't mine. I gave him back to you and you were never the wiser. I was that whore.

If your man glanced my way, I was going to thank him with my own personal brand of gratitude. I would let him take me the way he wanted. When he was done, I gladly returned him to you. He may have asked to see me again, but I would never do it.

They all came to me willingly.
Every.
Single.
One.
I simply extended the invitation.

CHAPTER One

Summer 2005

I HAD JUST SPENT the last few minutes scoping out my next invitation at the laundry-mat. He had been begging for any crumb of attention his object of affection would show him. He was hungry. I could tell by the way he was groping his girlfriend and looked at her as she playfully ignored him as she tended to her clothes. His eyes roamed her body with longing. She was petite with perfectly cropped brown hair and matching brown eyes. He slid his hands around her waist and she gave him a quick smile, then scolded him and removed his hands before resuming her duties. He was tall with dark blond hair and eyes I could not tell the color of, a jock's build with half hidden tattoos under his white t-shirt. He was hungry … and he needed my help. His hair was longer than business cut and it turned me on like no other. He attempted again to ease her into him with his hands on her shoulders and she once again refused his advances.

Time for the invitation.

I took a pair of my best panties out of the washer and put the rest of my clothes into dry. I casually walked their way with my wet panties cupped in one hand and some change for the drink machine—that was directly behind them—in the other. I purposely caught his eyes and he smiled. He was still behind his girlfriend, taunting her with his hands. I licked my lips then gave him a broad smile in return. His jaw tightened and he wrapped his arms around her again, this time achingly slow as he burned a hole through me.

Hook.

I turned to give all my attention to the machine, as if it was more interesting, and could feel his stare. I quickly glanced back and saw I had his full attention. Showtime.

I put the quarters in the machine as I scratched at an imaginary itch on my thigh, just below the hem of my red and black checkered mini-skirt. I continued to scratch at it until fake curiosity brought my gaze down to the unaffected area and lifted my skirt up further to inspect. Two seconds. A quick peripheral glance told me I still had him.

Line.

That was all it took and my skirt was back down. I pushed the button for a Coke and stood back. Instead of bending at the knee like a lady, I bent over completely so he could see I had nothing on. I hooked my undies with my finger so he could eye them and brought them with me to the restroom to slide them on. I coolly walked back out, popping the top of my soda. When I looked back at my prey, he was no longer engaged in playful musings with his love. He was now sitting behind her as she chatted him up, his eyes hooded and on me. I had him.

I gave him an innocent smile and turned back to my task. I spent the next twenty minutes of my time ignoring him completely. I folded my clothes neatly and made my way to the exit 'accidentally' dropping my entire basket as I opened the door. Two seconds later he was there helping me.

"I've got it, really. Thank you."

"No problem," he said, eyeing my legs. He grabbed a few of my tees and put them back in for me, then lifted the basket up as he held the door open.

"Jace, that was nice of you. Take it to her car," I heard his girlfriend sound off as she smiled at me.

"Thanks." I smiled back at the girl who had just unknowingly given me permission.

"You are so lucky to have a guy in your life."

"Yeah, he's the best." She cooed at him from where she was standing.

We made our way to my car and I opened the trunk.

"Quite a show you put on back there," he said gruffly.

"You see something you like?"

"Fuck yes."

"Here," I said, slipping him a matchbook I kept handy. It was to a pub that was three minutes from my front door. "Meet me here at nine tonight. I won't wait a minute past."

"I can't just—"

"You can and you will. Won't you … Jace?" I licked my lips again and gave him a once over, slowly taking in his body, imagining all the possibilities before briefly closing my eyes. I took the basket out of his hands and set it in my trunk and met his shocked eyes and gaping mouth. They were brown. Not my favorite color, but they would do.

"Nine, Jace. I wouldn't test me," I reiterated and closed my trunk, forcing him to jump back out of his daze. I could tell the wheels were turning. He was considering it. Maybe this one would surprise me and not show. I gave him one more courteous smile as I rounded my car to make our word exchange seem casual to his girlfriend's watchful eye, then jumped in my driver's seat as he walked back inside.

Sinker.

"Yeah, see you tonight, Jace." I laughed out loud as I started the car and felt the cool air hit me. I did not care that he was with the girl he would probably marry. He looked at her like he loved her, which is not the look I wanted. The look I wanted I would get tonight and all I had done to get it was the simple task of laundry.

AT NINE ON the dot I walked inside to find Jace waiting for me. I waved a quick hello to the bartender, Kyle, who knew me well. He nodded at Jace, knowing he was my next conquest. I gave him a nod in return and he shook his head in mild amusement. Jace was dressed up from what he had worn at the laundry-mat. I gave him my best smile and nonchalantly walked his way. Like all his predecessors, he looked around nervously, unsure of what he was doing.

"It'll be okay, Jace. I won't tell," I reassured him as I slid onto the bar-stool next to him.

"Drink?" he asked politely, still unsure if he should be there. His shirt was a blue button down with the cuffs rolled on each side. His jeans clung to him in all the right places. I had done well for myself today. I may have a loose libido, but I still handpicked each invite and gave a second inspection at our one and only meeting. I had walked away several times, but not tonight. Jace was an exceptional find. He had a coiling snake tattoo running up his right arm that was full of color and I found it sexy as hell. His smile, though unsure, was beautiful and his teeth were a solid white. He was clean. I never did dirty.

I had to ease his nerves and get some banter going if I was going to bring his best game out of him. This was his first time cheating on Ms. Cropped Hair and I could tell.

"I'll leave the drink up to you," I said, lowering my eyes. I patted his thigh and grazed my hand over his crotch—just barely—to get him started. This was going to be easy, but I preferred if they came with more confidence. He was instantly hard. Poor thing, he was starving.

"Looks like you could skip your drink, Jace," I whispered, studying the hard line in his pants.

"No," he said, giving me the look I knew was made for men; the look that said 'I am going to tear your ass up.' The look I craved. The look I needed daily.

I had to ask the question I always did. "What are you thinking?"

"Tequila." I stifled the disappointed look I felt until he surprised me. "Then making you raw."

Now you are talking, Jace.

"Patron," I smiled playfully, grabbing a lime from the condiment tray next to us on the bar, sucking it dry.

We took three shots as our eyes sized each other up in anticipation. A few lines of small talk and I was over it. I had no desire to know more than his name, and even that wasn't necessary. I gave him the come hither index finger as I grabbed my clutch. Tonight I was in snug fitting jeans that hugged my ass and long legs perfectly, a strapless black halter top that showed a huge amount of cleavage and expensive red high heels that I stole from my neighbor, Rory. She wouldn't mind. I would put them back before she noticed. I had the darkest shade of red lipstick on and I put my shoulder length auburn hair in a sharp ponytail so he could see as much exposed skin as possible. I made it to the stairs of my apartment around the corner without saying a word to him. He stayed a few steps behind me for one of two reasons. Either he was rethinking the whole situation, or he was thinking of ways to make me scream. This made me smile as I turned to look back at him. He did not return it.

"What is it with you?"

I froze at my bottom step. "Sorry?"

"You just offer me sex, no strings, nothing more, knowing I have a girlfriend and you still don't care?"

"You already had time to think about this, Jace. I'm not going to try and convince you of anything."

"I'm not backing out. I just want to know … why?"

"Let's just say it's the way I'm built."

"Like a man?"

I turned to him with a small seductive smile and said, "Definitely not."

I leaned in, towering over him standing on the first step.

"Can I at least know your name?"

"Nadine."

"God, that's beautiful. You are so beautiful."

"I'm also a sure thing. Save the compliments."

"Wow." He grinned at me now, his eyes still incredulous.

I gave him another small smile and leaned in closer, grazing my hand over the evident bulge in his pants, moving my fingers slowly back and forth. I heard his sharp intake of breath as he stared at me. I wanted the look. It was not there yet. I undid his fly, looking around to make sure my display went unnoticed. He placed his hands on each of the hand rails of the staircase. I saw his smirk disappear as I took him in my grasp, firmly stroking him as I watched his eyes dilate. He looked around in a daze, as if what was happening was not real, before finding my eyes again. There it was.

I carefully tucked his hard length back into his pants and ascended the stairs slowly, hearing him zip his fly and follow, his steps echoing each one of mine. He was so close I could feel his chest on my back at my front door. He turned me quickly and leaned in to kiss me. I took his mouth just in time to meet his tongue, feeling it glide across my teeth and reach deep into my mouth. He was good with that tongue, and I was ready to put it to use.

"God, you taste good," he whispered after releasing me so I could get my key into my door.

I made it three steps in when he grabbed me by the waist, bringing me flush to him, grinding his hardness into my back.

"Not yet."

"What? Why?"

"Do you want something to drink?"

"Hell no." He turned me to him and his lips found mine again, this time more greedy, less friendly. I wanted hostile and I was not about to settle until I saw I was going to get it. I pressed against his chest and he released me, the bulge in his pants more obvious, an intrigued and confused look on his face. I loved the way he towered over me. Tall men were my favorite; I loved feeling small next to them as I made them beg for it.

I kicked off my heels and slowly peeled off all of my clothing piece by piece, keeping his gaze and leaving the underwear I had put on at the laundry mat.

"Fuck," he said to me, walking my way. I put my hand up and stopped him and he cursed, frustrated. "What?" he snapped, but softened his tone repeating the question. "What?" Jace was not himself. He was almost there.

"Nothing. Just making sure you have protection."

He pulled a condom out of his pocket and I gave him a wicked smile. I took the few short steps to reach him, dropped to my knees and pulled down his pants, revealing his perfect erection. I grabbed it roughly with both hands and heard him gasp. I licked the moisture off the tip and heard him cry out a little. I took him inside my mouth and exhaled a moan simultaneously, making sure I had every single inch of him standing at attention.

"Jesus," he gasped again before saying my name, cupping my face until I felt more salty moisture enter my mouth. He was ready and I was dripping. Nothing turned me on more than a helpless man hard in my mouth, at my mercy. I gave just enough attention to keep him on the edge.

"Now I'm all yours," I said, recovering from my knees to meet his darkened eyes. I knew he would make good on his promise to get me raw. His jaw was set, his whole body tense. I had done my job, now it was time to reap the benefits. Without another word he turned me away from him. I felt my panties disappear as he tongue kissed my back. He stopped at the top of my thighs and kissed his way in between them, parting my legs as his fingers began to tease me.

"Further," he snapped, on the edge of losing his composure. I happily obliged as I felt more fingers enter me and cried out in pleasure as my orgasm began to form deep inside. I braved a look over my shoulder and saw pure fire in his eyes. This was going to be fun. He plunged his fingers in and out as I moaned and praised him. He continued rubbing and circling me as he ripped a condom wrapper with his teeth and spare hand. As soon as he fit himself with it, it was over.

He bent me over completely, as if he was picturing me back at the laundry mat. I gave a small smile knowing this was probably what he was thinking. I did not hesitate. I was about to get the best of Jace, probably better than the girl who claimed him as hers had ever had. I felt every hard inch of him as he buried himself inside. We both cried out in unison as he pulled himself out fully again, rubbing my center with the tip of himself before thrusting back in even harder. He took me down on all fours, ramming into me while caressing my ass and circling his fingers on my sweet spot with the opposite hand. This is how I loved it, this is how I craved it, but I needed a little more.

"I want to see your face," I told him as he circled his hips to make sure I felt every inch of him. He quickly turned me over and laid me on the floor, my legs hooked over his shoulders.

There it was, the look I was after. His eyes were intense, dilated, full of longing, hungry, and perfect, the look only a man gives when he is completely and utterly aroused and wants only one woman.

He was mine.

His pace was quickening as well as his intensity and I gasped as he used his finger to steal some moisture from me and brought it to his lips. As soon as he had a taste he withdrew himself from me and buried his face between my thighs, licking me from one end to the other, lapping me up and pushing his fingers in. He lifted my entire lower half and devoured me, licking and teasing, moaning as he worked me over thoroughly.

That was definitely the best of Jace, I thought as my orgasm shook me. I made sure not to claw too hard at his shoulders, wanting to leave no trace.

He brought his mouth over mine and hovered as he adjusted himself back to my entrance.

"Nadine," he breathed my name and covered my throat with his kiss. "God." He thrust himself inside again and slowly stroked in and out, my name on his lips, his hands covering my breasts in a caress. He slowed his pace to almost a dead stop, grinding every inch of himself into me with his hips. It was so good. Perfect.

"I want to come all over you."

"So do it," I murmured looking at him, taking in every second of his undeniable lust for me.

He picked up his pace until my pulse was pounding in my ears. I saw nothing but white behind my eyes as the second wave shook me. I finished in time to see him rip the condom off and scream out to me. I pumped my fist around him and cupped his sac to milk him of every last drop, feeling the evidence of him falling in hot droplets all over me.

I saw it in his face. I had just given him the best orgasm of his life. He was thankful. I gave him a knowing grin and excused myself to the shower.

"You can see yourself out. Goodnight," I called out from the bathroom before shutting the door.

Once out of my scalding shower, I fully expected him to be gone. At least I hoped he would be. But he was waiting for me on the couch.

"I didn't want to leave without saying goodbye. That's kind of messed up, Nadine."

"Look, I know it is. And I know I'm not your typical girl, but this was casual sex, which is all I truly wanted from you. So can we just call it what it is? Say goodnight and goodbye."

"You know I have a girlfriend but—"

"But nothing, Jace. That's what attracted me to you in the first place. I don't want to see you again."

"So this is over?"

"It was over ten minutes ago."

"Jesus, you really are cold."

"And you really are as good as I thought you would be, so thanks … and goodnight."

He walked toward me as I wrung my t-shirt in my fists, irritated already and praying he wouldn't try any harder. "At least let me give you a little bit more," he whispered in my ear as he pawed me in all the right places. I toyed with the idea, but dismissed it. I had the best of Jace. There was no more to get from him.

"No thanks, but I mean it, it was great." I stepped out of reach and turned sideways to give him a clear view of the door.

"Unfuckingbelievable." He seemed slightly irritated but shot a small grin at me. "I'll be thinking about you." He kissed my lips softly and turned to leave as I exhaled a breath of relief slowly so he wouldn't hear.

"Thanks, Jace." I gave him a genuine smile for not pressing the issue further and watched him walk out, taking one last peek at me, grinning and shaking his head. I got that a lot. None of it bothered me. The minute they left I was sure they were more worried about the guilt they were sure to feel. I counted on it. I counted on the fact that their current girlfriends would soon be treated better than they ever had, that they dove back into their current safe place and left me the hell alone.

Jace

CHAPTER Two

I HAD LOST MY job tonight because of Jace, but it was totally worth it. I had taken advantage of my boss one too many times. He gave me an ultimatum, either be there or stay gone. It was time to move on anyway. Maybe this was an addiction. Maybe I was wrong to think it wasn't. It had never come back to haunt me. I had never hurt myself or anyone else, unless they were stupid enough to confess, and so far so good. They were always attached, but it was always their decision. I suddenly envisioned myself in the Garden of Eden as Eve tempting Adam with the apple. I knew it was wrong. I knew it, but it didn't mean I wanted it less. It was a fun game with a happy ending, the players always changed and it never got boring. Why was this so wrong? Why? I loved to share my body, to feel wanted, to feel good. I had never thought of a man more than a day or so after our encounter. I wasn't incapable of loving a man. It just didn't appeal to me … at all. I liked the control my game gave me. Flowers, candlelight, it was all so pointless when the end result was always the same: sex. All the candidates I had were cheaters and I was the temptress, which made me a hypocrite, but I would rather be the other woman than ever be the woman who waited. That would *never* be *me*.

Did I feel guilty at times? Yes. But I didn't have the luxury of worrying about the backlash tonight. I didn't have rent. I hardly had a dime to my name. My stomach rumbled and I took what little I had saved for the bills and went on a gas station run to fill my tank, using the rest to make the grumble in my belly turn into a small moan. I should charge for being a whore. Life would be much easier.

Jace was still fresh and I needed to figure out my next move. For now I had his memory to keep my thoughts occupied; his mouth, his lips, I could still see the red on my knees and faint teeth marks. I reveled in the soreness growing between my legs as I made it home and drifted to sleep.

"DAD, I NEED some money." I gripped my cell with both hands and held it an inch away from my ear to save myself from his angry tone. I was still in bed and wanted nothing more than to hide from the world of bills I couldn't pay, but decided to suck it up and make the call.

"Dini, not again! What the hell is it this time?"

"Dad, look, I haven't asked in a while and trust me I wouldn't unless I needed it. I don't have rent."

I could feel the inevitable lecture coming on. 'Money doesn't grow on trees' or 'You are old enough to take care of yourself.' 'When are you going back to school?' and 'My money is mine. How much of it I have is none of your concern.' He was one of the most successful investment bankers in the country and worth millions. He had raised me to think for myself and told me my entire nineteen years that he 'would not be footing the bill for my life' and I 'would have to make my own way.' Instead, he surprised me.

"Dini, I have to make this quick. How much?"

"Sorry, Dad, a couple of thousand?"

"It's your birthday in a week, Dini. I will ease your mind this once."

"Thanks, Dad. I love you, and I am sorry I haven't been around more."

"I'm flying to France right now. I can't talk, but as long as you're okay. I have to go. I do love you, kid, but you know how I feel about you taking care of yourself."

"I know, Dad and thank you for not lecturing me."

"When are you going back to school?"

"Dad, I graduated."

"WHAT?"

"I sent you the invite a month ago. I took the early walk last week. I didn't want to make a big deal of it."

"Nadine, this was more than important for me to know! How could you not tell me?"

"I did, by invite. You should really get another executive assistant, Dad. Deidra is horrible."

Deidra was my Dad's current girlfriend and wanted nothing to do with me and everything to do with his money. Too bad for her my father was too smart to let her anywhere near it. He was new money and he was greedy with it. It was only after I had left home that his net worth had increased to what it was. We had spent years and years in a one bedroom apartment, both hating my absentee mother and scraping by. He had finally decided that he was done with the way of life he detested so much and worked his ass off to get to the position he was in now.

I missed the dad he was. He was attentive, caring and always around. He could make a dozen eggs into a million different dishes. I was thankful for the time we had nothing; at least then I had him around. He was a good father. No, he was a great father, but his job was done and I didn't blame him for enjoying his success or wanting me to have my own; though I did resent his new fortune for keeping me away from him.

We never vacationed when I was young. Oklahoma was the only place I had ever known. He was taking these amazing trips while I dined on gas station food. I knew why. I saw the struggle he went through to keep us afloat. He knew money was fleeting and was not delusional about the fact it could go as quickly as it came. He wanted me to be ready for life, for whatever came my way.

Most parents would hand their children whatever their heart desired if put in the position. My father knew that I would only appreciate my success if I worked for it. I finished high school at fifteen and started college immediately after. I earned a full scholarship, but pissed it away having fun like any teenager would, forcing my father to pay tuition when I decided to head back.

I am a very smart whore.

"I'll take care of you, Dini. Think of this as my graduation gift as well. Have some fun. I am so proud of you, you deserve this… wait … just a second… Honey, I have to go. It will be transferred before takeoff."

"Thanks, Dad. I love you. Call me when you get home?"

"Love you too, Dini. I'm so sorry I missed it."

"It's okay, Dad. Have a good trip."

I waited ten minutes before checking my bank account on my laptop and gasped.

"Impossible." I took another step forward and took another look at the amount. Yesterday I had six dollars, today I had sixteen thousand.

"FUCK ME!" I laughed and clapped, giving myself a moment before I immediately paid every outstanding bill I had. I wrote a check for three months' rent and slipped it into my landlord's apartment. I was FREE! Free of debt, free of worry, free of having to find a job for at least a month. For the first time in my life I had money, freedom, no obligations and not a soul to share it with. I ran across the hall to my best friend Rory's apartment and pounded on the door.

I had met her a month after I first moved in. I was just coming home from another one time rendezvous and saw her panicked face as she looked through her purse, desperately trying to find her keys.

"Fuck it all! Fuck damn shit piss hell!" she screamed as she pounded on her door.

I was at the top of the steps and had to stifle a laugh as she kicked at her door then slumped down in front of it, a hopeless expression on her face. She met my eyes and gave me an 'I am screwed look' as she shrugged her shoulders.

"Locked out?" I said, finding my door key and glancing back at her. "Sorry, that's obvious. Or maybe someone won't let you in?"

I turned to fully face her as my door opened. She had on a glittered dress and high heels. I liked her already for her filthy mouth and fashion sense.

"No," she giggled. "I live alone. That was a horrible display of 'I am drunk with a huge side of PMS.' "

This time I laughed out loud with her. After an hour of conversation and no real solution to her problem at four A.M., I invited her to sleep at my place until she could call our landlord.

That was two years ago.

I stood at her door now, pounding relentlessly.

"What the fuck?" I heard on the other side.

"Rory, open up!"

"Nadine, it's fucking eight thirty in the morning. You know," she said, opening the door as she finished her sentence, "I just went to bed!"

"Sorry," I kissed her cheek and ran inside. "I have great news!"

Irritated, she shut the door to face me, wearing only her thong and t-shirt. She was an adorable brunette with pink streaked hair, huge tits and a little body that didn't quite support them, though she supported herself with them. A whore with a stripper best friend, cliché enough for you?

"What? What!" she put her hands on her hips and gave me the evil eye.

"Pack and take a few days off. I'm taking you the hell out of here."

"What? Weren't you just banging on my door two days ago asking for money for gas?"

"My dad gifted me some money for graduation and I want to take you away … somewhere, anywhere, a road trip."

"I can't just leave. I have a job."

"You are a stripper. I know it doesn't come with a vacation package, but can you not take off?"

"I have bills and good for your dad. He's a dick and it's about time he helped you out." Her bitchy demeanor did very little to convince me she wasn't considering it. We both desperately needed this.

"No, he's not. I haven't really told him how I struggle. He has no idea. It doesn't matter. I'll pay your rent for a month. Come with me. I'm leaving today."

"You are crazy!" she said, pacing her apartment. I could feel her excitement at the possibility.

"I need to get away… I need this time to not … be me. Well, to be me but somewhere else. I want to be someone else for a few days, I guess. Please?"

It didn't take much. She put in a few calls and by sundown the car was packed and we were on the road.

"You know where we're going yet?" She had packed three huge bags and was stuffing the third in the back seat, due to the lack of room in the trunk. I shook my head as I watched her struggle.

"Rory we're just leaving for a week. We aren't moving."

"You never know. If I meet *him*, I am liable to drop everything." She winked as she finally got the large tote in with a heavy breath.

"You're not leaving me here to wither away, sister," I said, adjusting my seat as she made her way to the front.

"Never," she promised as she buckled her seatbelt. "So where to?"

"The ocean. I've never seen it. It's all I think about when I think of leaving this shithole."

"Florida?"

"Florida!"

"You know how crazy this is, right?"

"I know living to pay your bills is way crazier. Let's have some fucking fun before our skin turns gray and we rot."

"Agreed." I looked over to see her excited—more excited than I had seen her in months. Rory was my rock, my best friend, the only girl who understood me and what I did, loving me for who I was: another promiscuous girl who used her body for what she needed. She understood and never judged me.

She popped open her camcorder and pointed at me while I was driving.

"Day one with the craziest bitch to ever come out of Oklahoma. Where will we end up?"

I looked at the camera with a full smile and answered, "Florida first. Next is anyone's guess."

"Nadine goes to see the ocean take one." She closed the camera and turned to me, a dazzling smile lighting her face.

"What's it like?"

"The ocean? It's like smoking a joint in a hot tub. It totally relaxes you."

"I've never smoked a joint. You know that."

"Another first we will endure on this trip."

"I don't think so, sister."

"We'll see."

CHAPTER Three

W E SPENT THE first leg of our long drive talking about the things we wanted to do and screaming along to the best road tunes we could think of. As the GPS kept up with the miles we had left to travel, I let Rory get her sleep, leaving me alone with my thoughts as I drove into the night, with absolutely no view. Jace drifted through my mind just once.

I had nothing to worry about financially for the time being and that was a new feeling. I tried to focus on how I would start to put my degree to use and decided to make it first priority when I got home. No more minimum wage jobs. I had only two things my life revolved around: school and men. School was over, and the other, well… I tried to clear my head and live for the moment. In that moment, I was completely and utterly free of responsibility. Still, my mind drifted to the future I had not cemented, the uncertainty that would surely come when I returned home.

My mind drifted back to the number of men I had let have me over the last year.

Seventeen.

I was a whore who counted. Seventeen men. I hadn't ever had a year this bad before. Last year's count was eight. The year before six, and before that … before that … one. This was getting out of hand. I had no one to blame but myself. I spent more energy searching for my next lay than I worried about my future. Maybe I should just lay off this for a while, pun intended. Could I quit? Yes, yes I could. I was not addicted to sex. Was I?

I shook my head with disgust and quickly made peace with it. Guilt would not win this war; I was too excited to be where I was. As soon as we hit the Alabama state line I woke Rory up. We were close. The sun had been up for a few hours and I was exhausted.

"Pull over," Rory piped, the excitement lighting up her face.

"What?"

"Pull over. I'm driving the rest of the way."

I gave up the wheel willingly, and to my surprise, was woken up a few hours later by an amazing smell coming through the windows.

"What is that?"

"That's the smell of the ocean, Nadine. Isn't it amazing?"

"God, it's so different, it's…" I closed my eyes and breathed in deeply, letting the air reach me. A small euphoric feeling hit me that I was close to something … big. The excitement ran through me and the lack of sleep dissipated, replaced with my new found excitement. I was on the very first adventure of my life.

"It's so fucking sad you're almost twenty years old and have never seen the ocean. What kind of life is that?"

"It's not that big of a deal," I answered dismissively, knowing it was a lie.

I had watched all my childhood friends pack for their family trips, seen the framed pictures of them at Disney World and other exotic places. I would continually ask my father to take me so I could have my own pictures, my own memories to boast about. He would always look at me with a solemn face and promise someday. Even though he wasn't here today, he had kept his promise. Hadn't he? I began to feel the flutter of excitement in my abdomen.

"It is a big deal, Nadine. Put this on. We're close to Pensacola. I want you to see this beach first." I took the sleep mask from her hand and put it over my eyes, laughing at her gesture. She loved me enough to do this for me. I wanted this to be special. I hoped I wasn't making a big deal about nothing. The smell and the breeze became stronger and I could tell we were close. The car came to a stop suddenly and the adrenaline racing through me spiked.

Rory got me out of the car and took my shoes off. I heard the sound of what I could only assume were waves getting closer as my feet hit the sand. The sensation was amazing. I immediately wanted to take the mask off but Rory kept me from doing it. I heard her rustling with the camera as she steadied me with her hand and finally gave me permission to take it off. I was blinded by the sun first and shielded my eyes. Once they adjusted I inhaled sharply. The sand was a bright powdery white. I dug my heels further into it and examined my feet covered in it. The water was a mix of sparkling blue and green. I had never seen anything so beautiful. I heard the waves and felt myself start to sway to their rhythm as seagulls swooped overhead shrieking and diving through the air. I immediately felt moisture on my cheeks. I saw people surfing and holding onto kites as they whipped through the waves. My eyes drifted to movement in the sand near my feet and I saw a crab—a CRAB—scurry past me. I was in sensory overload and the only thing I could think was this was a big deal. THIS WAS A BIG DEAL! I ran.

I ran full speed into the ocean with my clothes on, not giving a damn what I looked like, not caring one shit what anyone thought. I had no fear as I ran full blast into an oncoming wave and felt the lukewarm water as it washed over me. I dove into wave after wave, turning back to wave at Rory who was laughing uncontrollably. I tasted the salt on my tongue as I ducked under a small wave and emerged laughing with glee. I felt the intensity of the waves as they knocked me off my feet and I landed square on my ass. Amazing, incredible, beautiful, profound. In that moment I felt an indescribable clarity, a sense that at that moment I was exactly where I was supposed to be. I turned to survey the vast expanse of water and stood in awe. I felt so small. I looked to my right to see a man staring at me oddly and I was so beside myself I started rambling.

"It's my first time in the ocean. Isn't it wonderful!" I cleared my eyes of the debris of hair and water and saw him surveying me. I had on my jeans, t-shirt and—oh shit—my purse was still wrapped around my opposite shoulder from the gas stop. He chuckled at my realization and I beamed at him, not giving a damn. I knew how insane I must have seemed and ran to the shore immediately, realizing I ruined my brand new tube of lipstick and that my wallet was soaked. It was worth it. I turned around to survey the sight one more time then ran to Rory, hugging her with a fierceness saved for those you love the most.

"Thank you. Thank you for making this a big deal." I felt more tears coming and heard her griping at me to get my soaking wet ass off of her.

Turning back around for another glimpse of the ocean in all its splendor, I saw the same man who witnessed me in the water toweling himself off at a nearby beach chair, smirking as he pulled it over his legs. I hadn't noticed in the water, but out he was way more appealing than I thought at first glance. Not going there, Nadine.

Seeing the ocean.

CHAPTER Four

"**G**OD THAT LOOKS good on you!" Rory said an octave louder than appropriate for the store we were in. I saw the heads of a snooty group of women turning to briefly look at us disapprovingly before carrying on with their task of judging others. I really couldn't stand more than a handful of women in my life. Men were so easy going, less dramatic. I had my favorite bartender Kyle to talk to and visited him often. The banter was always fun, even when he had a stick up his ass. Rory was the ideal woman to be friends with and I immediately took offense when one of the women stared at her a little too long with distaste.

"You want to lose that eye, bitch?" I ground out, irritated, my limbs on fire, ready to pounce. The woman openly gasped, placing her hand on her chest and I could see the 'well I have never' in her face.

"Keep on staring. I'll give you a two second head start." I smiled wickedly as she scurried off. The boutique manager cleared her throat and approached us. She too seemed to have an issue with us in her store. I knew it was because of Rory with her pink streaked hair and wild misplaced tattoos. I had an exotic look from my Brazilian mother. It was the only thing I could thank her for. I stood 5'9" to Rory's 5'5". It was if we were playing out a scene from *Pretty Woman* and I was nipping that shit in the bud.

"We will take both of these," I snapped as the manager approached and shoved my card in her hand. I had just bought the most expensive fucking bikini ever. Rory looked so happy in hers, I doubled my order.

"Nadine, you don't have to buy mine. It was just for fun."

"Rory, you and I both know these bitches probably don't deserve their luck. We deserve this. This is our time."

"It's me and you know it. You look like an exotic Julia Roberts, but prettier. I look like a stripper."

"Rory, you won't always be a stripper and screw them and what they were thinking. Honestly, if you don't know how beautiful you are, I can't help you."

"Enough with this mushy shit. Let's go sport these," she said, eyeing herself in the mirror proudly.

"Can't really do that now, babe." I nodded to the window as the sun started to make its decent. The manager came back with my card and a bag. I gave myself one last glance. It did fit perfectly. It was a deep red bikini that complemented my olive skin and barely held my boobs together with a straining metal clasps that matched the ones on the hips of the bottom. It fit my curves perfectly. It may damn well have been worth the price. I smiled and snatched the bag from the rude store manager who was still eyeing me.

"Really? It's 2005 lady. The fucking world is eclectic. Get a clue."

"Pardon?"

"Look, I understand you have to kiss the ass of the snobs who keep this place open, but why ruin a girls day by making her feel like shit for being in your boutique? The sign up front says open, does it not?"

The woman stood back, mouth gaping as onlookers watched me berate her. "Yes, it does," she said quietly.

"Not private boutique for judgmental rich bitches only?"

"Ma'am, I must ask you to tone it down."

"That's not on the sign, either. Don't worry, precious, we're leaving, and you can go back to burying your head in the sand," I continued as I stepped inside the dressing room and smirked at Rory's full blown belly laugh.

"Fuck's sake, Nadine, nobody did anything to you. When you figure out what you want to do with that degree of yours, you're going to have to tone it down."

"I hate women, Rory, I do. It's like I know what they're thinking when they look at me."

"Um, Nadine, maybe because you screw their boyfriends when they turn their head … idiot," she called, egging me on as I zipped up my jeans.

I laughed despite myself. "Well they deserve it."

"Who?" We emerged from our rooms at the same time and she met my eyes.

"I see how they treat their men. It's wrong. It's as if they could care less about them."

"Them or your mother?"

"No, not you too. Don't try and shrink me, Rory. I'm well aware I hate my mother."

"And you hate women because?"

"I hate my mother. There, I paid you in a bikini. I'm cured. Let's get the hell out of here."

"As long as you know, Nadine. They aren't all bad."

"I don't need them. I have you."

"Good enough for me, money bags."

"You loved me when I was poor, too."

"Yeah, but I love you more now." She smiled as I gave the love finger to the manager before we exited.

"Jesus, for a smart girl, you act like an idiot sometimes."

"I'm nineteen for one more week. I have time left to rebel."

"Nadine, something is up with you," she said, giving me a pensive look as we walked to the car.

"Maybe I'm just tired of the world shitting on me."

"I'm twenty-three and you're nineteen. I think I can tell you it gets worse." She rolled her eyes at me as she faced me over the car hood. I opened my door, happy to have done what I did in that store, even though I knew trying to act my age was pointless. I was way beyond my years, even at sixteen. I had conducted myself as an adult for as long as I could remember. I deserved a rebellious moment or two before civility was expected of me at all times.

"Bring it," I said with a devilish smile on my face. I turned to the store and saw the manager peering out the window. I narrowed my eyes and shook my head and repeated, "Bring it."

WE HEARD THE music in the tiki hut before we entered. It sounded like a mix of Stevie Ray Vaughn and Dire Straits—my dad's favorites. I immediately felt at ease. I nabbed a candlelit table as Rory went to the bar to get our first set of drinks. I never got carded. I looked older than my age because of my build. Tonight I kept it casual with a sundress and flip flops while Rory rocked her famous Gwen Stefani look—complete with ridiculous platforms and a leather skirt—and her hair in cute, pink streaked pig tails. She was into the rough and gruff men. I could always tell when it had been a while for her, she brought 'The Look' out. I am sure we must have looked a little strangely dressed in comparison. Oh, how I loved my best friend. I heard the now familiar sound of the ocean waves and studied the foam they left behind while letting the music move me back and forth, the song filling my senses. The day's earlier euphoria hadn't left me and I let myself go with it.

"Big Head Todd and the Monsters, *Bittersweet*," a voice sounded behind me at the next table.

I turned to see a pair of brown eyes, lips twitching in amusement at me. I felt my whole being shudder as I recognized him. It was the same guy who saw me jump fully clothed into the ocean and now had busted me swaying a little too enthusiastically to the music. I knew for the second time today I looked like an idiot, but smiled and thanked him.

"Thank you. I love it. It's beautiful." I turned back around in my seat, giving him a clear indication I wasn't interested in conversation.

"Soooo … today was your first time in the ocean, huh?"

Shit, where are you Rory? I turned to answer him and found him with a shit eating grin on his face. It annoyed me.

"Yeah," I replied quickly without enthusiasm. Short answer means go away dude, I thought as I glanced at Rory at the bar. He was with friends who were talking amongst themselves but had turned around in his chair, staring directly at me, either oblivious or completely uncaring about my brush off. I laughed at his boldness. Guys rarely, if ever, approached me without invitation.

"This song is a little old for you, isn't it?" I asked, truly interested.

"My dad loves this song."

"That's a nice coincidence. I was thinking the same thing. My dad would love it."

Rory approached with shots and beers and I again dismissed my intrusive new friend as I turned to her.

"Where are you from?" Damn it, dude! I gave Rory the wide eyed 'I don't want to be bothered, why won't he fuck off?' look and she nodded.

"Oklahoma," she answered, taking a look at him behind me, her eyes widening as she got a better look at him, then hitting mine as if to say 'are you crazy?'

"Not on this trip," I mouthed out loud, cutting myself off without realizing it. Wow. I was in recovery already, I thought to myself with a mental pat on the back. I laughed a little and felt his chair move across the floor closer to our table.

"What are you not doing on this trip?" he asked curiously.

"Getting into trouble," I said openly and with contempt. He wasn't taking the hint and Rory didn't care. I could detect the small amount of drool on the side of her mouth.

"Rory, shot?" I prompted, lifting my shot glass.

"Give me a sec, ladies. I'd like to join you in this toast."

"You weren't invited." I turned around, fully delivering the words harshly.

"May I pleaseee take a shot with you ladies?" He smiled now and I couldn't help but notice the dimples on either side of his cheeks, or how his long dark hair feathered around his face. I again hesitated drinking him in and instantly felt a pang of want. He lowered his eyes to meet mine, already halfway off of his chair to head to the bar. I took a sharp intake of breath at the intensity of his gaze. No, no, Nadine. No, no, no, no.

"Sure." Shit, I meant to say no.

"I'll be right back. What's our poison?"

"A slow comfortable screw," Rory replied, more flirtatious than I had ever seen her. When he got up, we both strained to check out the rest of him. Tall, dark, and hellishly built. That was the second time I had overlooked this man's good looks. He was the complete package with unfortunate brown eyes.

"Fuck me," Rory said under her breath.

"He's not even close to your type," I replied, taking in his broad shoulders and ass that sat perfectly in his tattered jeans.

"It could change. And why are you acting so weird? Normally you'd jump on it."

"That's where you're wrong. Do you see a girlfriend around?"

"We're on vacation, Nadine. Can't you make one exception? What's the deal with unavailable men again anyway? It's a sick fetish and you know it."

"It's safer for me, the way I like it."

"The way you like what?" he asked in my ear as he brought his chair to our table, taking a seat closer to me than socially acceptable.

"My best friend only screws unavailable men. It's a game to her. She uses them for sex and discards them like toilet paper." I saw Rory gasp at her admission and my eyes widened. I turned to see our new friend amused at Rory who had her hand clamped over her mouth and quickly began apologizing. I should have been furious. I should have thrown my shot at her. Instead I let out a huge laugh and lifted my shot glass.

"Well, here's to my best friend, the stripper," I added dryly.

Rory narrowed her eyes at me then smiled sheepishly and brought her glass up to mine. I turned to our company and clinked his glass before giving him my eyes, seeing nothing but curiosity in his stare. We downed our shots and I felt his arm drape around my chair casually as he leaned back.

"So you fuck for sport?"

"Wow, I never thought of it that way. Yes, I absolutely do," I said, picking up my beer and taking a sip.

"Wow, I've never had a woman come out and say that." His tone wasn't incredulous, buxt it was definitely surprised. I ignored his eyes on me.

"Technically, I didn't," I said, shooting small daggers at Rory who sunk a little in her seat.

"What's your name?"

"I am Nadine, and mouth over here is Rory. Yours?"

"Spencer."

"Cheers, Spencer," I said, grabbing the second shot he brought us from the bar.

"Let's drink."

CHAPTER Five

WE SPENT HOURS at the bar listening to their immaculate music, laughing, drinking and talking. Eventually we joined tables with his friends and all became acquainted quickly. He had come with a couple and another girl whose names escaped me. They were in refuge from Philadelphia and had decided on a whim, just like Rory and I, to escape. Why we had all chosen family oriented Pensacola beach was beyond us. We were all young and there were more than a few other beaches suitable for our age according to Spencer, who eyed me constantly over the table. I gave him small smiles here and there, but mostly ignored them.

Our night ended with a unanimous decision to skinny dip in the ocean, in honor of my first time. We laughed at each other as we all got naked, running full blast into the ocean, only the moon giving us a very small amount of light.

"This is kind of dangerous," I stated, but it was more of a question when a naked Spencer got within earshot.

"We follow the rules at home. Here we do whatever the hell we want." His tone was forced and I couldn't see his face, but I knew the venom was not for me.

"Agreed. Sorry about earlier. I didn't want to be rude. I didn't know you would be so…"

"So?" I could hear a hint of a smile.

"Easy to talk to?"

"Good enough. Were you afraid of me?" he asked, inching toward me. It was too dark out for me to read any expression on his face. I hated it.

"Well, hell no. Of course not. I'm not afraid of men," I said dismissively.

"No, not you."

"What the hell is that supposed to mean?"

"You use men for sport, sooo it's obvious you're not afraid of them."

"It's not like that. Screw it, it is like that. I give them an escape."

"You give them the most intimate part of you for nothing," he said in a whisper.

"I lied. You aren't easy to talk to and you're a total judgmental ass. You wouldn't say a damn word about this or even be interested if it was one of your friends. I came here to escape life, not be judged by a complete stranger who knows nothing about me." It was ridiculous. We were drunk and naked in the ocean and talking about my sexual habits. I splashed him in the face with as much water as possible and felt him grab me and pull me to him. It was awkward to say the least. He held me at arm's length and began quickly apologizing. I heard everyone screaming and splashing around but couldn't quite make out their faces. A small wave of panic shot through me.

"RORY?"

"I'm good," I heard her in the distance.

"Let go of me, Spencer," I said, trying to wade my way toward her voice.

"I'm sorry. I didn't mean to piss you off. You were open about it. I didn't think you would take offense."

"It's all true, whatever you think of me. It's true, Spencer, okay? Just think it, and don't say it."

"You could never know what I was thinking."

"I know that you just slipped up already. If you do it again, we can part ways. I came with my best friend and want nothing to do with my 'sport.'"

"Understood and look, I really didn't mean anything by it. I don't know why I said that. Truly, I am sorry. You've got to be the most beautiful woman I've ever seen."

"You can't see shit right now."

I felt something besides a human limb swim past me and immediately screamed bloody murder and made my way to shore. I saw four naked bodies come running toward me as I made it safe on the sand. I couldn't help but to burst out laughing at the flailing body parts as they got closer. I looked up to see Spencer standing directly above me, his shorts already on. I stifled the disappointment as he pulled me to my feet and quickly asked, "What the hell was that?"

"I don't know. I felt something swim past me. It wasn't big or anything, but it freaked me out."

"Jesus you scared the shit—" I saw a flashlight globe hit his chest and heard the boom of a megaphone.

"Nobody move!"

He might as well have fired a gun because we all scattered like roaches, fully naked and running for our lives while beach patrol on a golf cart chased us as we laughed hysterically. We yelled the names of our hotels to each other as Spencer screamed "every man for himself," and grabbed my hand as he found a small hole in between hotels for us to hide. We were panting heavily as I sucked in as much air as I could to calm down. Still laughing, I let it consume me. I had never felt so alive.

I leaned back against the wall of the hotel and saw there was a street light a block over fully illuminating me. I looked up to see Spencer more breathless than he was after we ran. I felt heat invade my body as he stood close to me, taking me in. I felt my breathing escalate as I did the same. He walked slowly toward me and placed his hands on either side of my head, peering into my eyes with a hunger that I was all too familiar with.

"There isn't a man alive who wouldn't take advantage of this situation," he whispered, inching toward me.

"Except for you right?" I shot back, hearing the fear in my voice.

"Fuck no. I was justifying it to myself." He was wrapped around me in seconds. I went limp when his lips came crashing down on mine and forced my mouth open with his tongue. His kiss was fierce and possessive.

His hands roamed every single inch of my flesh, my stomach, my bare ass, my nipples. His tongue caressed me like his hands did, slowly and thoroughly. He grasped my chin with his hand and tilted my head back, taking our kiss deeper. His tongue tangled with mine so smoothly and I felt the tingle between my thighs and moaned for him. He took the cue and pushed my back against the wall, bringing my middle to him. Stroking my face with the pad of his thumb, he let his other hand drift between my thighs. I sucked in a lung full of air when he reached my center while he plunged his tongue back in my mouth until I was dizzy and breathless. He stroked me gently, taking a single finger and rubbing it back and forth over the top of my sex, never going further. I heard his gasp when my moisture reached his fingertip, but still he didn't reach past. I readied myself for him and opened up wide, taking all he wanted to give before the realization washed over me.

He wasn't invited.

I was completely out of my element, surprised, aroused, infuriated and not in control. I pushed him away from me, gasping and needing space between us.

"Not cool," I panted, holding my hand up in a vain attempt to keep him away. I was panicking.

He brushed his lips with the finger with my scent and closed them briefly. I felt my body awakening at his gesture. My nipples were aching and my lower half begged for release. He opened his eyes and they bore into mine. Perfect. This would be exactly what I wanted to see. I was about to make a move toward him when he backed away.

"I'm sorry, I just couldn't... And you're so fucking beautiful, I had to touch you. God, that was wrong. I know that was wrong." He turned away from me and couldn't see my disappointment. I lashed out, still reeling.

"And you did, without my fucking permission." I was furious with myself for stopping him. I clearly wanted him, every inch of me was screaming for him. Still, I was more furious that it wasn't on my terms.

"You're right. You deserve better. So much better. I'll go get your clothes, but it may take me some time. Just wait here. I don't want to get caught. Wait, okay?"

"Whatever, just go."

"I am sorry I did it, Nadine. But I will never, ever fucking regret it."

"Clothes, Spencer, okay?"

"Going."

I must have stood there for an hour, scared shitless he wouldn't come back. I was naked and terrified someone would walk by. I was worried about Rory who knew better than to take off without me. This was bad.

Skinny dipping.

CHAPTER *Six*

M Y WORRY TURNED into relief as I saw Spencer approaching with a towel and my dress. I was crouched in a sitting position, too scared to sit my bare ass on the sand. I was starting to feel the pounding in my head and was no longer laughing. He handed me my dress and held up the towel so I could put it on.

"Thanks," I said, mouth shuddering now from being naked and wet, the whipping wind chilling me to the bone.

"I'm sorry it took so long. The damn beach patrol took forever to leave. They assumed we would be back for your clothes, guess they finally gave up."

"It's fine, thank you. I'm surprised you came back."

"Of course I would." He gave me an awkward smile. "Jack and Amy called my cell. Rory is with them and they're waiting for us at our hotel."

"Oh good," I said, not meeting his eyes.

"I'm sorry, Nadine. I shouldn't have kissed you and touched you like that."

"Whatever, I hadn't thought about it. I've been preoccupied, naked and freezing to death."

He gave a soft chuckle as I wiped off the excess sand from my legs and I studied him. Nice guy and harmless. He met my watchful gaze.

"What?"

"You take care of people," I stated.

"What?" It was almost a whisper as he came closer to me. I could see alarm in his eyes.

"You take care of the people in your life. I can tell. It's like second nature."

"How the hell can you tell that?"

"Just a gift I have."

"I might be really dangerous," he answered playfully, inching closer.

"No you aren't." I replied, certain.

"I take care of my dad."

"You look a little young to do that. How old are you anyway?" I saw his face tense and he grabbed my arm, steadying me across a huge mound of sand as we made our way toward his hotel. "Twenty-five."

He didn't acknowledge my first statement, so I left it alone.

"So who are Amy and Jack to you?"

"They've been my best friends since high school. They're incredible people and travel everywhere and drag me along once in a while."

"They seem nice." I felt at ease now walking along the beach in the dark with him. I still got excited every time I heard a wave crash into the shore. Oklahoma didn't exist. "And Ellie?"

"They hoped we would hit it off, but we didn't. They're dying to get me married. Not everyone has it as good as they do."

"Never Me."

"What?"

"I will never EVER do that to myself."

"Marry?"

"Hell no. It looks horrible. Like a job you have to do and pretend to enjoy. No fucking way."

"I won't argue that point."

We rounded the corner of his hotel and he grabbed me by the shoulders. "Let's hang out tomorrow."

"I don't know where I'll be."

"With me." He brushed my shoulders with the pads of his thumbs and I eased away.

"You are not invited."

"Yes I am." He smiled again, revealing the full beauty of his perfect face. I had never had a guy with dimples. They did something to me. He was not boyishly handsome; he was all man. His eyes were large and his lashes touched his checks when he glanced down at my body, which was pulsating and peaking in places under his stare. I instantly remembered the feel of his cool lips on me, his fingers grazing my body. I felt my breathing coming quickly and stopped myself from saying more. Outside his hotel I stared into his brown irises, letting my eyes drift down to his chest. It was perfectly bare and etched around him like someone had cut him from solid stone. They drifted further down to the swim shorts clinging to him. I wasn't taking this view for granted again.

"I am invited," he said with a grin as he watched me admire him.

I turned and dashed into the hotel, irritated with myself for giving him that much attention. We quickly made our way to his room. All eyes were on me first as I walked in. We all burst out laughing and telling our version of what happened after we ran from the beach patrol rent-a-cop.

"Flashlight cop, no gun, just a big flashlight. I see you, I see you," Rory laughed as she took a remote, pointing at each of us with it in jest. "What was he going to do, pile us naked on his golf cart and bring us in?" She roared again and we followed suit. This would be a story none of us would forget soon.

Amy welcomed us by putting shots in our hands. I tapped my glass with Spencer's and made the mistake of looking at him. His eyes swam with heat, but his mouth was curved into a sweet smile. Spencer was like nothing I was used to seeing. His dark hair hung loose around his forehead, barely sweeping above his eyes—eyes that were beckoning me to give him something—something I couldn't put my finger on. It wasn't the look I craved so much, it was … different. I pushed the thought down as I took the shot, letting it burn my thoughts out of me. The feeling in the room was one I hadn't felt in years. It was like we belonged together … and it felt like … like … family.

My intention was to grab Rory and leave, but we ended up taking shot after shot and talking until the sun rose. I was immediately taken with Jack and Amy and understood what Spencer saw in them right away. They were the happiest couple I had ever seen. It was infectious to look at them and even more infectious when they spoke. Ellie—the fourth in their group—was quiet and didn't say much, but matched us shot for shot and laughed along with all of us. She's not his type, I thought. She was too quiet for Spencer. That's why he's not into her. He needed someone with more personality. Poor Ellie, she had it bad for him. I saw her look at him more than once with 'the look.' Women, and the stupid damn curse of wanting what you can't have. I shook my head as I downed another shot.

"HAS ANYBODY SEEN the cat?" I heard Spencer groan next to me.

"What cat and quit yelling!" I groaned back in reply.

"The cat who took a shit in my mouth while I was sleeping."

The whole room erupted in laughter as I peeked at him on the bed next to me. He took my breath away with his devilish smile. I played immune and turned to face the wall, smiling at it instead. We had all passed out, strewn over the two king beds in their hotel.

"And so the day begins," Jack said as he smacked Amy's ass, getting an evil stare in response from her. Ellie walked around the room passing out ibuprofen and Gatorades.

"You guys seem to have it together," Rory remarked of their hospitality as she took her pills and popped them in her mouth, downing half her bottle.

We quickly rinsed our mouths and each took a shot of the liquor that made us sick and headed back to the beach. Rory went to get our suits from our hotel as I sat in a beach chair watching everyone else and my surroundings to wait for her. The sky was a deep blue, the sun the only thing to paint it. Today the water was a clear blue. I heard fifteen different songs streaming through radios and watched sunbathers rub oils onto each other. I jumped back as a seagull landed next to me on one of the vacant beach chairs. All I could think of was *Jonathan Livingston Seagull*, a fascinating book I read when I was young that blew my mind on life's endless possibilities. I truly believed some of its principles to be true. I pretty much based my future on the theory that if you accepted the world around you the way it was, you could never get to the next level. If you thought outside the box, the possibilities were endless. I had my father as living proof. But, as with any good book or piece of advice, I took what I felt was right for me from it and left the rest. I was sure there was a God, but I wasn't sure if he wanted anything to do with me. I made sure to listen for him.

"Hi, Jonathan," I piped happily, my headache now gone.

"We're naming seagulls?" Spencer asked as he approached for a towel on the beach chair next to mine. Every single time I looked at this man it was like taking a hit straight to the chest. His hair held the moisture from the water at the tips in drops of perfection that framed his perfect face. He was a damn wet dream and his lips were moving, asking me a question. What was he asking? His body was making the Oklahoma whore in me want to attack, his smirk ruining my stability. Oh, the seagulls.

"They are all Jonathans."

"One name for all of them… Hmmm, will you name your children this way, too?"

"It's a long story, about a book really."

"I've read it, 9th grade English."

"Well, what did you think?"

"Not what you do," he scoffed, drying himself off as Jonathan flew away.

"Save it. I don't want your negative thoughts ruining my good mood."

"They aren't negative."

"Sooo what?"

"You think the idea of levels is true?"

"Why not? Higher consciousness, progress, knowledge is power, brings you closer to God. What's wrong with that?"

"The book says nothing about God."

"I take the advice I want to in this life. You should, too."

"By taking yours right now? I'll pass."

"Why? Why so close minded? All the greatest thinkers who walked the world adapted to this theory."

"What theory?"

"What's your problem with being open minded? Thinking about what you truly want and asking for it out loud?"

"Nothing. No, not nothing. I just don't think it's realistic to believe if you open yourself up like that it's all sunshine and rainbows."

"To each their own, you total pessimist. You are ruined already, and so young," I said, mocking him with a grin.

"You are the baby. Nineteen? I thought you were at least in your twenties."

"Everyone does. Let me guess, Rory the mouth told you."

"Yep. I also know you have a birthmark on your ass shaped like an apple. I missed it last night."

"Sorry, pal."

"I'll see it."

"The hell you will."

He leaned in close, holding his towel. "You don't want to challenge a guy like me, Nadine."

"Oh, you clearly have no clue," I said coyly, rising off of my chair to meet Rory for my suit. "You can't win."

His hand clamped around my upper arm and he brought me to him, face to face. I looked at him with the same determination he returned. "Game ON," he whispered. His eyes told me this would be fun, but his wicked smile said he might have been telling the truth.

Shit.

I took his fingers and released his grip one by one and whispered back, "Your funeral."

I turned and narrowed my eyes at Rory. Shit, shit, shit, shit. I had just given Spencer an invitation.

"I am going to kick your ass! " I yelled at Rory who was fast approaching me. Rory turned around abruptly with both suits in hand, wild eyed with fear and leaving when she saw the menace in my walk toward her. I burst out laughing as she ran from me and I tackled her into the sand. I heard Spencer howling with laughter behind us.

"Rory," I said, keeping her locked to me on the ground while she laughed, "I love you, bitch, God knows I do, but could you please stop giving the enemy ammo?"

"Who's the enemy?" she giggled. "Spencer? Oh, he likes you."

"When the hell did you have time to unload that mouth of yours?"

"You were the first to pass out last night."

"I won't be tonight." I kissed her cheek and pulled her up with me as we dusted the sand off and headed to the closest place to put our suits on.

I felt Spencer watching me from the sea as I approached our newly adopted crew. The water felt like heaven and the sand beneath my feet soothed me. I let the waves move my body with their rhythm. It was intoxicating and so was the man approaching me.

"So you graduated college?" he asked as he waded through the water casually, bringing the water to and away from him as he knelt eye level with me.

"Yes, but I'm here to have fun, not talk about life levels or school or work or my 'sport.' "

"I'm just trying to get to know you."

"You know enough." I made a splash at Rory who was standing a few feet away. I smiled at her and her incessant, never ending mouth entertaining Jack, Amy and Ellie.

"You really love her don't you?" I snapped my head up to see Spencer eyeing me with that look. It was full up to of something so ... genuine. I looked back at Rory who had them all in tears with her bullshit antics. Lord knew what story she was telling now.

"Yes, I do. She's my family."

"I can tell."

"It's no big secret, Spencer. Rory is the only real friend I've ever had. So what's with you? What's your story? You know my name and what I look like naked."

"And about your birthmark, and that you're a total dork," he added amused.

"Fine, you got me."

"A drop dead gorgeous dork."

"Deflecting," I said playfully.

"I am, aren't I? That's a lawyer term by the way," he said, absently peering over my shoulder to take in the view.

"I am well aware of that fact. Damn you are good at deflecting," I said, peering into his eyes that he quickly covered by lowering the sunglasses that were on his head. Damn.

"I'm a lawyer."

"Ewe," I said, scrunching up my nose.

"Ewe?" he repeated my words, offended.

"Lawyers disgust me."

"That's a hell of a thing to say," he said, a small smile forming on his lips.

"You ruin hard work. It's a filthy profession."

"What? Why do you think that?"

"Nothing. Jesus, do you really want to play with me, Spencer? Might as well quit now because I am good at grilling."

"I see that." He made his way toward me and lifted his sunglasses off, giving me his full attention. He whispered his next words. "Your mouth is a nightmare, you know that?" He studied my lips and I inhaled a breath as he slowly slid his glasses back into place. I suddenly wanted my own pair.

My quip was late, but I said it anyway. "That's a compliment, sir."

"That figures."

"Avoiding the question, counselor!"

"What was the question?"

Shit, what was the question? He was close, too close. The question, Nadine. It was your question, you idiot!

"I said you know enough about me, what's with you?" I was proud of myself for remembering the exact question and regaining my senses. I really hated and loved the effect he had on me. It was completely foreign, but nice.

"Fine, my full name is Spencer Thomas Diamond. I was born and raised in Philly and I hate cats." There were nothing but dimples in his smile.

"COME ON!"

"My mom is *the* socialite of the Philadelphia scene. My father is a musician. I'm an expert on anything music. My taste is endless. I can name any song that plays on the radio. I have an insane amount of patience because, as I reveal this to you, I want to rip that bikini off your body."

I laughed at him and dove into an oncoming wave. He grabbed me and gave me a sweeping kiss then put me on his back where I spent the afternoon latched to him as he dove into wave after wave. I don't think my laughter stopped. I don't know how long we were there. But what I do remember is the look Rory gave me and her nod that she was still having the time of her life. It was a feeling of freedom in that ocean. A feeling of elation, of family, of total happiness and every single one of us shared the same smile.

Tidal Leap Frog

CHAPTER
Seven

W E ATE LUNCH at a small diner close to the water. I tried to concentrate on the task of finishing my food as I eyed Spencer across the table. He popped a fry into his mouth and chewed slowly, and appreciatively retuning my hungry gaze. I couldn't help but to notice his brown eyes had turned a golden hue as his skin got darker from our day in the sun. His face was perfect. I couldn't find a flaw, though I looked for one relentlessly. He had a small scar above his left eye, and though some might see it as a flaw, I found it sexy as hell. His thick lashes accented the breathtaking golden specks that seemed to have an effect on me like nothing else. I rubbed my shoulders as a chill swept through me and felt my stomach tighten with more than hunger for food. His arms were perfectly toned and bulged only slightly beneath his tee. I found myself letting my eyes drift as far down as the table in front would let them. His tee clung to a perfectly manicured chest and abdomen. I had already seen the perfect picture of small but defined hills and valleys that made their way down to his—

"What you thinking, Nadine?" Jack mused at me as Spencer smiled at him and raised his eyebrows, turning to me waiting on a response.

"I'm tired. And I think I got a little too much sun," I said dismissively, cursing myself for letting my attention stay on Spencer long enough for anyone else to notice.

"Is that all?" Spencer smiled and the dimples that looked out of place on him almost distracted me to the point of not answering. He had no flaws.

"Sorry, did I miss something?" I said rudely, snapping at the fact they wouldn't let it go.

"Nope," Spencer replied sweetly. "I'm pretty sure you got everything."

Jack chuckled as I felt my face go up in flames. I was thankful when Rory piped in, saving me from further embarrassment. Where was the 'in control at all times' whore I relied on so much? I cursed her absence.

"This has got to be the slowest service I have ever had! Nadine why the hell would you leave a two hundred dollar tip?" Rory said as she studied our check and held the money up exasperated.

"Look at her eyes, Rory. Haven't you noticed? They're swollen. Probably from crying. She has counted and recounted her tips every ten minutes since we got here. She's obviously worried about money."

Spencer stopped in mid-sentence while talking to Jack to turn to me. "How did you notice that?"

"It's just… How can you not?"

"I would have never known… Look she's doing it again," Spencer said as if he didn't believe me the first time. The whole table turned their attention to the waitress counting her bills as if they would magically reproduce in front of her. When she finished her count she hung her head.

"Everybody put in all you can," Spencer ordered, putting a stack of twenties in the pile. Everyone, including Rory who smiled at Spencer and then at me, grabbed every spare dime they had and stuck it in the pile.

"You are amazing." I turned to Spencer who gave me a smile with clouded eyes. His gaze was close to the look I so longed for. I found it odd that he gave it to me now.

I felt embarrassed at his remark and did my best to keep my smile to myself. "Thanks, ya'll. I bet her day gets better," I said, grabbing my purse.

She walked up to us and collected the money. I motioned for everyone to leave the table quickly, but glanced back as we headed out the door. She was jumping up and down at the bar waving the money to the bartender. I smiled and turned to follow the rest of my company and ran right into Spencer who caught my mouth.

He kissed me sweetly and when I returned his kiss he devoured me. My heart beat spiked and I was instantly to the point of no return. He picked me up underneath my arms and I wrapped my limbs around him. When he pulled away he continued to hold me to him as he peered at me, catching his breath. His gaze on me, but distant at the same time, it was if he was seeing something I wasn't.

"I don't think I'm going to survive you," he whispered.

"I don't think you should keep starting something you won't finish."

"I don't think you know who the hell I am yet." He grinned at me with challenging and confident eyes.

"Likewise."

He leaned in again, holding me to him, and I felt impatient eyes on us.

"YOU TWO CHILL!" Rory screamed from the passenger side of Amy's SUV. "God, who has the hose?"

"Keep going," Jack said comically, "Amy and I could use a little something new once in a while." I laughed as I slung my legs down to be free of Spencer and saw Coke spray the side of Jacks face, completely drenching him. I looked to Amy as the culprit holding her empty to go cup. Jack simply smiled, blew an air kiss at his wife and got in the SUV while Amy slung words of insult at him. Spencer burst out laughing and Ellie stood shocked.

Rory rolled her eyes and waved us on. "Come on, asshats. It's beer thirty!"

"I have never been called an asshat," I said, musing at Rory who was really coming out of her shell to our new found friends.

"First time for everything," Spencer said, grabbing my hand. I winced at his gesture and shook my head. He bowed out with grace.

BEING an asshat

CHAPTER Eight

W E SPENT OUR night doing body shots and laughing hysterically at a rip roaring drunk Ellie who did her best to act sober. She took two shots to our every one in a vain attempt to be more personable and to get Spencer's attention—which was completely on me. I tried not to indulge him, though it wasn't my nature to do so. I wanted to spare Ellie. She was a nice girl and I could see Spencer and my displays today taking a toll on her confidence. I was relieved when one of the better looking guys at the bar approached her and kept her attention. It meant I could finally focus on the guy chipping at my steel will minute by minute.

I would glance at him every once in a while and catch his long black lashes lying on his cheeks as he laughed. I would glimpse at his dimple filled smile. I took note of the way his long hair drifted just over his eyes and hung close to his ears. I was drawn even more to the way his eyes would light up when he became more animated. I loved the sound of his voice, the way it moved me and soothed me at the same time. Every word he spoke led me closer to him, though I didn't move. He was funny and witty and seemed to know how to keep us all at attention. He was a man's man and a ladies' man.

During the course of the night, I felt myself inching toward wanting to invite him. Even if we were playing a game, he had a way of triggering my appetite, and little by little I could feel my temperature rise with each brush of his knee against mine, each subtle swipe of his fingers over my arm. Every time he took a body shot off of me he lingered with his tongue and kept my eyes focused on him. He gave me subtle winks when he knew he had me aroused. He knew my body well, though he had never had it. He was completely in tune with me and knew it.

Now I was lying on the bar, legs spread, Spencer in between them, hitching my sundress close to the top of my thighs as he towered over me. My temperature rose as he took the shot from the bartender and licked my index finger before lining it with salt. The shot rested on the flat part between my chest and neck and the lime was strategically placed in my mouth by Rory. God I loved that girl, but I would be damned if I didn't sense she was on his side. Amy and Jack were doing some pretty heavy petting a few feet away at the table and Rory had excused herself to check out the jukebox, leaving me with Spencer and his next shot.

"Got you all to myself, Nadine." I had to stifle a moan as his eyes took inventory.

I spit out the lime. "Could you hurry this up? I feel like it's going to spill."

He grabbed a fresh lime from the condiment tray, placing it in my mouth.

"You really don't want that do you, Nadine?" He clicked his tongue with his teeth and I rolled my eyes. We were the last people in the bar. No one was paying us a bit of attention. I looked to the bartender who was counting her till. I was like a fly in ointment. Well, a willing fly.

"Stay still, Nadine. Don't move."

I felt his hands slide up my thighs to my hips, taking my dress hem with them. I felt the shot wobble as I sucked in a quick breath. There was no way I wasn't going to spill the shot. I quickly protested.

"It's up here, Spencer," I scolded through the new lime, but was not convincing.

"No one is watching me," he said quietly. He took his time licking the salt off of my finger as I took in a sharp breath. His eyes met mine and I saw the corners of his mouth turn up in smug satisfaction. I needed a fix and he was my only out, but I would be damned if I gave him any other indication he was ruining me. I was absolutely determined to keep my raging flesh hidden until I felt his hands slowly and tenderly stroking my hips as he leaned in and took the shot with his mouth and tilted it up quickly, taking it all. I watched him swallow in awe as his hands moved swiftly, massaging my sides and playing with the strings on my panties.

"Spencer!" I scolded, but sounded ridiculous through the lime. He leaned in, sucking the lime and my bottom lip. When he had his fill he tossed the flavorless rind on the bar next to me, still keeping his hands at my sides, and leaned in and kissed me deeply. I moaned into his mouth as he thrust his tongue inside and time stood still. Fuck the world and everyone in it. I wanted this man. I reached up and stuck my hands into his thick hair, letting his tongue taste while his lips massaged mine. When he pulled away I was panting and I could tell he was very close to losing his own self-control. The rise and fall of my chest showed him just what he did to me.

"Tell me I win and I'll put you out of your misery right here, Nadine."

"Screw you, Spencer," I hissed, my frustration and arousal apparent.

"Oh, I intend to. I've tasted you already and I want more." He quickly brushed his finger over my sex and slipped a single finger under my panties, making me gasp, and brought it to his full bottom lip, tasting me. He slowly roved his tongue over it and closed his eyes. Opening them again he pushed his center into me. I felt him hard against me and whimpered.

"Fucking delicious, Nadine. I could bury my face between those sexy fucking legs of yours right now."

I pushed at his chest as I noticed Rory coming our way.

"Stop right now. Rory can see." I could barely get the words out when his mouth came down on mine again. He gave me one final thrust of his tongue and closed our kiss. I rose up off of the bar quickly and noticed not a soul had a clue of what he had done to me. My body was on fire, begging me to tell him he had won. His smug grin told me he was in control.

"What's up, ya'll? Last call over? Shit I just put a dollar in the jukebox."

"Rory, let's go." I was furious. I darted my eyes at Spencer who was smiling arrogantly and licked his lips.

"Okay, but what's wrong, Nadine?"

"Nothing. I want to leave. I need to go." There was a horrible ache brewing between my thighs. I needed a shower. I needed sleep. I needed chocolate. Even worse, I needed Spencer inside me. Only he could deal with my true issue and I suddenly hated him for it.

"Don't go away mad, Nadine," he said from behind me. I jumped at his low voice and breath tickling my ear. I made a beeline for my car and he didn't follow. Fine, he won that round and screw him for it. I felt a strange draft from beneath my skirt and stopped dead in my tracks. My eyes widened and I quickly realized he had done more than taken his shot. Nadine, this is what he wants. Walk away! It went off in my head like an alarm. If I lost my temper, I would lose the game. Even worse, if I demanded what I wanted from him I would have to admit I lost. A slow smile crept up my face. I felt the night's drinks kick into overdrive. He was bold. I recognized that part of him in myself and it only made me crave him more. Still, he wasn't getting away with this.

"Back so soon?" Spencer was smug in his victory as he sipped his beer in front of Jack and Amy who were settling their bill. He had both of his arms hitched on the bar, his body facing mine as I walked directly in front of him and held out my hand. He put my panties in my hand and gave Jack a wink. Jack shook his head and went back to fussing with Amy who had suddenly insisted on tipping way more than what was normal. I smiled at that and turned to Spencer with a practiced ferocity in my eyes that I used often.

I grabbed Spencer's hand and took a finger into my mouth, sucking it down and letting it tickle my throat, then two, leaning in on him and taking them deep. I grabbed my clutch from behind him with my spare hand, grinding myself into him with my hips. I pulled back and glanced at his face and saw his mouth gaping and felt him hard against me. As cheerfully and casually as I could muster, I replied with a smile, "I just forgot my clutch." I gave his hard length a firm graze of my hand before I turned around to Amy and winked. She winked back. "Night, guys. See you in the sand box tomorrow?"

Jack laughed at Spencer and grabbed his beer from him, downing it without any protest. Spencer, who recovered quickly, replied, "Wouldn't miss it."

I have sleight of hand too, Spencer. Game on, I thought as I smiled at the door walking away.

Body Shots

I SPENT THE next day on the beach alone. I had spent the last two nights drinking and had slept a small part of the day away. Rory was still in bed and I grabbed a book at a little beach boutique. I couldn't focus on my book and spent a majority of my time peeking around and hoping to see Spencer approaching, but it didn't happen. I decided I had been neglecting my time with Rory anyway and went back to the hotel to let her know I wanted a date for just us girls. I found the entire crew in my hotel room.

I hid my elation that Spencer was there looking amazing in a plain black tee, shorts that hugged his body perfectly, and flip flops. I couldn't justify any of my fascination for a man I hardly knew, but justified that once I had him it would quickly be over.

I waved to Amy and Ellie who were fussing over the remote.

"Looks like you got some sun, Oklahoma," Jack said as I took a bottled water out of the fridge.

"Yeah, it was so peaceful today." I gave Jack a smile. He was cute in his own way. Still as pasty white as the night I met him, though it seemed impossible due to our amount of sun play. He had short cut blond hair and dark blue eyes. Amy could pass for his sister instead of his wife.

"So … Nadine, don't get mad, but I told them they could smoke in here. You know, weed. "

"Why would I get mad? Just because I don't do it?"

"Ever?" Spencer said behind me in amusement.

"No, I've never done any drugs. No intention of doing them."

"Weed is pretty harmless," Spencer said, eyeing me.

"Who are you to play Devil's advocate, counselor?" I quipped.

"Not this week, the counselor part I mean," he said, undressing me with his eyes.

Rory laughed and added, "Oh God, Spencer. I've tried to tell her a million—"

"I'll hit it." The whole room looked at me like I had just fired a gun. "What? We're on vacation. I'll try anything once, unless I don't want to. And I'm up for it." I felt Spencer eyeing me as I dug through my clothes for a change. When I found my evening outfit, I looked at Ellie. "Do you smoke, Ellie?"

"No, I wigged out when I did. Be careful."

"I'll be right back." I could feel my heart accelerate as I walked past Spencer who grabbed my hand and guided me into the bathroom as if I didn't know where I was going. He shut the door behind us.

"I missed you today." He took my mouth so quickly I didn't have time to answer. His arms were around me then and I melted into his kiss. I quickly remembered the aggravation of the night before and protested with my hands pushing his chest.

"I don't know what you think is going on here between us, but I'm really just trying to have some fun," I said, breathless and hating myself for it.

He leaned into me with his body and I felt him hard against me. "We are playing a game." He smiled and I lost even more composure.

"Everyone is out there and knows we're fooling around."

"I just wanted to tell you that I missed you today. And for someone who fucks for sport, you sure aren't acting like it." He gave me a dimpled filled smile and tapped my nose with his index finger. Was I cute to him? Oh no, this wasn't going to work.

"Not that it's any of your damn business, but I don't really showcase my private life in public or otherwise. In fact, until I met you, Rory and a bartender were the only ones who knew that about me. Look, about our game, I'm not so sure I want to play anymore. Maybe we could just be cool and hang out."

"Why, are you mad about last night?"

"Yes and no. Smooth by the way."

"I wanted to keep those panties. Seriously, I didn't mean to upset you. And now I just wanted to see to unfinished business." He took me again, this time with no mercy. He took my sarong off and stood back, eyeing me in my bikini for several moments until he slid an arm around my waist, pulling me to him.

"I'm going to get between those thighs, Nadine, and you are going to beg me for more. And when you do, I'll rub it in the right way by fucking you senseless and making you wish you had given in sooner," he said, kissing my neck and stroking my back with his hands. I reached into his jeans and felt his length and heard his groan as he tongued my neck. I instantly wanted to drop to my knees, but pulled back to watch his reaction to my fingers. I wanted the look, and what I saw took my breath away. His head was tilted back, and his eyes were closed. When he finally opened them, they had turned into a pool of liquid black.

"Fuck," he moaned as I stroked him over and over, making his hands roam, frantically grabbing my chest. I stopped quickly and stood away from him. My heart stopped when he turned those eyes back on me, a wicked smiled crossing his lips. I hadn't won this round, either.

"Finish it," he ordered, making my sex twitch.

"No way," I said slowly, dragging the words out as I enjoyed his discomfort.

I undid my top and lowered my bottoms, keeping eye contact. A small smile played on my lips as I tossed the bottoms at him, seeing his face fall as I jumped into the cold shower. I heard the door open and close a few minutes later. I took my time getting ready thinking this round might have gone to me.

My sundress was form fitting and long. It hugged my every curve and showed a small amount of cleavage. I swept my hair to one side in a braided bun and put on my darkest shade of red lipstick. My sun kissed skin made my clear blue eyes pop. I wanted nothing more than another go at Spencer, but this had to stop. The longer I stayed away from Oklahoma, the less I felt like the girl who left there. I was done playing. At least I was beginning to feel like I was. I walked out ready for whatever they had planned and was met by Rory.

"Ready for this?" She eyed me with worry. "You don't have to." I saw her nod to Jack who had just finished wrapping what he called a 'pristine' joint and handed it to Spencer.

"She's not smoking," Spencer said dismissively. I narrowed my eyes. Bossy bastard.

"The hell you say, sir! I made the decision. It had nothing to do with you," I said, giving him a hard look. He lifted his hands up in amused defeat as he walked toward me.

"Take one drag. See how you feel. It creeps up on you," he said while inhaling a large drag, doing a double inhale that I had seen so many people do and found so sexy. He passed it to me and I looked around the room to find everyone staring at me.

"I'm not a guinea pig. Stop staring." All eyes diverted from me to the hotel TV as I did what Spencer said. I took the joint, inhaled and immediately started coughing.

"I said easy, fireball," he said, laughing at me and handing me a bottled water. "That's good for now." He took the joint away and passed it amongst the rest, minus Ellie who scrunched her nose up at the smell filling the room.

"Let's go eat," Spencer announced, walking toward the door. We all followed as Rory sprayed the room with her best perfume and turned on the a/c, shutting the door behind her. She gave me a quizzical look and I just shrugged my shoulders, telling her I wasn't fazed by my small hit. I kept up with the rest of them, but felt my legs quickly turning to Jell-O as I tried to keep the pace. I suddenly felt a wave of something hit me and immediately felt the urge to sit. I tried to mask it as best I could, but quickly began to panic. This can't be how it feels to be stoned. This was … bad. I sat in Amy's SUV trying to make sense of it, to get it together in my head. They were all standing outside with the car doors open, debating on where we should land tonight for what had become our new routine. I took deep gulps of air to calm myself down and ended up panting instead. I was out of control, mind racing at a ridiculous speed. I couldn't think straight. Something wasn't right.

"Guys," I panted as they all laughed amongst themselves. When I got no response I tried again. "Guys," I said a little louder, not wanting to cause too much of a scene. I thought I could control my panic, but my next plea for help came out in a scream. "Guys something is WRONG!" All eyes were on me.

"Oh shit," Spencer said, rushing to me. "It's okay, Nadine. It just crept up on you." He turned to Jack. "She is wigging."

"Fuck," Jack said as he rounded the SUV to approach me.

"I need to go to the hospital, now. This isn't right. Take me, now," I demanded. As soon as the words left my mouth, every one of them, including my best friend, burst out laughing.

"This is not funny. Rory, help me. Something is wrong." Rory slowed her chuckle and I was still gasping as my mind raced. This wasn't right.

"This is why I do not smoke that shit. Total paranoia," Ellie said with a serious tone.

"It's not a normal reaction. It's just weed," Spencer defended.

"I NEED SOMEONE TO TAKE ME TO THE HOSPITAL NOW!"

"Nadine, look at me." I was still hyperventilating and refused to meet Spencer's eyes. I was absolutely terrified. This is not how I wanted to go out. Great… Death by joint.

"Nadine, baby girl, look at me." His tone soothed me slightly and I met his eyes. "It will pass in a little while. This is not the norm, but it happens to a few who smoke it. The buzz is a little too much to handle."

I burst into tears and tried to reason with him. "I am dying, right now and you are ignoring me!"

He laughed at me and wrapped his arms around me, pulling me to him. "You are not dying, I promise. It's just not a good buzz for you."

"This is bullshit. Rory, take me to the hospital!" I pleaded with her as I became furious that no one, not even my best friend, would take me seriously.

"Nadine, no one has ever died from smoking a joint. " She tried to maintain her calm, but lost the battle. Jack and Amy were hysterical and I looked to Ellie for help, but she too couldn't contain her laughter.

"It's okay, Nadine, really," she assured me as her chuckle slowed when she saw the terror on my face. I trusted Ellie, then. I don't know why, but I knew she wouldn't lie. I pushed Spencer away from me and grabbed Ellie's arm, bringing her to sit next to me in the SUV.

"I felt the same way," she whispered to me. "I know how you feel, and I promise I won't let anything happen to you, girl." I looked in her eyes and saw the worry and sincerity.

"Good. Just help me through this shit, and when it's over, I'm going to get these assholes," I said with more venom in my voice than intended and they all heard me. Spencer went down holding his stomach and laughing until it was almost impossible not to join them.

"Mrs. Wiggins," Spencer cooed to me as he took the seat behind me. He began rubbing my shoulders in an effort to get me to relax and within a few minutes it worked. The haze I was under was slowly disappearing and I could take all the air in I desired. I burst into laughter at my own reaction and glared at everyone who turned to gauge why. They were still the enemy as far as I was concerned. What I was sure of was that was my first and last joint.

Weed of
death

CHAPTER *Nine*

T HE BEER AT the restaurant we landed in tasted amazing. I drank half the pitcher before our food arrived. I dealt with their snide remarks and gave them all the love finger every so often. I kept Ellie next to me and decided to grill my new friend. Whether she knew it or not, I felt safer with her around.

"So you like him," I said, nodding toward Spencer who was absently running his hand through his dark locks and laughing with Jack.

"Is it that easy to tell?" Ellie answered, lowering her head.

"No, he can't, but I can," I said prodding her to open up. "If you want me to I will back off. I've never done it before, but I would for you."

"He's so into you. It seems you both are. I can't ask that of you."

"Does it bother you?"

"It did. But now?" She looked again at Spencer. "I think I just wanted to screw him, honestly."

I let out a laughter filled gust of air and replied, "Me too, I think."

"He makes for a nice view, but look around." I did and saw a guy at the bar eyeing Ellie while his friend kept eyes between Rory and I. Ellie made a cute girl wave and her prey smiled. She smiled back and that was all it took. A few minutes later the three of us girls received shots and took them, lifting them to the tall dark and handsome distractions not at our table. In mid-shot between toasting them and the glass reaching my lips, I noticed Spencer's eyes flash with pure jealousy. Nice. And I didn't even try. He dismissed me and continued taunting Amy with his playful banter.

Once our food arrived, I was on a mission from God to fill myself. I knew this was the appetite of a stoner and indulged. I ate at least two pounds of crab legs in record time without looking up and pushed my plate away, letting a beer burp accidentally escape me.

"Whoops." I looked up to see if anyone had heard it and saw Spencer and Jack holding their watches side by side.

"Seven minutes! Two pounds in seven minutes!" The whole table roared with laughter at my expense as Ellie motioned for me to grab the excess crab dripping from my chin. I felt the heat fill my face as they put their watches back on.

"You guys suck," I said, hiding my smile with my hand.

Spencer caught my eyes and gave me his dimpled filled grin and that look. I loved that look, whatever it was. I lowered my hand and smiled at him fully. He clutched his heart and grabbed his beer taking a long slow sip, his eyes telling me what I knew to be true. This would have to come to a head soon. We both wanted it too much. Spencer broke our gaze to answer Jack who was questioning him about something at home.

"No way in hell I'm stopping whatever this is you two have going," Ellie whispered to me. I gave her a small smile and looked back at Spencer who already had his eyes back on me and his beer lifted. I held mine up giving him an air clink and put it back down.

"Thanks, Ellie, for taking care of me," I said, giving her a half hug at the table.

"I didn't do anything," she said, her short brown hair falling into her huge green eyes, a sincere smile painting her face. She lowered her voice and whispered, "But I'm glad you're better now."

"You were a friend to me when I needed you, which is more than I can say for this shit head." I nodded Rory's way and she immediately took offense. I continued my assault. "Bitch, the next time I have a panic attack and I tell you take me to the hospital, you take me to the hospital, got it?"

"Oh shut up. I knew better." She dismissed me as she winked at the guys from the bar who were now standing directly behind Ellie and me. I saw Spencer stiffen.

"Ladies, it appears that you might not all have dates."

"They do," Spencer said with finality. "So fuck off."

"Spencer," Ellie warned. "You will have to excuse my friend. He is a caveman with no manners. I'm Ellie."

"Derek," the shaggy haired brunette said, taking her hand. "Should we go to the bar and do a few shots?"

"Sure," Ellie said, sticking out her hand further to let him help her from her chair.

"How about you?" The next guy sat beside me, taking Ellie's seat, giving me a great view of what he had to offer. He was a little too short with wavy brown hair and blue eyes—nice eyes. I smiled at him and started to answer when I heard the boom in Spencer's voice.

"What the fuck did I say?"

"Sorry, man. Is this your girl?"

"No I'm not," I said, glaring at Spencer who was standing behind and above us.

"The hell you aren't," he said, lifting me from my chair into his arms. In an instant I was being carried away over his shoulder and laughed whole heartedly as I pounded on his back to let me down. When he finally did we were on the sand, the sun setting behind him. Our smiles faltered and only one word could come from my lips.

"Spencer."

It was more of a question than a statement. I had never taken the time to get to know any of my invites, but I knew better than to think this sexual pull was normal. Every time he looked at me my senses reeled, my body ached in places he had already touched. He was most definitely invited. This was so out the norm for me, I couldn't say anything else. I would have to let him take the lead and that in itself was a huge leap from my comfort zone. Instead of thinking any more about it, I decided to just let it happen.

His eyes were pooling dark and it took my breath from me. I looked down at my hands, which were balled in fists on my dress, and he tilted my chin back up to keep his gaze.

"Twenty-five years old and I can't bring myself to say what I want to a beautiful woman." He rubbed my cheek and took my lips with a tenderness I wasn't used to.

"Spencer." I moaned in unison with him. "How do I know you're not just screwing with me?"

"What do you think, Nadine?"

"I really don't care, I guess."

"Maybe then I won't take you until you do."

He shut my mouth with his and drank me in completely. I was drunk on his kiss and his arm slid around and cradled my waist. Every touch seemed so natural and so right. His kiss was deafening, though the only sound around were the waves playing their melody. His tongue was so gentle and dipped sweetly into my mouth over and over. I felt the moisture between my legs and began to ache for him. It was getting to be too much for me to handle. I took his assault and leaned my body into him, pressing my chest to his. Telling myself that this may be just another ploy at getting the best of me and worse enjoying it, I ripped my lips away.

"This isn't how I usually do this."

"Maybe times are changing for you."

"And I think I want them to." Shit. He saw me regret my admission and I saw a curious look on his face.

"When was your last boyfriend?" he asked, rubbing my bare shoulders in a hypnotizing way.

"I've never had one."

"Never?"

"No, well once… maybe… kind of." Our voices were in whispers as if we were trying to keep a secret between us.

"Kind of? You were his or you weren't?"

"I wasn't. I don't care about that stuff. It's not my thing."

"Your thing?" he asked harshly.

"I'm not comfortable with the … relationship stuff. It's not me."

"Oh, really? So when I kiss you, you feel nothing?"

"No."

"Ah, got it." He let go of me quickly and turned away to start walking toward the restaurant.

"Where are you going?"

"To lick my wounds. Coming?" He turned back to eye me. The sun was finishing its decent, washing us in a haze of purple. It was absolutely beautiful.

"Don't take it personally or anything. I like you and you're so much fun."

He turned to fully face me and made it back to me in a few quick strides. I felt my body being pulled to him in one quick movement as his lips crushed mine and my breath completely left me. He took me down to straddle his lap as his ass hit the sand. Then his hands were everywhere while his mouth kept mine and our hunger mingled perfectly. I was moaning uncontrollably and it didn't go unnoticed.

"You are starving, baby." I felt his fingers trace their way from my thigh up to brush my sex and I moaned again in appreciation. "Tell me, Nadine, what do you feel now?" He licked my swollen lips as he kneaded my ass with both hands.

"Good," I breathed, grinding myself onto the stiffness in his pants.

"Not nothing?" He cupped my breast under my sundress and roved his fingers over my nipple, gently coaxing me.

"Ah," I let out in a shuddering breath. Every inch of me was on fire at his touch. I was trembling with need. Still, I couldn't see him. And worse, I couldn't see his eyes.

"Ah, is not nothing." He moved his other hand over my panties, rubbing up and down over my tightening sex. "I know what you need, Nadine." He stroked the lace barrier up and down, taunting me with his voice and I gasped again as his tongue coaxed my lips open and our kiss deepened. I lost the ability to hold back as his fingers found their way underneath my panties. I grazed my fingernails over his back. He felt my warmth for him as his tongue thrashed wildly and I matched it with my own, much more aware now that the control belonged to neither of us.

"Fuck," he whispered as his own composure left him and he entered me with his fingers. I was so close to the edge and rode his fingers while he took all of my mouth and rubbed my chest with his spare hand.

"I might have to take you right now. I can't wait."

"So don't." I licked the tip of his ear and felt the tension building as his fingers moved quicker inside of me. He rubbed the moisture over me, circling my arousal over and over. I braced myself.

"Get a room!" I heard Rory yell in the distance. It should have felt like cold water splashed over us, but I was too far gone. Spencer started to withdraw his fingers and I wrapped my arms around his neck and pulled us chest to chest.

"Don't stop," I pleaded.

"They're standing too close," he replied, his tone just as pleading and desperate.

"Please … don't stop." I felt his fingers resumed their pace again and I kept my body covering his. I exhaled as I came slowly riding his hand and let go of my moan in his ear, "Coming." His fingers moved more quickly as I rode out the orgasm.

"We'll be right there," Spencer said loudly, holding up his free hand.

"Again," he ordered, licking my lips, outlining my gaping mouth as his fingers dug deeper inside me and he circled my already sensitive bud.

"I can't." He kissed my neck with a fever I was sure was in his eyes and I was missing it, damn it. He was biting and sucking hard at my nipple he had freed with his mouth as I quickened my pace. I let the sensation of what he was doing wash me over and rode his hand until I felt a second and more intense wave hit me.

"Ah," I exhaled into his ear again.

I felt what had to be an unbearable erection beneath me as I collapsed into him as he wrapped his arms around me tightly.

"Jesus," he breathed as he kissed my sweaty forehead, my neck and my lips.

We sat for only a few moments, collecting ourselves. I became increasingly aware of just how public our display might have been and cringed. Though it was completely dark now and we were alone on the beach, I had been taken completely by the heat of the moment and lost total control.

"What about you?" I asked as we straightened ourselves up to try and save face back at the car. I was pretty sure they could see the outline of what we were doing if they looked.

"I felt everything," he said, visibly trying to catch his breath as we made our way back to the SUV.

Purple Haze

CHAPTER Ten

W E ALL WERE taking our time rousing from our sleep. Another drink filled night had left us paralyzed in bed. We ordered room service and took turns showering. I found Spencer staring at me as I ate my breakfast of biscuits and gravy. Jack, Ellie and Amy were at the table chatting away while Rory showered. I looked up and saw Spencer with pure determination and an agenda on his face.

"What?"

He leaned into me, grabbed my finished plate and brought me to lay on his chest, his back to the headboard.

"You know exactly what I am thinking about," he said as his lips slid over my hairline.

"Our game?"

"No," he answered softly. "The way it felt when you came, Nadine." I could feel the longing in his voice. I felt it too.

"If we were alone, I could give you what you need, Spencer."

"Where's the challenge in that?" he whispered, his breathing burdened as he turned my head to face him and took my lips in a slow kiss, tracing my mouth with his tongue. "I can't take much more," he said as he bit the lobe of my ear.

"We're becoming quit the exhibitionists." I smiled wickedly, slipping my hand under the covers to stroke his length. "I can finish you off right here." I tightened my grip on his impressive erection and felt him on the edge, his body tense. He didn't give me a chance to ruin him. He quickly removed my hand and brought me down on the bed, fully kissing me for everyone to see.

"You two are getting your own room in New Orleans," Jack said with a slight amount of disdain.

Spencer ignored him, finishing his kiss and looking into my eyes. "Good idea," he grinned, leaning over me with a smile. It was only then that I realized that Jack had mentioned New Orleans.

"New Orleans?" I croaked, my voice hoarse from Spencer's over attentive stare.

"Yes, we're leaving today and we want you to come."

"I'm in!" Rory shouted from behind us, freshly showered.

"Why New Orleans?" I asked anxiously.

"Why not?" Spencer mused, leaning in to pull my shirt down over my bare stomach. He winked at me and I quickly lost my train of thought. He sat us up and held my back to his chest.

"So will you come?" he asked seductively in my ear while rubbing my bare thighs with a give and take motion of his hands.

"Like we all ride there, leave my car here? Kind of stupid considering we go home that way," I said turning to look at Rory.

"This is a road trip within a road trip. It doesn't have to make sense," Amy taunted. "Have you ever been to New Orleans, Nadine?"

"No, this is my first trip outside Oklahoma City."

"That's ridiculous," Ellie said, giving me a sympathetic look.

"I agree, that's total bullshit," Jack said, grabbing the dishes from everyone, stacking them on the hotel tray.

I kept my eyes on Rory's hopeful face. "You're the boss on this trip, Nadine." I smiled at the leeway she was giving me and turned to Spencer who looked at me hopeful.

I looked around the room at the set of faces and quickly realized I was nowhere near ready to part with my make shift vacation family. As insane as it was, I was already smitten with them all.

"Let's go."

SPENCER AND I sat in the last two seats of Amy's SUV. Rory seemed happy to give me up. In fact, it seemed she had done everything in her power to push us together. Spencer impressed us all by naming every song that came on the radio and by the time we were an hour into our trip, he hadn't failed to name a single one. It was amazing. Rock, rap, R&B, it didn't matter.

"God, that's awesome," Ellie said, turning back to grin at Spencer.

"Yes, yes, I am awesome," he chuckled, turning his baseball hat around so that the bill was in the back. Oh, oh dear God. I was instantly turned on and had no idea why that had done it. I once again began to study his profile as he named the next song and all I could think was he is … beautiful. This man was beautiful. His thick lashes, strong nose, masculine jaw. Even the bob of his Adam's apple as he spoke through perfect full lips had my heart pounding. His shredded hair was dark brown, bordering on black and feathered perfectly around his hat. Beautiful is what Spencer was. There was no other word.

He turned to me and smiled and I felt a wave of embarrassment flow through me. This must be the third or fourth time he had caught me staring at him. I remembered my invites and their attraction to me, but I never remembered being this attracted to them. I needed to feel Spencer—to see the look in his eyes when he took me—then this fascination would be over. I was sure of it.

I looked away from him as I stared out the window. It was a cloudy day, but we were all in good spirits and excited about our next leg of vacation. Spencer made us all laugh as he rolled his eyes and named the song on the radio adding with a low murmur, "Britney Spears."

"Oh yeah, fucker? Name this song," Jack challenged as he changed the radio to AM and Spanish music burst through the speakers. Amy punched Jack in the arm from the passenger seat as we all burst out laughing.

"I like this song," Spencer said "He's taking her heart for his own." He looked at me and I rolled my eyes and rested my head on the seat behind me. So he was fluent in Spanish, looked like a Greek god, was polite, smart, intuitive and had the hots for me. I hate him. "I am a lost cause."

"No, you're not," he whispered, rubbing my leg with his finger and lifting his brow. "You are not," he said more forcefully.

"Well it's not my heart you're after is it, Spencer?" I said coyly and licked my lips.

"Wow, talk about master of deflecting." He grinned at me and I looked out the window.

I WOKE UP, not realizing I had been tired, and stretched as much as I could in the car seat. I looked towards Spencer who was deep in thought.

"What are you thinking about?" I asked seductively before I noticed his frown.

He looked around and saw that the girls were talking amongst themselves and whispered to me, "My dad. I've tried calling twice and he won't pick up."

"Why would he not be okay?" I whispered back, looking around and seeing that I couldn't have been sleeping long. Amy was a camel and her new bottled water was still full. "Why are you so worried?"

"He's a really nasty drunk, Nadine," he said, looking at his phone as if it would ring at any moment.

"Oh." I didn't know what to say, so I said nothing.

"That's why you surprised me the other night when you said taking care of people is second nature to me." He dialed again on his phone, got no answer and cursed in frustration.

Spencer kept his next confession low, for only me to hear, as Rory and Ellie talked about what they wanted to do in New Orleans. "I take care of him by picking up the pieces of his fucking nightmarish aftermath. He's a failed musician, or at least he thinks so. He's the best I've ever seen. He's a pianist and watching him is unreal. He can actually play fourteen instruments, but he's a master at piano. He thinks he's punishing himself with his drinking, but he actually punishes everyone around him."

I felt a tug in my chest as I saw the sadness in his eyes.

"So let him deal with his own demons. He'll just weigh you down. You're twenty-five, right?" He nodded. "Don't you think it's time to fly the coop?"

"He got worse this year when he discovered my bitch of a mother was having an affair. Like most musicians, he's passionate and he was always very clear where his passion lies: his music, me, my mother. If you could have only seen him when he was young, so full of life, so much charisma, he could keep an entire room entertained." I smiled because that is exactly what Spencer could do to a room. I knew this about him and had only known him for a few days.

"Call him again," I said, nudging him with the side of my body, hoping it seemed encouraging.

"I don't know why I'm telling you this." He looked panicked, almost desperate.

"You're worried, and you know enough about me. Call him."

He flipped his phone and dialed. He put his hand on my thigh, rubbing it with his fingertips. He looked at me while holding the phone to his ear and gave me a worried look, as if to ask me if it was alright his hand was there. I gave him a little nod. He began to rub further up, moving my sundress, and I shook my head quickly, bringing it down as he revealed his dimples and his eyes lit up. I didn't know whether it was me or the fact that he finally got an answer on the other end.

"Dad. Damn it, Dad, I told you to answer the phone every time I called!"

I heard his father's voice slightly on the other end and Spencer cracked up at his reply.

"Well, now that's an excuse. Put Mom on the phone." There was a short silence and when Spencer spoke again his tone had changed.

"You are keeping your promise?" I saw his face flare in anger. "Kind of hard to trust you, Mom. I am trying. I can't do much if I have to worry. I know he's your husband. Fine. Please pick up when I call." He flipped the phone shut and looked at me as if he had just broken free. I saw a weight come off his shoulders I hadn't noticed was there, which was unlike me. He brushed his lips over mine and whispered a low, "Thank You." I shrugged, gave him an 'I didn't do anything face.' I saw the difference speaking to his father made and knew then that he loved him deeply. His mother, however, he had a huge distaste for. That we had in common.

"So you hate your mother?" I had to ask. This was too damn coincidental. It seemed we both adored our asshole self-absorbed fathers and hated our mothers.

"No, I love her. I guess I hate her as a person."

"I'm not fond of my mother, either."

"That's an understatement," Rory said, turning to give us her undivided attention.

"I hate my mother because she hates me," I defended. "I was a burden to her. She was always bitching she 'never had time for her man because she had to take care of a brat.'" I laced her statement with a hint of her accent. "My father hated her, too. It's open and shut. She was a horrible and selfish woman. Still is as far as I know. My father stopped bringing me to her when I was ten."

"My mother is the same way. If her agenda doesn't fit whatever you are doing, it's not an option for her, even when things are important. I guess we both have selfish mothers."

"And fathers," I added. "Could have been worse," I muttered, bored with the conversation.

"Doesn't bother me, either," he said, as if reading my mind.

"You are both screwed in the head, and I'm the stripper," Rory commented matter-of-factly, turning around in her seat to face the front. Spencer and I burst out laughing and I thumped Rory's earlobe with my fingers. I saw her grin on the side of her cheek.

God, how I loved Rory. Every time I bitched about my parents I felt bad about bringing it up in front of her. Out of everyone I knew, she got it the worst. Her father had killed her mother right in front of her. He came home for dinner, pulled out the gun, shot her in the head and turned it on Rory as she sat at the dinner table. Rory said she only said one thing to her father when he aimed it at her. She told me she had thought about screaming and crying, begging for her life, and she almost did. Instead, she didn't make a sound. She simply stood up from the table and walked toward her father who was holding the gun, pointing directly at her. She was only nine years old and knew she was going to die. So she said what she had always wanted to say to him. "I didn't ask you for anything."

He stood there holding the gun to her head, not saying a word. He turned it on himself at the last minute, leaving Rory orphaned or 'better off,' as Rory put it. The shit she must have gone through. The things she saw. The fact that her father had screamed at her and her mother every night for years about the fact that he had to support them. It was a nightmare she only spoke of twice since I had known her. Rory, so full of life, so optimistic, was my hero. I had nothing like that happen to me and I felt jaded by the world already. I knew having her around would somehow rub off on me. And to an extent it had.

I became an optimist right along with her, except when it came to matters of the heart. I had to shake my thoughts of her standing there with a gun to her head away from me. I felt an uncontrollable shiver run down my spine accompanied by an involuntary shake.

"You have a ghost moving through you, Nadine?" Spencer said, the corners of his lips turning up into an amused grin.

"What?" I asked, slightly dazed.

"You know, when you shiver like that. It's an old wives' tale that a ghost is running through you. By the way you were moving it looked like the ghost of James Brown."

"Who is James Brown?"

"Oh, oh you're kidding, right?" Spencer asked hopefully.

"No, no clue." He did sound kind of familiar.

"She's nineteen, Spencer," Ellie reminded him.

"Tragedy, just when I forget how young you really are." He shook his head back and forth.

"Okay, so are you going to tell me? And I turn twenty in a matter of days, you ass."

"No, I will not. If you want to listen to nothing but the music of the 80's, 90's and up, that's you poisoning your own brain."

"Fine, I will figure it out."

Ellie and Rory giggled in front of us, obviously knowing who Mr. Brown was. I needed to know who this James Brown was and fast. No one was making a damn fool out of me.

Amy and Jack fought over the music again as we all talked nonstop about what we wanted to do and see in New Orleans. Amy made Jack listen to Mariah Carey and Luther Vandross sing *Endless Love* on repeat as punishment. Apparently it was their prom song. We laughed the first two times and started groaning when it became unbearable, threatening to jump ship. Amy laughed and laughed as Jack winced when she turned it up at the most powerful point and sang at the top of her lungs.

"Diana Ross and Lionel Richie's version is way better," Spencer said to me.

"Friends can listen to *Endless Love* in the dark." I giggled.

Spencer looked surprised at my knowledge of the song and then realization hit him that I was quoting a movie. I listened to Spencer speak the entire scene from *Happy Gilmore* that I had just quoted and I sat there in awe until he finished.

"Movies, too?" I said amazed.

"And books. It helped me prepare for law school."

"You are a total freak, Spencer Diamond."

"And you are a nerd, Nadine Rhodes," he countered playfully.

Conversation drifted from movies to food to our first sexual encounter. Jack told everyone to describe their first time in one word. We all laughed at Rory's two word reply, "hairy ass." Some of us protesting the picture forming in our heads as she spoke in great length. When it was my turn, I opened my mouth to say the word I had carefully thought of. "Normal," I said then paused.

"I guess normal?" I looked at Spencer for reassurance and he gave me an inquisitive look.

"Define normal," Spencer said, urging me on. Jack was pulling off the highway to a restaurant we had all decided on a few miles back. I saw him eye me in the rearview mirror.

"Do tell, Nadine," Jack said curiously.

"We dated for a month or two and when I had just turned sixteen. He was nineteen and I felt I needed to impress him, so I dressed the part. I put on a pink teddy and set my bedroom up in candles. He came in, ripped my teddy off and took me." I was too embarrassed to admit it was my father's room and mine was actually a horrible couch I had outgrown years before.

"Ripped your teddy off?" Spencer said, his face turning pale.

"Not like that. He just didn't stop to appreciate it. I guess he didn't like it or something. Anyway, he climbed on top and you know the rest."

"No, we don't," Rory said, turning her full attention on me. "You never told me this." I gave Rory the wide 'shut up' eyes and I continued.

"I wanted him to say he loved me. You know I was young and stupid and thought it mattered. So I said it to him and he just… I don't know, ignored me. He ordered me to lay down and you know." I got lost in thinking of the details and completely forgot I was in a car filled with people. "He had on this long shirt. I remember thinking it was the length of a nightgown. I wanted to make fun of him for it, but it was almost as if he was angry. He wouldn't kiss me or touch me like he did when he took me out. He wouldn't even take off his clothes. He looked at me like I was stupid when I told him I loved him. If you want the truth, he looked at me like he hated me and I was a waste of time.

"I didn't want to keep going, but I was already there and naked so I just let it happen. He climbed on top of me and I remember feeling ripped. Ripping—it was if he wanted to hurt me. I realized as he was grunting over me, I didn't like him at all. He was sweating so badly it was dripping all over me. It wasn't fun. I never heard from him again and I was glad. I'm assuming most girls' first time is like that. Awkward, uncomfortable and … bad."

"No," Rory said, her eyes filling with tears, "not like that, Nadine."

I looked up and the whole SUV was staring at me. Ellie's eyes were wide and she looked to Spencer who I studied next. "No, Nadine. That's not *normal*," he said quietly.

"Oh, no, no, no. Hell no. You guys stop looking at me like that. It wasn't rape and I am not so damn stupid I wouldn't know the difference. I know what the definition is, okay. I dressed up for it and I knew what I was doing. I never said the word no. Get those looks off your faces. Let's go eat. This is way too serious—too heavy. My first time was with a complete asshole. It's not news."

"You heard her, let's go." Jack beckoned and everyone followed, climbing out of the SUV though they were quiet.

I turned to Spencer whose eyes were way too loaded with questions. He wasn't moving from his seat to let me out.

"Smart people can reason their way out of anything," he said, opening the door to let the air in. "Tell me about the last guy you were with. What was that like?" he asked softly.

"Um, no."

"Try to tell me something." He looked at me with sadness in his eyes.

"Jace… He was good."

"Normal?"

"Yes, Spencer, normal. God, if you're going to make a big deal out of this—"

"Give me the details."

I climbed into his lap and straddled him. "Forget it. It's not a big deal."

"Okay, so if it's not give me details about Jace," he said, pulling my arms from around his neck. He wasn't going to let me deflect.

I opened my mouth to speak but couldn't think of one thing to tell him. I turned my head to the side and went completely blank. My anger began to swell and with it came my words.

"Don't shrink me, Spencer." It was a warning I hoped he would adhere to.

"You can't remember, can you? You don't want to remember. Don't you think that's a little odd?"

"Time to eat, Spencer." I felt the bile in my throat. God, how could I be so damn stupid to tell everyone that story?

"You can remember every detail of the day that asshole ripped your virginity from you years ago, but not the details of a guy you slept with a few days ago?"

"Yes, counselor. Two nights before I met you, if that's your question. I am not hiding anything."

"Are you safe with them? The guys you sleep with?"

"I always use a condom and … I can't have children."

"What?" he asked, cupping my chin and bringing my eyes to his. I met his with no emotion. It didn't bother me and I wanted him to see it.

"I can't have kids. My first gynecologist trip confirmed I couldn't. There was tissue from damage and other stuff."

"Jesus Christ."

"Look, it wasn't all that bad. He didn't hit me or demand I give it to him. He was rough—too rough. I just assumed that's how it was. He was just uncaring and rough, okay? It was consensual. I invited him."

"He intimidated you to make sure you would give it up. It's not okay, Nadine. It fucked you up."

"No, I chose this lifestyle and that's a choice I make every day. I do it to myself. And let me remind you again that I am trying to change that and you are really not helping." I rubbed myself over him, licking his ear, relocking my hands around his neck.

He took me off of his lap and brushed his lips across mine.

"I am not some victim!" I said, furious with him for making it seem so. I felt the lump in my throat and the pain of his rejection seared my flesh. Fuck this, all of this. Why the hell did this guy even care? Two days ago he was lifting my panties off in a bar.

"I can't just do this with you… Not like this."

"Oh, but it was fine when you were finger fucking me like crazy on the beach last night, or did you forget?"

"Jesus, Nadine, I have never wanted a woman so bad in my life. But let me make this clear, no matter how convenient this all is, you being the way you are and also that you are so beautiful and so fucking sexy, trust me my dick reminds me every five seconds, that doesn't make it right. It's there for me too, but there is always a choice to act on it."

"So you don't want me now? Why? Because I'm a poor pathetic whore? A slut, beat up?"

"That's just what you think and don't put words in my mouth, Nadine. I think you are incredible." He jumped out of the SUV, blocking me from doing the same as he turned to face me, pinning me to my seat.

"But pathetic. So we can't have fun now, right?"

"That's not it!" he said, pacing next to the truck while I glared at him.

I was defeated. I had no more to give. I lowered my voice to a whisper. "I haven't told Rory that I can't have… You know and it really doesn't bother me, so if you could just do me a favor and keep that between us. I don't know why I told you any of this. And I'm not lost on your comment that I'm fucked up. I know what I do is not the norm, but what happened didn't scar me.

"Spencer, you are wrong. You need to accept the fact that some women consider the affection and flowers pointless. We are built differently. Call me the Grinch of love, buddy. My romantic heart is three sizes too small. If you can handle that, we can have some fun. But if you can't, feel free to roam about the cabin. Ellie has eyes for you, ya know.

"I would truly love it if there were a reason I felt this way. I would totally love it. Maybe then I could relate more to other woman on some level, but I don't. You see it as some sort of glitch in me. I see it as this is the way it is. It doesn't bother me, don't let it bother you. Now, can we please go inside and try to have some fun? This is absolute bullshit and you are pretty much a complete stranger and know way too much about me."

"Maybe sometimes we need to bare our souls and see what we see in the eyes of strangers," he said, reaching for me. I dodged him and retreated back into the seat, staring at my toes.

"You want to know what I see?"

"No." I gave him a small smile as the terror crept up on me. I didn't want to know what the man who had completely consumed my senses in a matter of days thought of me. He was talking himself out of an invitation. If it was any indication of his reaction to me right now, he thought I was a lost, stupid and pathetic slut. I had no way of ever convincing anyone I knew what I was doing when I seduced these men. I am a villain. I am a villain and I enjoy it. Or I did. It had only just lost its flavor recently. It didn't mean my appetite was gone, it meant I was ready to move on. I was still guilty in every sense of the word. And the girl who had spent a lot of time and energy taking what didn't belong to her and toying with it was still very much a part of me. I wondered then what the next step would be. How I would move on from my routine when I got home. Everyone wanted to see the good in me and here I was in a parking lot with an invitation having to explain myself for the second time. I was beginning to regret my decision to come. I looked at Spencer who surveyed me from head to toe.

"I see a girl who had her innocence ripped from her by trusting a total piece of shit she wanted to love and who got hurt and decided to heal herself the wrong way."

"Nice. Jesus, are you done?"

"I see an insanely beautiful woman who wants to try again but is too afraid to admit it."

"WRONG! Listen, baby, I'm all yours for as long as this trip lasts. You can do whatever you want with me and I won't fall apart, I promise. Honestly, Spencer, it's not in me to be that girl you think I am. I hate all of it. I don't date. I have never been courted. I like sex. It's that simple. I can also do without you calling me beautiful."

"What the hell is wrong with calling you beautiful?"

"It's not a blessing, Spencer, it's a curse. I've been hated my whole life for looking the way I do. You think a beautiful woman doesn't know she is beautiful? Well I have news for you, she totally does. Even the women who don't flaunt it, they know. I can tell you half the time they don't flaunt it because they have been punished for it, and by other women. It's not a blessing at all. I would trade this face and body to be anyone else on any day to save the years of shit I had to deal with because of other woman and their eyes on me. I didn't graduate early because I wanted to. I did it to avoid them." Son of a bitch! I had to get out of here. This was way too much. Why didn't I just tell him my blood type and middle name? Why oh why couldn't I shut the hell up? I have never told ANYONE these things. I didn't want his damn pity. I wanted sex and all I was doing was revealing myself to him— revealing way too damn much.

He pulled me to him and refused to speak until I met his eyes.

"I also see a woman who is starving for the right kind of attention, but would never know because she's never had it."

"And what about you? Why don't you turn that finger inward?" I asked with a shaky breath.

"That's for you to do. You are my stranger." I looked to him and saw the look that only he gave me. It wasn't filled with pity or sadness, just recognition.

"Don't fall for it, Spencer. I'm not an innocent woman. You couldn't live with the things I've done."

"I'm doing just fine knowing what I do. I just can't do this thing with you and be okay with it, Nadine."

"What thing? We haven't done anything and this is different," I said, catching myself admitting too much. Again.

"It is, but I can do better."

"Better?"

"Come on." He lifted me out of the SUV and set me on the ground, keeping my eyes. "Let's eat." I could see his wheels turning and I let the conversation die as we joined them at the table and all eyes drifted to me. Great.

WE SPENT THE last leg of the trip quiet. We were all tired. Spencer placed his headphones on me and I looked at him puzzled. He smiled and took my magazine from my hands. He brushed a finger over my lips then roved his fingertips over my face, cupping my chin and tracing his thumbs along my cheek as the song started to play.

"I can do better," he mouthed as the song filled my ears.

"What in the hell is this?" I laughed as he grabbed the MP3 player and gestured for me to just listen. I turned my head to look out at dusk through the trees. Jack picked that exact moment to let the window down as the song filled my senses. It was old. I knew that. I had to stifle a giggle or two when I began to listen, but soon I was completely immersed in the melody, the words. It was beautiful. I felt the breeze lift my hair and turned to Spencer as it flew all around me. It was amazing. Spencer was amazing. He knew how to fill my senses with a simple song. This man was so ... cool. I smiled at him and nodded my head and his eyes gave me that knowing look. I watched the sun peek through the trees as Van Morrison sang about the mystic. My heart began to beat faster as the song got more intense. I loved it. I instantly loved it. I didn't know what intrigued me more about Spencer, the way he looked or the way he was. He had that ... that... Whoever the hell this man was, I was so thankful he was the one sitting beside me in that moment.

It occurred to me that Spencer was being just as honest with me as I was with him. I shook my head as he slipped his hand in mine and he took it away. I kept my eyes out the window. We had said a lot today, but now I knew he had decided to share something else, another part of him. Music spoke volumes for him when he couldn't and I secretly loved what he was saying.

Road trip confessions into the mystic

CHAPTER
Eleven

I T WAS NIGHTFALL when we arrived in New Orleans. We checked into the same hotel, this time getting three rooms so we could all sleep comfortably and Jack and Amy could have some much needed alone time. As far as the question lingering if Spencer and I would share a room and let Rory and Ellie have the other, we let it linger. The girls all dumped their luggage in the same room and got dressed together. Ellie insisted I try on a red dress she bought the previous day, saying it showed too much skin. I tried not to take it as an insult, seeing as how I had her height beaten by at least a few inches. It would be ridiculous on me, but as soon as the material sank on my skin and I looked in the mirror, I let the argument fall away.

"I knew it," Ellie gasped as she motioned the girls to come look in the bathroom. It was made of silk and flowed perfectly around me. It hugged my every curve and was just long enough to go mid-thigh.

"She looks hot, nothing new," Rory said, walking off uninterested.

"God, Nadine, you could be a model," Amy said sweetly, peeking around Ellie to compliment me. It was the perfect dress to christen the Big Easy. I laughed at the thought. Maybe Spencer wouldn't be able to resist me in this one.

"Thanks, Amy, Ellie. I love it. How much do I owe you?"

"A full confession when you get Spencer naked." We gave each other a knowing smile and Amy blushed and walked away.

"Amy?"

"Yeah," I heard her say as she rounded the corner, sticking her head back in the bathroom.

"Can I ask you something?"

Ellie winked at me and walked out of the bathroom, giving me alone time with Amy. I turned to her. She really was what I could only describe as a doll. Though she had Jacks pale skin and blonde hair, her lips were perfectly shaped and overly full. She looked like a blonde Snow White. Her hair was perfectly set around her face and she had a small dainty figure. Her skin was creamy and flawless. She would never know how jealous I was of the way she looked. She would never believe me.

"What is Spencer like at home?"

"The same, I guess. We don't see him a lot. He takes care of his dad and barely has time to juggle the few cases he takes. Stressed, definitely more stressed back home. So you like him?"

"It's obvious I do. I'm just not sure why."

"Trust me, honey, he has blazed a trail across Philadelphia of women who ask themselves the same question. He was always beautiful. Always. Anywhere and everywhere we go they drop like flies and when they recover its total mayhem. I couldn't help but overhear the talk the last couple of days. If you're a girl who likes her fun, you have met one hell of a man to play with."

"Wow, so he's the whore of Philadelphia?"

"No, not anymore. He was. I think his age and his father and the fact that he hasn't been able to start his practice have tamed him. Not in a good way, though. He could be doing so much more by now."

"I'm sorry I bothered you. I was just curious."

"For the record, I like you. I wish I was a little more uninhibited at times. I try, especially being married, but I guess I'm just a stick in the mud."

"Don't sell yourself short, Amy. They never show what happens at the castle when the prince wakes Snow White up."

She started laughing uncontrollably and then asked incredulous, "I remind you of Snow White?"

"Yes," I answered plainly.

She seemed touched at my answer and patted me on the shoulder. "You know I handpicked Ellie out for Spencer and I had half a mind to be a real bitch to you at first, but this is better. And we love Rory."

"Thanks, Amy, really. Thank you." There was no other way to say it. At home we felt like a couple of outcasts, here we felt at home with our new friends and travel companions.

"Just … give him hell, Nadine. He deserves to finally get a dose of his own medicine. He has tortured a few close friends of mine. It's been fun to watch him squirm around you."

"That's something I'm extremely good at." I winked at her and she smiled and shook her head.

I let my hair down and straightened it perfectly. It had lightened a little in the sun in some areas but remained a dark, deep red in most. I put on a tall heel and some glitzy fashion jewelry one of the girls had lent me, including a necklace that hung in doubles clear down to my waist. It was very 'New Orleans' from what Ellie said.

Less than an hour later we met the guys at the hotel bar. Jack took one look at the job I had done on Amy and tried to walk her back up to the room. She laughed hysterically at his reaction and he planted his hand on her ass and kept it there. Spencer was turned away from me talking to Ellie when I took the bar stool on his left side and ordered a dirty martini. I tossed it back and started with the olive. When he finally turned to me he did a double take.

"Nadine." It was a prayer. I winked at Ellie behind him as I turned fully on my swivel stool to face him.

"Spencer." I stood up, ignoring his mouth which was slightly ajar.

"Where should we go first?" Ellie asked, the excitement evident in her voice.

"Pat O'Briens," Jack said, keeping his hand on Amy's ass as Ellie joined me to walk in front of Spencer. I turned to find Rory engaged in a flirty discussion with the bartender.

"Rory, we're leaving."

She leaned over and whispered into his ear and he nodded enthusiastically then turned to me with a smile waving us off, but not before ogling me from head to toe. A curse, I thought. There is no way I would tell Rory what that asshole had just done seconds after she probably propositioned him. God, how I hated that, but it also made me a hypocrite. If it was someone else's date, I would have jumped on it. I shook my head in disgust and grabbed Rory's hand.

"Love you, Rory. Ready to have fun?"

"Yep and I brought the camera!" I saw her check the battery as we all groaned.

I hadn't seen an inch of the city and I felt the excitement hit as soon as we exited the hotel. I also felt the humidity. It didn't matter. We had entered a different world.

Our hotel was right next to Bourbon Street, so naturally we made our way there. The bright neons caught my attention as well as their strange contrast to the age of the city itself. It was almost circus like with an old world feel. It was surreal. I felt the excitement pulse through me and I paused to take a deep breath, noticing Spencer had stopped as well. I turned to him and gave him a huge smile that he returned. Jack and Amy were tourist veterans of the city so we followed their lead, stopping first at The Cat's Meow and then to what Jack named the world famous Pat O'Briens.

There were two huge bars on each side of the crowded room. The middle was filled with cocktail tables with literally no room for dancing, though people were trying their best. I was in total sensory overload. It looked like a scene from the movie *Gremlins* that I had watched as a kid where the bad Gremlins take over the bar and are swinging from the ceiling. The bartender on our side of the bar screamed at us to "Order now." We all thought quickly, and as soon as our drinks were delivered, she jumped on top of the bar and kicked off karaoke by singing with the bartender on the opposite side. It was an old eighties song I recognized.

"Lame," I said shaking my head.

"Don't knock this music. It's what our parents fell in love to," Spencer whispered in my ear. He was almost fully flush on me and I had been so preoccupied with the sights and sounds of New Orleans I was only now taking him in.

He had on jeans and a black short sleeve shirt. He smelled like soap and heaven and had a fresh shave, making his dimples more obvious. I didn't have time to appreciate it because I was pulled up onto the bar by the bartender who had just finished her song. Spencer helped, getting a good handful of ass as he assisted her in her struggle to get me up. The whistling was ridiculous and my entire crew didn't bother to help me with my screaming protest. She called me out immediately.

"It's 80's night, baby. What's your flavor?"

I shook my head no vehemently and heard a room full of protests. I attempted to get down but was stopped by the bartender.

"Sing or get out bitch," she spoke directly into the mic, humiliating me as the crowd cheered for my slow execution.

Whoa. I looked around quickly and realized it must be the norm. I had better get with it and pick something quick. I gave her the only song I could think of, a song my mother played over and over on the record player when I was little. She jumped down and set up my song. A line of guys came up to me offering shot after shot, which I gladly took off their hands. By the time I took shot number four, Spencer was taking them out of their hands, angrily shaking his head no. He gazed at me with shock and awe, and with that look I felt more confident. I saw Rory rip out the camera and gave her the love finger as the first rift of the song came on. I looked to Spencer who mouthed Blondie and I nodded at him as we shared a little moment. Next thing I knew I had a mic in my hand, my shots hadn't hit and I was up singing *The Tide Is High*.

They booed me profusely, so I did what any woman with a shitty voice would do. I made it sexy. I started moving around, swinging my hips back and forth, dancing like I was balancing bananas on my head. I really had no talent for dancing, either. The crowd went wild when I started swaying. My shots hit after a minute or so and I began to really belt it out, trying to win them over. I had a crowd of guys follow me as I stepped over the tip jar and made my way around the bar. I sang the last thirty seconds to Spencer, who was smiling so broadly at me his whole face lit up. He chuckled as I imitated the voice squeak at the end of the song. I jumped onto him and handed the mic back to the bitch bartender.

"That really was the worst thing I have ever heard. You sounded like a dying Jonathan."

I laughed as he let me down and I looked to Rory who seemed to be messing with her camera and gave me the thumbs up. Ellie was pulled up next and started belting out Joan Jett. Ellie was on a bar, in New Orleans, singing. What a different damn world we had entered. When Ellie's song was over, she was held up by waiting admirers. Jack and Amy had managed to find a table covered in used glasses and we all gathered around sipping our drinks. Jack refused to let Amy out of his sight unless she had to use the bathroom. Even then he watched like a hawk. Amy would be having a good night. I laughed as Rory and Ellie walked with her to go.

"What's so funny?" Spencer asked, noticing me looking on at the girls.

"Snow White's going to get a spanking tonight. The good kind." I nodded toward Jack who was watching for his wife long after she was out of sight. Spencer nodded as if he understood and toyed with Jack who was looking slightly uncomfortable.

"Amy is setting up wood all over the place tonight, bro."

"Fuck you, Spencer. That's my *wife*."

"Sorry. Just pointing out that she looks pretty damn good."

Jack just smiled as he caught onto his friend's goading and threw a stray bar peanut at him.

"So this is New Orleans, huh? Like one huge party," I said, addressing Spencer.

"It's more than that. Much more. There are two sides. I'll show you."

"My own personal tour guide?" I leaned in and watched him watch me.

"I can't call you beautiful and it kills me. What can I call you?"

"Nadine."

"Nadine," he said appreciatively.

"I've had four shots, Spencer. You match that and we might be able to tackle the scenarios going on in your head tonight."

"Your wish is my command, but first let me show you something." He walked me a few feet toward the back and I saw it immediately. It was a water fountain that had flames flowing throughout. I was instantly intrigued. He opened the French door that led out into the courtyard where it sat, very out of place—a huge cup of water and fire standing at least fifteen feet tall. There were lanterns lit, burning against the building in the distance. It was surreal, like we had stepped back in time, and yet everything surrounding us was modern. It was an odd mix and I loved it.

"It's amazing what can happen when you say yes," I said, letting Spencer know I was thankful for the invite to New Orleans. I studied the fountain, enthralled that something as simple as that brought me so much joy. "Two different worlds," I repeated and turned to Spencer who eyed the fountain next to me.

"I'm going to hold your hand now, Nadine, and you're going to let me," he said, never taking his eyes off of the water filled with fire.

"I told you, Spencer, I don't need that stuff."

"Well I do."

I let him take my hand and hold it. He gently rubbed his thumb over the top and I felt all my numb nerve endings from the shots come alive. This man… This man has got it. Whatever it was, he swam in it, drank it and resembled it. I was instantly ready to invite him again.

Rory burst through the door screaming, "I'm next. Billy Idol, bitches!"

"Oh dear God," I chuckled as Spencer led us through the crowd to witness Rory's horrible rendition of *White Wedding*. No matter how hard I tried, I couldn't concentrate on anything but Spencer's hand that never let go of mine all night. We drank until the early hours and the girls and I hooked arms, claiming our undying love, as we took turns throwing up on the way back to the hotel room we all gathered in. The guys simply laughed as our love fest continued until the room was quiet. I was not going to pass out tonight. I had actually sobered up a bit after my spill at the corner of Bourbon and God knows where.

I furiously brushed my teeth and made sure Ellie and Rory left to take the other room Jack and Amy weren't occupying. Spencer look confused as he turned around and saw we were alone, then a slow smile graced his face. I walked toward him—kicking off my heels along the way— in what I hoped was a sexy saunter. It wasn't. Because halfway through the sentence I was going to say, which was "Tonight game over," I only got through "Tonig— before tripping over Amy's huge suitcase and smacking my head on the fridge door, going down like a ragdoll.

Spencer was hysterical and concerned at the same time, if that was even possible. He couldn't get the alright out of 'are you alright?' and I moaned over and over at the throbbing in my head from the fridge. He brought me to face him and I had tears streaming down my face from laughing with my head in the carpet. He gripped my shoulders and sobered suddenly.

"Are you really hurt? Nadine?"

"Yes, Spencer. I mean no, I'm fine." I was humiliated. This would not make Amy proud. I had failed to teach the whore of Philadelphia a lesson. Instead, I was a laughing stock. Spencer lifted me to my feet and hugged me to his chest, which I hated. I pushed away from him and tore off my dress in one swift movement. That shut him up. I lifted his t-shirt, pulling it over his head and pulling it over mine. His eyes were heated, but not enough. The look was not coming tonight. Not with him picturing me spilling my shit in that hotel room. Damn it. He seemed to understand and flipped on the TV. He walked over to the king size bed, pulled back the covers and laid down, cupped the back of his neck with his hand, then patted next to him in an invitation to join him. Oh this was bull-shit, I thought as my thoughts began to blur. I was still too drunk. I laid my head in the crook of the arm that he offered as he covered me with the nice cool comforter. I could feel the ache in my feet began in unison with my pounding head, but the bed made up for the discomfort quickly as I melted into his scent and the comfort of his arm. I heard Spencer mouth his disappointment with a "Damn it" and smiled as I drifted off.

Karaoke
a fountain of fire
luggage cock block

CHAPTER Twelve

THE NEXT MORNING I woke up to an empty bed and saw a note from Spencer on the dresser.

> Tease,
> I hope you didn't trip trying to retrieve this message. When you wake up, join the girls. Jack and I are out getting breakfast.
> PS You are a horrible lay.

I laughed out loud and threw on some comfy pajama pants and a loose fitting bra. I had no intentions of doing anything today, though I knew we only had a few days left. I swallowed an entire water bottle and headed to the girl's room, finding them all huddled in one bed, moaning and bitching. I fit right in, lifting the covers to join them. Rory raised her eyes to me and I quickly shook my head with a disappointed no. I hadn't gotten the goods from Spencer. She smiled briefly then lifted her hand to her head with a groan. We sat in silence mourning our brain cells and watching *Thelma and Louise*. We barely looked up when Jack and Spencer came in toting a huge amount of breakfast.

"Thanks, guys," Amy said, her voice hoarse as she lifted up only to grab whatever food was in the bag and shove it in her mouth.

"Baby, you can have whatever you want today." Jack beamed at her with a knowing smile.

"Silence is golden," Amy chimed. "And the curtains, draw them immediately." I gave Amy a knowing smile as she blushed. I had given her a few tips on how to drive a man insane last night. I was sure she had used them all.

The guys looked at each other as Rory, Ellie and I grabbed a handful of the breakfast sandwiches and began to devour them. Spencer gave me a wink and brushed my leg with his fingertips as he stood next to the bed.

"The girls are useless today, bro," Spencer said, eyeing me as I stuffed half a sandwich in my mouth.

"Guys, go and don't let the door hit you where the good lord split you," Ellie said, muffled only by her sandwich. We all cracked up and motioned them on to leave us in our misery. Spencer gave me a look of remorse as they left us to wither away. At noon we slowly emerged from our coma, all of us passing out immediately after Thelma and Louise took their plunge. We all woke with one thing on our minds: a shower.

We had three rooms so I went to the one Spencer and I shared the night before and claimed it. Rory was fast behind me, bitching that she wasn't paying for the room so she would suck it up. I laughed at her still whining as I stripped. I felt great, better than great. I would take it easy on the booze tonight, so I could be hard on Spencer. I had a goal and had no intentions of going soft on it. After my shower, I heard Spencer talking to Rory, so I decided to play dumb and come out wearing nothing. I saw his eyes widen and Rory's knowing smile as she muttered something and took the bathroom.

"Thanks for last night," I said, wrapping the towel around me, seeing his disappointment.

"Why don't you come over here and thank me."

He was sitting in a desk chair, looking heavenly in shorts and a white t-shirt. His legs parted slightly and he patted his lap. Everything about his demeanor made him irresistibly dangerous.

"No."

"No?"

"No."

"Well that's a terrible way to thank a man," he said with a small amount of humor in his voice.

"Sorry," I said dryly, feigning indifference.

"Get over here," he said in a commanding way and I was instantly hot.

I dropped the towel again, sliding on my skimpiest pair of lace panties, leaving my breasts bare and slid a flowered sundress over my head.

"No."

"Nadine, you are going to regret that."

I smiled and walked over to the table, picking up his iced tea.

"Love it. Can I have it?" Without waiting for an answer I sucked it dry making a slurping noise.

"You will pay for that, too."

"Wow, looks like I'm in trouble." I giggled as he wrapped his arms around my waist and dragged me to his lap.

"So flowers on top and the devil underneath?"

"Pretty much sums it up."

"I understand your game, girl."

"Are you ready to play today, Spencer?"

"Baby, am I ever." He slid his hand up my thigh, making no attempt to slow himself, and reached my panties in seconds, circling me and making me cry out suddenly. He nibbled on my lobe before sticking his tongue into my ear. "You're wet already." I moaned louder, still hearing the water going, and knew we were safe. I waited on his next move.

He kept circling, bringing me to the point and then slid his hand underneath my panties, dragging my slickness over me. I turned my head and bit his shirt, grabbing a little skin with my teeth while furiously rubbing my ass over his erection, up and down as he circled me. His breath was just as ragged as mine. Still teasing me with one hand, he used the other to roam my chest, cupping my breast and pinching my nipple gently. I moaned out to him as his tongue flicked in and out of my ear. Neither one of us was winning this round; it was time.

I turned on him suddenly and sank to my knees, freeing him. I took a little time to admire his hard length. I showed my appreciation by taking him fully in my mouth. Within seconds I was swallowing his hardness completely and saw him exhale as he titled my chin up to meet his eyes. There—already—was the look I craved. He reached in his pocket and grabbed a condom and ripped it with his teeth. I studied his sex in awe and found myself sad at the loss of the sight of him as he fitted himself with the condom. I gave him one quick stroke of my hand and climbed onto his lap and positioned myself. He grabbed my hips, ready.

"Jesus," he breathed across my parted lips. I put the tip of him in me and heard the water shut off. Spencer cursed a string of obscenities as I let out my own, sliding my underwear in place as he fastened his throbbing back into his pants.

"You are so going to pay," he said as he stood up quickly and walked out of the room.

I was too consumed with what almost happened to laugh at his quick retreat to relieve himself. It had been too much. I was all too tempted to follow and let him take me somewhere, anywhere, the elevator, the staircase, a freaking bathroom. Truth be told, we were both enjoying this amazing game of cat and mouse, but enough was enough. We were total idiots at this point for missing any chance we had at being alone. I was positive we were now in agreement.

I would make sure tonight there were no interruptions. The ache inside my thighs had me uncomfortable and bitchy. Rory circled the corner and met me, flaming and puffed up.

"Damn, Rory, you couldn't take a longer shower!"

"Well, looks like you struck out again, Nadine." She laughed. I picked up a brush off the bed and smacked her ass with it hard.

We spent less than an hour on our appearance and met up with everyone in Jack and Amy's room. Once we all gathered again, we headed to the nearest place for crawfish. Apparently, this was the place to get it. I wasn't fond of the idea. As we sat ordering beers, I was having second thoughts. I knew what they were, but they didn't appeal to me. Not at all. I had taken it easy on the beer as Spencer sat across from me, screwing me every which way from Sunday with his eyes and I did the same.

"We should do it again, what we did last night. Exactly the same way," Jack snickered, eyeing his wife.

"Shut up, honey. Really, if you don't, it will never happen again," Amy said, her face lighting up. I gave her a knowing smile and looked at Jack who seemed to be glowing. Wow.

"I don't freaking think so," Rory and Ellie muttered simultaneously at the recall of their pounding heads this morning. I was smiling along with them until an entire trough of crawfish was dumped onto the table before us. They had heads, and eyes, there were *eyes* on the damn things. NO, NO, NO.

"Hell yes," Jack said, digging in and taking one by the head and sucking it dry. Everyone looked excited and I quickly stood up.

"I…" I stifled a gag. "I won't be able to join you for this one guys. Those look really… Ya'll enjoy that. I'll be at the shops. Call me, Rory." I covered my mouth as I ran from the table and as usual, everyone laughed at me.

"Oh come on, honey. You can inhale crab legs, you've got this," Jack said, his voice growing distant as I got the hell out of there.

"How about a burger?" Spencer said, catching up with me.

"Jesus, that's disgusting. I will eat a rare steak, but I damn sure don't want its eyes on me when I do."

"It's not for everyone." He laughed as he led me out the door.

"He sucked the brains out of that thing, Spencer!"

He laughed again at my disgust and grabbed my hand. I looked up to him and chuckled. I saw a clock over an awning in front of us that read five o'clock and was quickly saddened. I had lost half a day being hungover. Not worth it. I made a mental note to chill out. I saw a sign directly beneath the clock that made me smile.

"Come on." I dragged Spencer across the street and he eyed me with a smirk as we made our way into the store.

"Voodoo?" His lips twitched in amusement as we reached the door.

"Why the hell not? I mean no I don't practice, but it's fascinating, isn't it? The dark side." I wriggled my eyebrows and he laughed as we stepped up into the mustiest smelling shop I had ever been in. It reeked of sweat and incense, the latter trying to mask the stench, but doing a horrible job. My distaste for the smell echoed on my face and I turned to see Spencer's nostrils flaring as well.

There was a lady behind the counter turned around watching a tiny TV. Some voodoo shop, I thought. All it had in it was tiny trinkets that looked to be commercially made. This was a tourist trap. Only an idiot would endure the smell to buy a replicated mini voodoo doll. I looked at

Spencer and nodded for the door, but our unspoken quick escape plan was interrupted.

"Oh, chérie, sumthing you looking for?" The woman's hair was white, like ghost white, like the color of chalk, and tucked underneath a frumpy knitted hat. It must have been at least a hundred degrees outside. I tried to keep my fascination with her appearance to myself. Her skin was the exact opposite of her hair, dark as night and looked to be as smooth as silk. Her eyes were a color I couldn't describe. I had no doubt when she was younger she was never left alone. She had a dark look about her, but the tone of her voice was genuine, sweet.

"No, just browsing."

I gave Spencer an apologetic look as we were forced further into the store to save face. I began closely looking at a shelf full of ridiculously marked ingredients for spells and rolled my eyes. I started browsing through books titled *Voodoo for the Modern Man* and *Authentic Voodoo Rituals*. They might as well have read IDIOT, you are an IDIOT for believing this total bullshit.

I was sure the Voodoo practice was real, but nothing in the shop was. It got me no closer to the dark side and I was a little relived. I was both fascinated and afraid of the dark side. I once bought a Ouija board just to turn around and throw it away an hour later. I was fascinated by evil, or the evil that people do. I studied every single notorious serial killer as a young teen, trying to figure out what made them tick. Voodoo, witchcraft, and all of the other elements that were depicted as evil had nothing to do with any of those cases. They were simply insane, and their nature was evil, and typically methodical. It had nothing to do with believing in anything. Still, all facets of what was considered evil fascinated me.

After a few painful minutes of browsing as the woman watched both Spencer and I carefully, I turned to thank her and she turned back to her TV, not giving us another glance. I walked to the door to find Spencer frozen at the threshold, a look of pure terror on his face. I followed his eyes to find him staring at a black cat who was clearly irritated. It was hiked up on all fours, tail high in the air ready to pounce. The cat was huge. It had to weigh at least twenty-five pounds. Spencer was paling by the second and I heard the cat's hiss.

"Ma'am, your cat seems to be terrifying my friend." Spencer's head refused to look away. He didn't move, but he was clearly going through the scariest moment of his life.

The lady approached the cat and with the wave of her hand it went completely lax and disappeared behind a shelf. I was now free to laugh and I did so with so much ferocity, I couldn't stop. Spencer turned on his heel and hauled ass out of the shop and I followed, howling and choking. When we got outside he was completely covered in a layer of sweat that didn't have a damn thing to do with the humidity.

"You don't hate cats, you're terrified of them." I went into another raging bout of laughter.

It took Spencer a few minutes to recover. When he finally did, he started in with a string of curses and then directed his anger toward me. I backed up, still laughing, my hands up as he cornered me into the shop's wall.

"You see this scar?" he said, pointing to the one I noticed over his eye a few days ago.

"Yeah so, a cat did that?"

"Fucking A right a cat did that. T-Rex, our family pet. I was into dinosaurs when I named him. Anyway, that was the worst animal on earth. He attacked me while I slept!"

"Okay, Spencer, it's over. I'm sorry I dragged you into the scary cat shop."

"Not fucking funny, Nadine. Quit laughing!" I let out another chuckle and grabbed his hand.

"Sorry, it's just you don't seem the type to be scared of much."

"Yeah, well have a cat scratch your face up at six years old in the middle of the night and see how you feel about it." He chuckled a little, but I could tell it wasn't really genuine.

The gang joined us for a few hours of sightseeing, but Amy and Jack retreated back to the hotel after a while at Jack's insistence. I heard her playfully refuse him as he fully grabbed her ass in plain sight as they walked off. Amy turning back to say they would meet us for dinner.

CHAPTER Thirteen

I WATCHED A HORSE drawn carriage slowly move past us, mesmerized. This was truly a dream. I looked at Ellie who was totally unaffected by the insane display of architecture and history. She was messing with her phone and talking to Rory. I couldn't figure out why they weren't as captivated. Did they not see the beauty of this incredible city? Spencer smiled at my reaction and grabbed on to the back of the covered carriage, gave me the shush finger, then waved me to join him. I was not quiet.

"Are you crazy?"

He continued to wave me on and I was losing ground quickly. I looked at Rory who gave me a knowing smile.

"Well of course I'm going to do it."

"Meet you at the hotel at dusk?" Rory asked.

"Done."

I took off running and watched Spencer's eyes light up as he saw me getting close. I could hear the tour guide talking to the couple inside the carriage as I approached, trying not to giggle as Spencer hauled me up so delicately it would seem like I was just another bump in the road.

We toured behind the carriage for a good half hour without people drawing attention to us. They seemed entertained with our sneaky tour. I smiled at Spencer who looked at me with a mix of mild amusement and hunger. I traced his lips with my finger and kissed him for the very first time, surprising him and taking his tongue into my mouth to suck it sweetly. We were interrupted seconds later by the Creole voice of the tour guide as he apologized to his passengers.

"Whoo wee, sorry about that folks. It's definitely a job hazard."

We couldn't figure out what he was referring to until seconds later the horrible smell hit us and we saw a trail of horse shit underneath us. To our absolute horror we burst out laughing uncontrollably and had to make our escape while still hysterical. Spencer landed firmly and held out his hands as I held my stomach and wiped my tear filled eyes and jumped quickly. We saw the couple who had paid for the tour peek out with their bodies twisted and give us a wave. No one ever got pissed in New Orleans it seemed. I laughed and waved back at the couple then looked at Spencer who was no longer laughing.

"You look the best like this, Nadine."

"Like what?"

"Off guard."

"Thanks?"

"You're welcome." He pressed his lips to mine and wrapped his arm around my shoulders, walking me to the sidewalk.

We spent the next hour grubbing on hot dogs and walking around The Quarter. Something in Spencer had … changed. Something had awakened in him. With each hour that passed in New Orleans he had become more alive. He kept grabbing my hand to mildly assault me with feverish kisses in a corner, behind a tree, in an abandoned alley. His kiss grew more intense with each display. I could feel the vixen in me about to step up to the plate. For now I would take whatever he offered. Soon, I thought. I had to have him. I reminded myself this might be a game, then scorned myself for thinking otherwise. I didn't care what it was. Spencer had my full attention and I had his.

"So tell me about your dad," I said casually as we strolled through the streets with absolutely no destination in mind.

I saw him cringe and then hesitate. I felt like I had sucked the fun out of the entire day with my words and regretted them, but looked at him expectantly anyway.

"You remember the movie *Arthur* with Dudley Moore?"

"Vaguely."

"Well he's like that, but not the funny version."

"Oh." I studied his face for a minute and decided to pry a little more. "You are too damn young to be taking care of him already. Your life should have started years ago, or what should have been your life. Why can't you walk away?"

He looked at me as if he was disgusted. "It's so easy to judge, huh, Nadine?"

"No. I'm really not, I swear."

"I've already given up on him, Nadine, but I can't let go. He's the only person besides Jack and Amy in the world that I love. Anyway, let's talk about something else."

"Not yet."

"Drop it." It wasn't a question, it was an order. Instead of pissing me off it intrigued me. I was close to getting what I wanted.

"You can't even properly practice law. I overheard you telling Jack, and Amy told me as well, because you're too busy scraping your father off of the streets of Philadelphia. How long will you let this go on?"

I could see him visibly shaking now, his anger beginning to show on his face.

"I am your stranger," I said softly.

He looked at me puzzled, then remembered his own words.

"Yes you are." He moved in to kiss me and I turned my head.

"Deflecting," I chimed a little too forcefully.

"Nadine, leave it alone. It's not a problem I can solve with the snap of my fingers."

"If you do nothing, nothing changes," I said, offering him the truth.

"Again, with the levels shit," he muttered, pretending to be distracted.

"It's not shit. It's all true. And it's mostly common damn sense, Spencer. Don't make fun of my principles because it's convenient for you. Now you give me one truth about this and I will drop it."

"One truth?" He knew exactly what I was asking, so I didn't bother helping him.

"You heard me." I pressed in.

I saw him pause with an automatic response on his lips and change his mind.

"No," I said loudly, making him squirm a little, "I want to hear exactly what you were about to say."

He looked at me exasperated and finally gave me an answer. "If I stop, he will die."

"That's part of it," I added "What's the other part, Spencer? The truth?"

"He will die anyway." His voice was shaking now and I could see he was angry at me for it, "No matter what I do."

He walked away from me then to look around for his escape. There was none and I wanted him to see that. I also wanted to show him that I was there, so I grabbed his hand and laced our fingers and saw the surprise on his face. He gave me a soft look, one I hoped matched my own. I was hoping that he didn't see sympathy, just someone who cared. God, why did I care?

"Spencer, I could never turn my back on my father, either, but I know this much. If he loves you like a father should, he has already worded your escape to you a thousand times, hasn't he?"

I saw a single tear roll down his face and he didn't hide it. It made him seem even more human to me. I grabbed it with the tip of my finger and waited for him to respond.

He gave me a simple, "Yes."

"And what was it?" I saw torment on his face as he looked around. This man was showing me his most vulnerable side and I didn't want to screw it up. I felt my chest fill with lead as he finally faced his fear.

"Let me go, son."

He held his head up and fisted his eyes, stifling his emotion, and I quickly walked him onto a quiet street. Once there, I walked away from him to let him gather his thoughts, wrapping my fingers around an iron gate to view the well-kept garden behind it. Several minutes later, Spencer wrapped his fingers around mine and I could feel his chest behind me. It was slow and paced. He was calm.

"I'm sorry I pushed you," I whispered.

He said nothing for a few quiet moments then turned me to face him, keeping his hands around the gates, locking me in.

"You are the perfect stranger," he whispered back, brushing my lips with his. I started shaking as his eyes bore into mine. "My perfect stranger."

He lifted me onto the brick wall just below the iron gate and forced himself between my legs. He ran his hands up each one of my legs, up my thighs and underneath my shorts, stroking his thumbs on my inner thigh, just a hair from my panties. A sharp intake of breath had my lips parting as he stared into my eyes, his thumbs stroking me stoked my desire. I braced myself, expecting him to move his thumbs further, but he hesitated, soaking in my need for him, reveling in it. I couldn't speak. I couldn't protest or beg. I was completely lost in the stroke of his thumbs and the heat emanating from his body and the look of pure lust in his eyes. It was the look I craved and so much more.

He continued to stroke the delicate skin and I felt my wetness and urged him on with the tilt of my back, but he stayed relentless in his pursuit to completely undo me. I kept my hands firmly planted next to me and gasped as his thumbs rubbed only once over my sex. Still he said nothing. He had reduced me to nothing with the stroke of his thumbs and the look in his eyes. I waited for him to speak first, but he remained silent. He wanted my submission, and right now that was the only thing I wanted to do. He leaned in and brushed his tongue along my lips while simultaneously brushing his thumbs across my sex. I let out a low moan and he backed away, lowering his thumbs to again stroke the inside of my thighs. The act begin to gnaw at me as the moisture between my thighs and the pulsing in my sex began to eat at me. He had no intention of freeing me.

He leaned in again and I turned my head, grabbing his hands from underneath my shorts and giving them back to him before forcing him away from the wall so I could escape. He let me out of his grasp and I got a few feet away when he grabbed me and flattened by back to his chest. He moved my hair out of the way and darted his tongue in and around my ear.

"Don't get testy."

"Don't flatter yourself, Spencer. Are you all done? Was that your best shot?" The words were a perfect choice, but the delivery was way too breathless and buried any chance I had of saving face. This round, like the last, and the one before that, had gone to Spencer.

His grin was almost as tempting as his touch. "Come on, beaut—Nadine, let's go get the girls. I think you've had enough of me."

He grabbed my hand again and I quickly realized all I wanted was to be alone with him, just a little longer. It was already dark and I had told Rory I would meet her. Frustrated, happy, tired, even hungover, there was no such thing as too much Spencer. Either way, this was the last round he was winning.

CHAPTER
Fourteen

WE MET THE crew at the hotel and Rory brought me to one of the empty rooms for a little alone time and debriefing.

"Rory, I'm sorry. I keep leaving you."

"Oh, screw that. I've never seen you so … entertained. Anyway, there is a reason why I brought you here."

"What?" I asked, curiosity piqued as I took in the excitement on her face.

"You know that bartender? The one downstairs?" she said excitedly, pulling out the makings of an outfit. I felt a story coming.

"Yeah, so are you hooking up?"

"Yes, tonight. I can't wait. God, he is so hot. His name is Rafe and he's taking me to a secret spot, you know for locals."

"Can you trust him, Rory?" I said harshly, making sure she knew I would worry.

"I know, I know. But you know where he works and what his name is, plus he seems harmless. Well, he might bite if I ask him to. It seems like he may have a little to offer a girl." She waggled her eyebrows up and down and excitedly turned on her heel for the bathroom after laying out what I was sure was an outfit suited only for Catwoman. This one must be new.

I shook my head as she started singing in a horrible octave the minute she hit the water. With Rory occupied, I quickly came to the conclusion I had a job to do and it was time to focus. I hadn't been that girl in almost four days and it was time for her to come out to play. Tonight, I wasn't going to win a round, I was going to win the game.

I felt the day's wear on me but pushed through as I picked out the tightest form fitting white dress I could find. There was a huge circle in the chest, heavily exposing both my breasts, and hung just a few inches short of exposing everything underneath. It had puffed sleeves reminiscent of the 60's, so I pulled out my thigh-high solid white go go boots to finish the look. Half an hour later, I had my hair tousled perfectly in a way that screamed 'I was just screwed but could go for another round.' I put a bright pink gloss on, added heavy shadow and I was ready. I turned to Rory for the okay.

"I know, you hate telling me if I look okay, Rory, but tell me anyway."

"Seriously, Nadine, Spencer is going to lose it. He doesn't have a chance."

"That's exactly what I wanted you to say."

"Well, then I did good." She grinned. "What about me?" I couldn't help but admire her perfectly manicured body in her skin tight cat suit.

"Honestly, you look hot, but like you're going to a Halloween party as Catwoman without the tail."

"That's exactly what I wanted you to say." We laughed and hugged until Rory pulled back to study me.

"You've been so happy on this trip. You smile all the time. You're even dating!"

"Not dating, playing a game," I said, studying myself in the mirror and excited for once to have the body I did. Batter up bitch, I mused. "It's just a game. But I like him, Rory. He's so cool and fun and funny."

"It's called dating. God, are you sure you're a college graduate? Let me explain something to you. Dating is a game, Nadine. It's a horrible game of Roulette. You have this little ball, let's say this is your heart, and you throw it out onto this scary wheel for all the world to take a piece. You have a one in thirty-six chance of landing on your number. Your chances are slim to find the right age for you in the first round, so you automatically lose. When you actually hit the right number, then you have to worry about landing a black or a red. Black being the good eggs and red being the obvious bad eggs. You following me?" I nodded, amused and dying for the rest of this explanation.

"So typically the girls like you and me go red all the way. If you had dated you would know this by now. These reds are the bastards with no clue how to treat a woman and are amazing in the sack, but they will screw your best friend when you aren't watching. He will max out your credit card while you wait for the next orgasm and you will love it … until it inevitably ends due to the fact that he's a red. The reds are overall nasty bastards, but they're the ones girls like you and I crave.

"Okay, now black is predictable. This is the guy that will hold your hand and tell you you're pretty, buy you flowers, introduce you as 'the one' to his parents. The black works hard for a living and will never make you wonder where he is. This is the good guy."

"Thanks for the explanation, babe. Really, did you think just because I don't date I wasn't aware of the difference between a bad and a good guy?"

"No, I don't think you know you're looking for the green."

"The green?"

"Yes, betting on the green. It's also called 'believing in God' in gambling terms. The green is a mix of both black and red. He challenges you in every way. He is the one who tames girls like us."

"Rory, where the hell do you come up with this shit?"

She simply zipped up her boots and gave me a knowing smile.

"Well, thanks for that, Rory. But seriously, this is a guy we met four days ago on a beach who lives in Philadelphia where he will be returning to in three days, so I really don't see this as dating."

"It's a step in the right direction at least, don't you think?" Rory looked at me hopeful.

"I think if we'd had one chance to sleep together in the last four days, you and I wouldn't even be entertaining this at all. It's sex. Simple."

"They should have named you after de river," she said in a horrible accent.

"What river?"

"De Nile." We both chucked as we gathered our purses, putting our lipsticks and cash in.

"Seriously, overthinking things ruins shit. I don't even know why I brought it up. Just have fun with him. But as much as you're resisting the good about all this, the stuff that has nothing to do with sex, it's there. The good is there, Nadine, and it's showing all over both your faces."

"He is different."

"Compared to what or to who? See that's my point. You have no clue. Stop fucking and start dating. Then you will really understand what you have going on."

"What?"

"Look, I love you. I don't have your book smarts or your amazing body, or your freakish way of observing what no one else can, but what I do have is a clue when it comes to this. Just … trust me and go with it."

"Okay," I said, nodding my head toward her and letting the word drag.

"Good, now I am going to have sex."

"No fair and I have to have feelings?" I said, mocking her lecture.

"No, you have to throw your little ball," she said, shutting the door behind us.

Amy and Ellie were headed down the hall toward us and let out cat calls as they approached.

"Good God you two look like you're ready to make a *Star Wars* porno," Ellie let out without thinking. Rory and I looked at each other and burst out laughing. Ellie had an apologetic look on her face as Amy scolded her.

"Sorry, it's just you two don't look…"

"You both look amazing, and surreal is what I think my idiot friend is trying to say," Amy said, eyeing Ellie with menace.

"I really didn't mean it to sound…"

"Ellie," Rory said loudly— always so loud this one was—"say what you mean and don't worry about how the rest of the world will interpret it. Seriously, unless you mean to be ugly or rude when you say it, don't worry about offending everyone. You'll be eating shit for the rest of your life if you do. I am flattered and I plan on making a *Star Wars* porno tonight. I'm leaving Leia here with you two so I can go do just that. Night ya'll."

She turned to me giving me a knowing smile and kissed Ellie square on the mouth, shocking her. Sweet Ellie jumped at the contact and then kissed her right back, making her lips smack at the separation. Rory patted Amy on the ass and walked away. I shook my head back and forth with a chuckle. Ahhhhhh, Rory.

"She has no idea how cool she is, does she?" Amy said, watching the elevator door close on her.

"None," I said, smiling proudly. "Shall we go girls?" I said excitedly. I was dying to get my sights on Spencer.

It had become routine for us to get ready separately and then meet up for what I guessed was the big reveal. I think we did it for Amy, honestly. She was becoming more loose lipped, her clothing a little more scant with each outing, and her and Jack seemed to be thriving because of it. Amy was a school teacher at home, but tonight she was a rock star's wife. Her petite body looked amazing in a little black dress and red stilettos. I was proud of her.

"Some heels you got there, Amy," I remarked as we made our way to the elevator.

"These are the shoes I always pack and never wear." She winked at me.

I was already smitten with the girls, but fell over to the love side with Amy and Ellie at that moment. They knew I was no saint, no one to look up to. They knew about my lifestyle and still they accepted me. I was sure in three days I would be miserable leaving them. I sized up Ellie who had gone all out in second skin jeans, pumps and a tight fitting tank. It seemed like tonight we were all on a mission.

We agreed to let the guys go early so we could take our time getting ready and met them at a crowded bar on Bourbon. There was a huge circular bar in the center of the room and cocktail tables on the outskirts. People were lined all around the bar, some dancing, others just waiting for their next drink.

"Let's dance first, ladies, then we can find them," I shouted as we waded our way through the unruly crowd. Usher started screaming *Yeah* and I felt my hips move as we continued to walk. Amy lifted her hand, pointer finger in the air, and led us out to a part of the floor with the most space. Ellie stood frozen as Amy started dancing and I joined her. Ellie, still a little shell shocked, began to move slowly and was instantly claimed by the guy behind her who grabbed her hips, pulling her to him. She wasn't able to see his face but chuckled at the fact he was so bold. She looked to me with a 'should I let him dance with me, is he hot' look and I gave her a thumbs up, because in truth, he was.

Amy and I were bombarded seconds later by two men who seemed to have no problem grabbing what they saw fit. I smacked a hand off my ass sweetly as I looked at my new partner and gave him a little no no gesture, but continued to dance with him until the song was over. Amy was close to full on slapping her dance companion when Jack burst through, grabbing her hand, showing her now confused partner her wedding ring by raising it to his face for clear view. Amy laughed as Jack bitched her off the dance floor and I zeroed in on Spencer at the bar.

His eyes were hot on me, but there was a beautiful blonde next to him speaking in his ear. She was making his dimples show. I hated the way I felt right then. It made me sick. This was jealousy. I knew what it was and why I was feeling it, so I decided to drink it away. I gave Spencer a sweet wave and headed to the other end of the bar. I didn't want to interrupt whatever he had going on. Plenty of fish … blah … blah… I was jealous as hell. I mean raging mad. He wasn't my boyfriend, we hadn't even had sex. I did everything I could to keep my gaze away from the end of the bar. I never let my eyes drift once. Spencer was definitely a red. RED. I hated him instantly for making me feel anything resembling jealousy. I avoided this shit. This is why. Confirmation, right there at the end of the bar, talking to a blonde with a ridiculous body.

"Whatcha drinking tonight?" The drawl in the voice told me I just landed myself a cowboy. Please let him be hot. I turned to my right, surprised to see a clean cut blond haired suit with a cowboy's voice. Even better. I gave him the come hither smile and nodded at his drink. "What are you having?"

"Old fashioned."

"I'll have one, too," I said sweetly.

He lifted his hand in the air for service and at the same time got a little closer to me. I surveyed him from head to toe while he was distracted with the bartender. Tall, hot, confident, he was a strong candidate for an invite. Maybe he was a red and could give me what I needed.

"Are you here with anyone?"

I suddenly felt guilty, but shook it off quickly. Spencer was nowhere to be found, and without Rory I was on my own. Ellie was still on the dance floor getting whiplash and I was sure Jack and Amy were having a heated discussion on her new behavior. I smiled at that. Another good night for the Mrs.

"Nope, no one."

He smiled and revealed a perfect set of teeth. I could smell his cologne and it was faint but pleasant. This guy took care of himself. We quickly started conversing and two drinks later we were getting quite comfortable. Spencer walked by solo, eyeing me as though what I was doing disgusted him. I gave him narrowed eyes and shrugged my shoulders, focusing my attention back on my new cowboy who was named Martin, oddly enough.

A few songs later, the music came to a sudden stop and the crowd was asked to step away from the bar. The lights went dark and the crowd protested. I felt hands on my waist and was pulled back into the crowd of onlookers.

"What the fuck are you doing?" Spencer's voice was like venom in my ear. There wasn't an inch of space between us. I felt the outline of his chest on my back and the heat from his hands on my hips.

"Having a good time with a new friend."

The crowd was still protesting as the bar was eerily dark. A single disco bulb lit the ceiling and the crowd erupted in praise. Then another and another until the ceiling was completely full of multicolored reflective light. It was beautiful, but I was having a hard time enjoying it. Spencer was not happy. Good. Both of us were jealous.

"Spencer, I saw a woman whispering in your ear and gave you space to make your play. I don't interfere with stuff like that."

"You think I wanted to fuck that woman?"

"I have no idea what you want," I whispered harshly.

He turned me to face him and I saw wrath in his eyes. It was the look. I instantly melted, rubbing my thighs together as I waiting for his next words. This was getting really good really quick.

"You're enjoying this?" Shit, he read me. Okay, new tactic.

"Look I came, I saw, you were busy, I got company. Can we drop it? You've obviously scared him off." I looked around for Martin and didn't see him anywhere. He definitely was a red.

"LADIES… GENTLEMEN, please don't be gentle, I like it rough!!" I looked up to the fattest man in drag I had ever seen. He hadn't bothered to hide his huge gut. He was covered in boa feathers and had on a tutu. And how the hell he had managed to get into high heels was beyond me. He had painted his face much like Tim in the *Rocky Horror Picture Show*. Things were getting downright freaky in New Orleans tonight.

"I am bringing the finest bitches you have ever seen out here tonight for the Dress and Guess contest. I want you alllll to do your best to support them. Now holler for the ones you like and scream for the ones you love, ya hear me? That's how we'll choose."

Spencer stood beside me now, his anger still apparent. I didn't care. If he wanted it made clear I was his date, he should have motioned me to him instead of letting me walk away. His fault.

"I am not your girlfriend, Spencer."

"No, you sure the hell aren't."

"Fine. I was hoping tonight we could get along." I started to walk away and felt his hand on my wrist.

"Stay your ass right where you are, Nadine."

"Now you're telling me what to do? I don't think so."

He gave me a look that could kill and my legs stayed put. The spectacle in front of us quickly took our attention. An entire line of women took up the circular bar, and the one standing directly in front of Spencer and I was captivating. Her hair was ridiculously long. Too long to be sexy, but it worked for her. Every single inch of her was perfect. My eyes traveled from her legs to her perfect small waist to her chest. Not only that, but when she turned to the side in her short and sassy sequined dress, her ass was amazing.

The disco lights illuminated her dress, making her sparkle from head to toe. What was most appealing was her face. It was truly beautiful, perfect high cheek bones and full lips. I was clearly not alone because Spencer stood looking at her, mouth gaping. She was truly that beautiful. I watched her closely, trying desperately to find a flaw. The girls rounded the bar, giving everyone a chance to take in their beauty. I watched her walk away from us and shook my head in amusement as I looked at Spencer.

"What is it, Nadine? She is gorgeous, probably the most beautiful woman I've ever seen."

He had to know that stung. I was sure he did. I felt the heat on my cheeks. He was still mad. Fine, I had an ace to play.

"She sure is, if you like men," I said, antagonism dripping from my voice.

"I would bet my dick on a stick that is not a man! Surely a woman as beautiful as you isn't afraid of a little competition."

"Well, I would hate to see your dick on a stick, Spencer, but how about a little wager for fun?"

"I'll bet anything. You're crazy. That's a woman. NO WAY is that a man."

"I win, you dance all alone on the dance floor, like I guess you expected me to do."

I was sure me accompanied on the dance floor is what started our little jealous tiff. His silence confirmed it. Talk about insecure. Pot, kettle, buddy.

"And if I win?" he said with so much confidence I almost felt sorry for him.

"Your call," I said, roving him in his plain white tee and jeans. Jesus, he would look good in a ketchup costume.

"You submit to me for a day."

"Fine."

"Whatever I say goes, Nadine."

"Fine."

"You're going to regret that."

"I'm not going to lose, Spencer."

The parade stopped and the announcer's voice came blasting through the speakers.

"Our guest judges have narrowed it down to five. If you weren't tapped on the shoulder, ladies, please leave the stage."

Our girl stayed put as the plot thickened. I had no idea how I was going to get this girl to admit she was a guy, but only seconds later I was saved the trouble.

"Okay, ladies. Lift them." The majority of the girls lifted their skirts, revealing everything underneath. The guys screamed and howled in appreciation. Our beauty smiled a devilish grin and lifted her glittered skirt, revealing a perfect pink penis. Spencer's curses were louder than those of the other protesting men and the gasps of the women around us.

"We have a winner!" The announcer stomped his way down to our beauty, handing her a trophy. The crowd cheered, including me who did rich girl golf clap inches from Spencer's nose.

"How the hell did you know?"

"The contest name was *Dress and Guess,* Spencer. Not to mention the walk, see." I nudged him to watch our lady in drag walk away. "It's practiced, not natural. And even though he had his Adam's apple shaved, I looked for it."

"That's crazy how you pick up shit like that." His anger was easing away from him as he studied me.

"Still the prettiest you've ever seen?"

"Shut up, Nadine."

"Get to dancing, Spencer."

As if on cue, the music started to play. It seemed I was running this night. I joined Amy and Jack at their table and Ellie introduced me to her distraction—it was either Chase or Gage, I couldn't hear. I turned to watch for Spencer to settle our bet. I caught him walking toward us and he stopped in the middle of some dancers on the floor. I suddenly felt terrible for him. What if he couldn't dance? Oh, he would hate me for sure. I didn't feel bad for long.

"Nadine, are you okay?" Amy chimed next to me.

I felt the sweat building on my forehead and between my thighs, but couldn't tell if it was me or the whore who was losing their mind. He moved with such precision, I couldn't maintain my composure. Jesus, it was the hottest thing I had ever seen in my life. I watched his hips move and looked around to catch the eye of every single girl in the bar staring at him in amazement. I felt my hands start to sweat as I started to answer, but Amy didn't give me a chance.

"Jesus, he's the best I've ever seen," Amy blurted out, just as shocked. Apparently, this was another hidden talent.

"Show off," Jack mused, laughing at Amy as he wrapped his arms around her, kissing her neck and gyrating his hips into her back.

"Fuck me," I murmured as a drove of women started making their way in his direction from all sides of the bar. He lifted his eyes to mine and I stood there, like an idiot, mouth gaping as he swayed his hips and moved his arms perfectly to the music. He gave me the come here finger and I instantly started moving my legs, in his grasp within seconds. He wrapped me into him, my back to his chest, dumbing down his talent to move our hips in sync. I saw the glare of half the woman at the bar and smiled broadly.

I lifted my arm, cupping the back of Spencer's neck, bringing his face to mine and his heated eyes to survey my chest. He slid his arms up and down my sides, over my waist, slightly brushing my chest but kept it clean. When the song was over he walked off of the floor, leaving me there breathless, but turned back to me a few steps away, his hand out.

He was screwing with me, again. This round went to both of us. And this time I didn't mind.

Beautiful girl with a penis
Thermal break down

CHAPTER Fifteen

A S THE NIGHT went on, I felt the tension in me growing for Spencer. Rachel, his new cling on, was practically wrapped around him. He continued to dart his eyes from her to me with a confident smirk as I sat there like an idiot waiting for him to do what I assumed he would do: give her the brush off. As he continued to make conversation, I gave up. I saw his hand stay on the seat close to touching her and I was done. This was complete and hypocritical bullshit. No wonder women in Philadelphia hated him. He was a shitty date, so to hell with throwing my little ball and all of Rory's advice. Spencer was a red. I waved goodnight to all of them and made my way out of the bar.

I spotted Martin talking to a girl at a table close by and grabbed his hand. There was no resistance whatsoever. He followed me and I took one last look at Spencer who was burning a hole in me. I gave him raised brows and an FU nod and turned to leave with Martin. I was not going to sleep with him, this I was sure of. It was time to push Spencer. And push him I did.

I heard Martin first as our hands were disconnected.

"What the hell, man?"

I turned to see Spencer's fury. He was inches from Martin's face.

"That's twice tonight you have touched what's mine. You want to try a third?"

Spencer was scaring the shit out of me, so I knew this guy was intimidated. I acted uninterested as I made my way out of the club. Seconds later Spencer's hand firmly clasped mine. He roughly jerked me out of the club and began walking in front of me. I followed, stumbling in my boots as our hands were still clasped, ready for the fight he was looking for. I had him where I wanted him.

"I do NOT belong to you," I said, still being dragged while he marched in front of me.

"Maybe I just don't want to watch you use your body as a batting cage!"

"What the hell do you care? Really, Spencer, I've only known you four days."

"I don't have to know your favorite color and what your first dog's name was to care about you, Nadine."

He released my hand and took off down the street. I called after him, stopping where I was.

"Spencer, this is ridiculous."

"It is. You have no idea what the fuck you're doing."

"What am I doing? Acting my age for the first time in my life? I deserve this! And really, you hypocrite, you have no right to be angry. I mean come on, what were you doing back there?" He turned to face me, walking in my direction.

"Talking, we were talking"

"Oh bullshit, that was payback and you know it." This time I walked away, but he grabbed my wrist roughly, turning me to face him.

"Stop it. Just stop it. It's okay for men to use women. It's *not* okay for you to use men. Deal with it. No matter how hypocritical, it's the way of the world and it's not going to change for only you. It's not okay, Nadine. It's fucked up. You can't treat men or women like pawns because you feel like it. You will not only lose every man you have, but lose the respect of everyone close to you."

"Rory loves me. She doesn't judge me."

"Yes, she does judge you and that's the sad truth. She blurted it out the night I met you both. You think that doesn't mean something?"

He had a point. He was right. She loved me anyway and I stated that to Spencer.

"And someday a man will love you anyway, too, if you give him more than five minutes. But for how long? You said you wanted to end this thing you do, so end it."

"I haven't done anything wrong!"

"You were about to!"

"No, I wasn't," I said in a whisper I was sure he couldn't hear, but he did.

"So that was all for me?" he whispered back, inching closer as he glared at me.

"Do you really think I'm that naïve? I'm completely aware of just how much you want me. Don't be pissed I have you where I want you. I manipulate. I get my way. I get what I need. It's simple."

He took huge strides towards me and I readied myself, but he walked past me.

"Where are you going?"

"I'm fucking done with this!"

"Of course you are," I said dryly, watching him walk away.

"I'm too old for this shit. I wanted to give you something you've never had, instead I want to beat the shit out of you."

"What exactly did you want to give me?"

I could still hear his voice, though it was faint. "Me."

"Well, you're right. I've never had that. And Pinky, as in *Pinky and the Brain!*"

"What?" he stopped at the corner. I saw a couple pause across the street to watch us fight. I inched my way toward him.

"My first dog's name was Pinky."

He turned again and started walking in the direction of the club.

"Red," I shouted after him, "it's a whore's favorite color!"

He stopped walking and turned again to look at me. I caught up with him quickly and grabbed his face, bringing my lips close to his. "And I'm sorry." I kissed him sweetly and felt his chest heave. He ripped my hands from his face and kissed me viscously. I quickly cupped him, stoking the fire. He cursed and picked me up, wrapped my legs around him and walked me down an alley, setting me on an old newspaper stand.

"Spencer, this isn't really safe," I noted as I looked both ways down the abandoned alley.

"No, it's not. You're the most dangerous woman I've ever met."

He ripped my panties off and kissed me roughly, pulling his mouth from mine and glaring at me. He took a finger and slowly slid it up and down my sex. All of my breath left my body. I was past aching, past needing, past wanting. My body was begging.

"Who are you wet for?"

I refused to answer him. I was on dangerous ground.

He shook my arms and held his face inches from mine. The street light shadowed the curve of his perfect jaw and I gasped at the look in his eyes.

"You, Spencer, it's you." I moaned as he began to circle me with his finger.

"Liar. It's not me you want inside you, is it?"

"Spencer," I gasped as he slid a finger inside. I melted into him and he shook me again.

"Look at me."

It was the look I craved, but not the look I wanted. Something was missing. I leaned in to kiss him as he teased and tortured me with one finger, then two. I felt my heart pounding and was panting. He refused my kiss and peered into my eyes. I grabbed his jeans and unbuttoned him, freeing the hard length that proved he was just as ready for me. I licked my palm and stroked his length, watching his furious stare soften slightly to over the edge desire for me.

"Spencer, you have to believe I want you."

He ripped a condom from his pocket, fitted himself quickly and shoved the entirety of his length inside of me. I was instantly full of him, gasping his name. He pulled back and eyed me as if the amazing feeling of us finally connecting only made him angrier. I was already on the edge about to fall off.

"Jesus… Fucking you is all I can do right now," he spit out hoarsely.

"It's all I want," I whispered in a low moan.

"You think you deserve this, Nadine?" He thrust into me like a madman and I moaned looking into his eyes, willing him to look at me.

He brought my legs to rest hooked over his forearms and drilled into me. He slid himself in and out, pounding his delicious length, making sure I felt every inch. He ripped the top of my dress, freeing my nipples and licked the hardened beads, leaving the rest aching. This was not for me, this was for him.

I heard his curse as he cupped my ass, lifting it further for better access and I moaned his name as I came. He continued his assault as I shook with the weight of the strongest orgasm I had ever had, looking deep into his eyes. The look was like no other I had ever seen and I instantly moaned at its arrival. He wasn't finished with me. Not even close.

"Did you feel that, Nadine?" he said, lifting me onto my feet, turning me around and bracing my hands over the shaky stand. He entered me again and brought his fingers around to my sex, circling me, and I came again instantly. He grabbed my ass with both of his hands, squeezing painfully as he filled me over and over, making me call out to him. He held onto my waist with one hand and cupped his other hand over my mouth, sticking his fingers in. I bit and licked them with my tongue.

"I'm just another one, Nadine, remember that. I mean nothing."

I couldn't help the hurt I felt at that very moment. I felt my eyes swell and heard him exhale and moan with his release. I took huge breaths as I looked around making sure we went unnoticed. We were completely alone. I was more frightened of the way I felt than I was of the dark alley in one of the most dangerous cities in the U.S.

I turned around to face him and saw the hurt on his face. I gave him a slow smile in retaliation for the hurt that was making its way from my chest to my throat. Tears threatened, but I refused to let them show.

"I thought I explained I only have a man … once." It was if I had slapped him without touching him. I was instantly sorry I said it.

I slid my skirt down and did the best I could to fix my top, but it was pointless. He walked me back to the hotel without saying a word. Our spell was broken. The whore had ruined it all.

He whispered goodnight to me at the hotel entrance and kissed my forehead as he turned to walk back to the club. I quickly made my way to the elevator, covering my chest. By the time I reached my room I was sobbing. God, I deserved this, but I would be damned if I wanted it served to me by Spencer. I scrubbed every bit of makeup off of my face and let the hot water run over me in the shower. I got into bed and ordered a ton of room service. I watched the clock, unable to drift off, but pretended to sleep as I heard the door open. I heard a sigh and knew it was Rory. I breathed a sigh of relief and sat up quickly.

"I forgot my key to the other room," she said, her cheery voice deflated. "I didn't think anyone would be here. It's only two."

Rory kicked off her shoes and climbed into bed beside me, grabbing some fries off of one of the plates.

"What the hell is wrong with you?" she said, surveying the mess of plates on the bed. I gathered them all and placed them on a table, reeling on her in anger.

"Thanks for the amazing advice, Rory. It went well." My anger was misplaced. I was wrong and I knew it, but I didn't care. I gathered the sheets on the opposite bed and pulled them over my head as I laid down again, my back to her.

"What the hell did I do?"

"Nothing, just let me sleep," I mumbled. The light next to me clicked on and I felt the covers being ripped from me.

"Oh, hell no. You aren't pinning this one on me, Nadine. Just what the hell happened?"

"Nothing, okay. Just … it doesn't matter."

"Oh, yes it does. Talk. You aren't sleeping until you do."

I turned on her and grabbed the sheet back. "I am not cut out for this game, okay."

"No, it's not okay. Tell me."

I sat up rubbing my eyes and glared at her. "What do you think happened? I screwed it up. He hates me. I showed my true colors and he didn't like them much. It's okay, though. He got off."

"Jesus, Nadine. Why do you do this to yourself? Why?"

"I don't know."

"So you brought out the best in him?"

"No, this is the first time I've ever brought out the worst." Though my body disagreed.

"Because he cares about you, Nadine." Rory sat next to me, now bringing me down with her on the bed. Her next words were in a whisper. "You know he wanted a little more from you than your body, Nadine. He made it clear by waiting as long as he did."

"I don't know how to give him anything."

"Just let go."

"I think it's too late."

"No, Nadine, it's not."

I grabbed her hand and apologized. She squeezed it and let go.

"You are my family, always will be. I love you, Nadine, but I can't always be the only real person in your life."

"I know," I said, not trusting myself to say more.

"How about you order me some fresh stuff to eat and I grab a shower and we watch old flicks until we pass out?"

"Sounds good to me," I said, instantly feeling better. I watched her rip off her cat suit as if it disgusted her. "Hey, wasn't someone else supposed to be doing that tonight?"

"Oh, yeah, that. Total nightmare. Total disaster!" She raised her hands to me in exasperation.

"What?" I couldn't help but chuckle at her dramatic flair. She had her cat suit around her ankles and kicked it off, muffling the beginning of her next sentence while she put on a t-shirt. "So we get to this 'locals spot' which only ends up being a shithole that serves cheap beer. I'm assuming now that is all he could afford, and I overlooked it as the drinks went down. We get hot and heavy and I liked him, he was actually pretty damn funny. We went back to his place and…" she lowered her head in shame. I chuckled again waiting for what I was sure was an epic tale.

"Nothing, the man had nothing. After a good half hour of making out I reached into his pants and there was nothing there." She lifted her thumb and pointer to me in an attempt to make an inch and lowered it until they were touching.

"He couldn't choke a Cheerio." I fell off the bed laughing as she cursed me to shut up.

"It was an infant penis." She joined me on the floor as we laughed until tears streamed down our faces. "I didn't even have to make an excuse. He knew. Poor guy. I ran out of there so fast. I felt terrible for him. I can't even imagine how he survives." She shook her head as she eyed me still hysterical and headed for the shower.

I ordered two more platters of junk and we kept each other laughing until we heard the door again. Ellie walked in inebriated and begging for food. She crawled in bed with us and we laughed at her tale about Gage who hadn't been honest about his girlfriend. Apparently she had no problem publicly humiliating him either and tried to take Ellie down. Ellie barely escaped with all her hair.

"Spencer took her off of me just in time," she said under her breath. She looked at me and I simply shook my head no as if to tell her to leave the subject alone. We lay in bed laughing about our nightmarish attempts with the opposite sex until sleep took us. It was definitely a night to remember.

Small penis and other disasters

CHAPTER
Sixteen

THE GIRLS AND I walked downstairs the next day and waited on Amy for a small girls only shopping trip. It was the only way I would agree to go. Spencer never came back to the room last night and I assumed he stayed with Amy and Jack or the empty hotel room. I couldn't afford to care. I didn't want to see him, to face him. I wanted Spencer to know nothing of my feelings for him, though I ached to look into his eyes, to see his smile. I ached for his conversation and his friendship. Of course I ached for the part of him that I still felt so deep inside of me. He was an amazing lover. I wanted more. I needed more. I was sure he hated me. I wasn't so sure by the way he treated me after our little tiff, I didn't feel the same. Hating him felt much better.

"Ready?" Rory chirped, happily downing chocolate milk.

"Sure," I said, bracing myself. The last thing I wanted to do was shop. I wanted to hole up in the hotel room and repeat last night. We started walking toward the shops at the lower end of the street and I felt Ellie's eyes on me.

"You guys go ahead. I need to talk to Nadine." She stopped me a few feet from the entrance of the hotel. Amy and Rory walked ahead never asking why, but I knew Ellie saw the emotion in my face. Damn it.

"Don't worry. I know how hard it is for you to talk about things that hurt you. I just want you to know Spencer looked destroyed last night at the bar."

"Fuck Spencer," I said in an unforgiving tone. Just as I said it, I turned to see him approaching. He stopped in mid-step when he heard my decree and caught my gaze. Well done, Nadine. Great job.

I saw his face contort and then calm washed over him. His smile was menacing.

"Yeah, game over, right?"

I felt my chest explode into a thousand pieces as I looked to Ellie for help.

"That's disgusting, Spencer," she snapped, grabbing my hand to walk away. As we walked past I turned my head to keep my eyes on his.

"It was her game." He smiled at Ellie, not quite meeting my eyes.

"He's right," I said, my eyes filling with rage. "Game over."

"Sup, Jack," he said unaffected, walking past us to join him on the hotel steps.

"Nadine, hold on. Just hold on." She grabbed my arm and pulled me through the closest restaurant and into the restroom. As soon as we were inside I burst into tears. I felt the sobs come in waves and let go of them one by one.

"He's just a guy I met a few days ago," I said, trying desperately to straighten myself out and failing at every attempt.

"You are a woman, Nadine. You care for him. You really like him and it seemed that way for him, too."

"I am an idiot for thinking this was anything more to him than a game."

"I don't think it is, Nadine. I may be wrong, but I'm almost positive he cares for you."

"It's over," I said, dabbing my eyes. "I act like a whore, I get treated like one."

"Tell me what happened." I gave her the story without too many details and waited on her to comment. I was completely vulnerable and to another woman, no less. I felt my anger grow at my lack of control.

"At least you admit you had some fault in this. He's an asshole" She wrinkled her nose as if she smelled something bad. "Hey, let's go get ridiculously drunk and eat fattening food and be total slobs."

"Ellie, you are the best." I hugged her. I actually freaking hugged her. My emotions were surfacing daily now. It was as if all that I had kept hidden was coming to the surface.

As if she knew what I was thinking she said, "We aren't all out to get you or take what you have to offer."

"I know. Really, Ellie, I'm beginning to realize the truth that really exists and the one I have made up in my head. I started this … shit, all of it. I have to figure out a way to end it on my terms."

I had spent so much energy avoiding people, avoiding relationships, avoiding life. It was becoming clear to me that my declaration of war on each sex for various reasons was pointless. Along with the bad, came the good. There was no stopping the fact that bad people just existed. I had let them win, shut myself off, kept all people out in the hopes of escaping the cruelty of pure human nature. I was a coward, and what I was missing out on far outweighed the pain I had to endure when I was younger. Ellie's new friendship spoke volumes to me. And Spencer, though at this moment was far from the good guy, was also a good reason to wake the hell up.

"I want to end it." I washed my face at her urging, waiting on her verdict.

"And you will. At least you know now it's not who you really are. You want my advice? I think you know exactly how to live. It's a moral compass you've been ignoring for a long time. If something feels wrong, learn how to listen to your compass. It's there for a reason. It's the same as when something feels right, Nadine, and Spencer felt right to you. It's time to listen again. I think you stopped listening. But you can't keep ignoring it forever. You are too smart for this. Now, come on, let's ignore both our compasses and get into some trouble."

I burst out laughing at the bold new Ellie who had emerged on this trip. It seemed we were all becoming someone new.

"OH GOD, I moaned, my head hanging off the hotel bed. My vision centered finally and everything I saw was wrong side up.

"Ellie?" No answer. God, what happened? How did I get back to the hotel? Where the hell was everyone?

Still on the bed with my head hanging, I heard the bathroom door open and a fully naked Spencer coming my way. With my vision wrong side up I could still fully appreciate every single thing I saw. He had a perfect ass, thick muscular thighs, not to mention a delicious distraction I could spend an insane amount of my time on hanging heavy between them. I had to fight to keep from losing my head. My mouth was instantly dry at the site of the perfection he was. I moaned and brought my hand quickly up to my head to play it off as a headache.

"Great job today, Nadine. You could compete with my father as the world's worst drunk." I watched him start to dress and wanted to protest. Once he had on boxers, he brought me two ibuprofen and a Gatorade. I pushed the pills away but took a huge drink, the cold liquid soothing my throat. I was either not hungover or still slightly drunk. I was pretty sure it was the latter.

"What did I do? And why are you here? What time…" I looked to the clock and saw it was only seven P.M. Burning the image of his bare ass in my memory, I took a glance at his eyes. They were full of contempt. "Is Ellie okay?"

"What didn't you do? Ellie is fine and is recovering as runner up. Your bar tab was two hundred dollars. Just yours!"

"I'm sure I paid for it. Right? I'll take care of it. Look, I don't need a babysitter and I damn sure don't need the look you're giving me right now. We started out friends, we did what we did, now we hate each other and this little excursion is over. I'll take Rory home now. Have a nice life," I said, picking up my bag. I turned to grab some clothes and ignored his stare. Shit, I couldn't remember a thing. I suddenly felt terrible that Spencer had spent time cleaning up after me. I hated myself then, if only for that reason alone. I felt the guilt lodge in my throat and silently prayed my emotions would stay in check. I wanted to turn to apologize, but I kept packing my bag. He jerked the dress I was folding out of my hand.

"Do you ever think about anyone but yourself?"

"Haven't had to! That's the whole point. I don't have to. I can be just as selfish as I want."

"Well like it or not, princess, you have an entire troop of people to think of until we get back to Pensacola. So take it easy and do us all a favor and be a fucking wallflower for a few days instead of the train wreck you are."

Remorse quickly turned into anger and I couldn't hold it in. I threw my Gatorade at him and saw it land all over his fresh white t-shirt and face.

I stood nine feet tall now and made the quick steps to him. "I am NOT going to be a punching bag for you. I am NOT going to apologize for pushing you last night because you were being a total bastard. And I will not ever let you make me feel like this again!" I said, pushing his chest. It was moot, he didn't budge an inch.

"Nadine," he said, grabbing a towel and wiping the Gatorade off of him. He was eerily calm … again, like he was this morning. "I don't want to ruin everyone's trip because of the stupid shit we did. Let's just call a truce and call it what it was, a big mistake."

I had to take a deep breath. I was beyond furious and hurt. "Don't care. Don't want to hear your point of view, really. This is why I use men. Their dick matters, not their opinion." I turned on my heel and felt myself being jerked back onto the mattress.

He was on top of me, his face twisted with anger. "You don't mean half of what you say. Never do. You have it all figured out, huh? You are clueless, Nadine." He roamed my breathless chest as he held my wrists down painfully.

"Just stop. You think you're intimidating me but you're just pissing me off. I do not like being held down unless I ask for it."

His eyes flashed as his face twisted further, his gaze bored into mine. He stayed above me, his eyes taking me apart piece by piece. I felt my eyes fill and saw his face soften.

"Did I hurt you last night? Just tell me if I hurt you."

"I'm over it. I've come to expect it. This is why I hate emotions. They're useless."

"I meant physically," he said, his shocked expression telling me everything.

Shit.

"Get off of me," I whispered, trying to disguise my shaky voice.

"Nadine, please talk to me. Are you telling me you care?"

"Get off of me, Spencer."

"No, tell me the truth. Let me see you. Just one minute. Just give me thirty fucking seconds. Let me see you."

"Stop it, please," I pleaded with him, my eyes spilling as my chest heaved. His wet hair tickled my temple as he held his lips inches from mine and his eyes melted my resolve. I turned my head and was unable to stop the next round of tears from coming.

"Look at me, Nadine. I will never forgive myself for the way I took you last night. Ever. I hate what I did and what I said. I told you I could do better and I tried. But you pushed me so far. God, how I wanted you … and still want you. I'm tired of this shit. No more games. You're an infuriating pain in the ass, and one I can't stay away from."

I gave my eyes to him and let go. I felt the wall come down as I took his lips and exhaled a tearful breath. I couldn't hold it in anymore. "I want you", I whispered in between kissing his lips softly. "I don't want to fight. I want you, too, Spencer." I quickly realized he wasn't kissing me back. "Spencer?"

"How do I know you're telling me the truth, Nadine?"

He was searching my face, my eyes. I couldn't believe he was unsure of who I was. I was laying it all out for him. I had led him to this point of not trusting me. I had no one to blame but myself.

"Look at me," I said, fresh water running in a stream down my face. "This is me."

He covered my mouth with his kiss and we moaned in relief. I was naked in seconds. Spencer sweetly devoured every inch of my flesh as his kiss drifted up and down my body. I met his lips and felt him hard against me as his mouth trailed down over my chest to my naval and ending at my throbbing center. He spread me so gently I was almost surprised when I felt his tongue work in a slow sweet circle. I looked down and saw his eyes hot on my reaction and then turn their attention to my aching. He blew cool air on me and then slid his finger inside and I gasped. "It's perfect," he whispered, his eyes fixed on his finger. He made a circle with his tongue and whispered again, "God, it's perfect."

He kneeled on the floor and brought my whole lower half to him. I held onto the sheets for dear life as he licked and teased me with his tongue, bringing me to the edge and stopping before I went over.

"Spencer," I pleaded. He grinned wickedly and diverted his eyes back to my sex. I stared at his long lashes on his cheeks in awe of how beautiful he was as he slid his finger in and urged me on with it.

"Spencer, please, let me come." When he continued his torture I began begging. Only when I was drawn so tight one more tug of his finger would push me over the edge did he let up.

"Damn you!" I said as I rose off of the bed on my knees, chest heaving, fury evident on my face.

He gave me a heated look and took down his boxers and my mouth watered. I dove for him, shoving his entire length into my mouth and heard him groan. I felt his fingers trail their way down my back as he lifted my ass his way and entered me again with them. I looked up with my mouth full of him to see the appreciation in his face. He was staring at me as I let him thrust inside my mouth while he pulled me closer to the edge with his fingers. I pulled his length out and ordered him beneath me. Once he was covered in a condom, I straddled him and pinned his wrists.

"Don't touch," I said, gliding my tongue over his lips. I took the tip of him inside and saw his eyes dilate further.

"Tell me," I asked sweetly, "what you want?"

"What you do," he answered.

"That's not how I do this. I need to know how you want it."

"Why?" he said curiously, a smile playing on his lips. He took one of his hands away from my grasp. I let another inch of him inside and saw the smile disappear. He licked his index and his thumb and lightly pinched my nipple with them. I almost lost it.

"How … do … you … want … it?" I could barely get the words out. I was close. He stroked the skin over my sex and looked me right in the eye as he placed his thumb over the throbbing.

"I want you," he whispered, lifting his hips so more of him eased inside.

I slammed myself down onto him, feeling all of him. He ripped his other hand free and brought them to my waist, pressing them down as he moved his hips with mine.

"Oh, God," I moaned in unison with him.

"It's so fucking good," he said, looking up at me with his mouth gaping. Intense, delicious, overwhelming, and absolutely perfect, we were both gone.

"Spencer," I whispered, my voice shaky. I had lost control and was riding him faster and harder than I even thought possible.

"I'm right here." His voice led me to the edge and I went over, gasping and bucking like my life depended on it. Then it all went away in a wave of pure ecstasy. I looked him in the eyes as my body shook from my toes to the top of my head. My release and the look on my face seemed to trigger him close to his and he shot up, laying me down beneath him, thrusting and saying my name with each one. I held his eyes briefly, and for the first time ever, closed them when he finished, because he took me with him.

"Nadine?" His voice was distant though he was right above me. I had more than enough going on in my head. "Nadine?" he whispered a little more firmly. "What is it?' he asked as he trailed his kiss from my chin to my taut nipple. I felt the evidence of him all over me, and I still wanted more.

"Again," I demanded as his lips left my nipple and formed into the most beautiful smile I had ever seen. I was in no joking mood. "Again," I demanded as he reached my lips and finally gave me an answer I wanted.

HE STROKED ME roughly from behind over and over, circling his hips and stopped suddenly.

"I'm not going to come, Nadine." He pulled me to him, my back to his chest and whispered, "I have you senseless, wouldn't you agree?" He slid his hands between my thighs and I fell apart as another wave hit me. I'd had so many I stopped keeping count. We had been at it all night, or he had. It was the most amazing torture I had ever endured. We turned our phones off, only stopping to shower and even then I wasn't safe.

He grabbed and squeezed my throat. "You like it rough, we know that," he whispered to me and I felt my sex clinch around him. He squeezed my throat again in warning. "Let go." I immediately obeyed.

He pulled his length out of me and walked over to the dresser and cleared it off with the swipe of his hand. He came back to me and picked me up, bringing me over to the dresser and placing me on my knees, bringing my hands up to hold the mirror. I could see me fully naked and Spencer behind.

"Watch," he said, running his hand up my thigh in between my legs. His touch was so gentle, I ached for more. He clutched my sex with his whole hand and gently circled it, turning in one finger then two, then he spread me so I could see. The level of heat I felt at that moment sent my entire body into flames.

"You see this?" he said, taking my bud in his fingers and running my moisture over it. I let out a moan and closed my eyes. "Open them, baby. See what I see. I want you to see your face when you come."

He tilted me further toward the mirror as he entered me from behind. I watched him slowly disappear inside and saw his eyes hot on me as he reached around to touch me again. I was on the edge already. Spencer let go of my sex and grabbed my chin, forcing me to look as I fell apart. He picked up his pace, pounding into me as I let the wave go. Taking his thrusts down to almost nothing, I looked into the mirror to catch his eyes.

"Now, you get everything else." He touched me so softly it brought a small sob to my lips as he slowly slid himself in and out, caressing me with his hands, roving my chest, my nipples. Every part of me was on fire for him.

He wrapped an arm around my waist and pulled me to him as he looked at me in the mirror, kissing my neck as he made love to me. I could see him perfectly enter me. Every inch of him was perfection. I was full and I was exhausted, beyond exhausted, but would never tire of him.

"Do you like this?" he whispered as he slowly and methodically slid himself in and out of my opening. I moaned as an answer and reached up, thrusting my hands in his hair behind me.

"Beautiful," he said, studying us and the way we fit together as I took his length and he caressed me, stroked me, loved me.

"Please kiss me," I begged. He tilted my head and captured my mouth as he slowly pulled himself from me and swept me into his arms back into the bed. He stared at me before he came down on top and

I sighed as his mouth found mine again. He entered me slowly and I cried out to him. It was the most comfortable and beautiful sore I had ever felt.

"Again," I said as his mouth again curved into the new grin I craved.

"TELL ME ONE strange thing about you."

"Like what?" I asked, amused at his question.

"I don't know… Are you ever a weirdo? Do you eat bugs when no one is looking?"

"Eat bugs?" I chuckled at his question.

We were face to face, lying on our stomachs, and I had never been so sated in my life, though his touch was stirring me again. His smile was playful but his eyes followed his fingertips and I could feel the same ache from him that echoed in me as well. I had to stop this madness! It was morning and we hadn't slept. I studied the curve of his bicep, the way it bulged out a little fascinated me. His hair was swept away from his face and fell short of hitting his pillow and I loved it. I could spend hours soaking in his golden eyes and his thick black eye-lashes. I wondered if he had any idea how he truly looked to other women. He grinned at me then, his dimple filled smile. Sure he knew. I grinned back at him.

"Come on, Nadine. Everyone has a little weirdo in them." He slid his hand from my shoulder down to my bare butt and rubbed it sweetly with his fingertips. "Give me something."

I thought long and hard, then heard the familiar thump in my ear on the pillow.

"When I was a little girl, well…" I stopped and buried my face in my hands.

"I will not make fun of you, I promise." I watched him and knew he was full of shit. Whatever I brought out would forever be held against me. I went on anyway.

"Well, you know how you can hear your heartbeat at night sometimes when you lay your head on your pillow?"

"Yeah," he whispered, distracted by the circles he was making with his fingertips on my back.

"Well, I used to be afraid of the dark, and to make matters worse, I had it in my head that the sound of my heart beat was actually footsteps."

His fingers stopped. "Footsteps?"

"Yeah, so instead of reasoning my way into not being afraid of the dark, I scared myself even worse by inventing the footsteps of a man who was coming for me."

He said nothing as he brushed the hair from my face, soothing me. I wasn't used to it. It made me so nervous I started rambling.

"Anyway, to cope with that I sent him on errands, long ridiculous errands." Spencer's brows lifted as he smiled at me. I continued, knowing I sounded like a total lunatic.

"I knew if those footsteps stopped that meant he was going to get me and that my time was up. So I would give him orders. I called him Darkman because he never had a face. He was pretty much in my mind a silhouette, a shadow. It scared me so badly," I felt another James Brown shiver run through me and continued, "so I would tell him 'Darkman you have to walk to China and back twenty times.' Stupid things like that. I remember once telling him he had to walk every single foot of all the oceans."

"Darkman?" He wasn't laughing at me, but I could tell he was on the verge. I felt my face heat.

"Yes, anyway that's one of my weird things."

"So do you still talk to Darkman?" he said amused.

"No, I don't talk to my damn heartbeat, Spencer. I was a little girl. But little did I know how true it was."

"What?"

"That when he comes for me, when I can't hear his footsteps on my pillow anymore, my time is up."

"True."

"So now you think I'm a total weirdo." I turned my body so he

Kate Stewart

could fully see me in all my naked glory. He roamed my body from head to toe with his eyes in appreciation and I gave him a broad smile.

"No."

"Why not?"

"Because that was actually kind of beautiful."

I reached out to touch the scar over his eye. I traced it with my fingers and then pressed my finger to my lips and back to his scar. "You're a weirdo, too. I think I will get a cat when I get home."

I laughed hysterically at the face he made and even harder when he pinned me under him, demanding that I take it back.

Pillow Talk

CHAPTER
Seventeen

WHEN WE FINALLY emerged from the hotel room we were met by an irritable Jack who had taken up the slack the half day we had slept. Dusk was upon us as we all gathered for dinner. The girls gave me knowing looks, but reserved judgment. They were happy because I was happy. Ellie and I exchanged a few excited whispers as we walked to dinner. I looked back to Spencer who was talking to Jack and eyeing my ass appreciatively.

"Thanks a lot, asshole. Do you have any idea what it's like trying to entertain three women?" Jack said, giving Spencer hell for his absence.

"I know just how to entertain the ladies. You could learn a thing or two, Jack," Spencer replied and I swear the direction of his voice was pointed at me. Ellie giggled and Amy glared at Jack.

"We weren't that bad. We went to five places," she cooed at her husband.

"More like thirty-five," he mumbled.

"Jack Redmond Sawyer, I will kick your ass if you say one more word about how we bored you all day," Amy said, scorning him playfully.

"I love this city," Jack replied unaffected. "It brings the damn hellion out of my wife." He caught up to her, scooping her up as she yelped. "What are you going to do to me, Mrs. Sawyer?"

"Mmmm … kiss." She leaned over and planted a fiery kiss on him and he pulled away gasping. "See what I mean, Spencer?"

Spencer laughed at their banter, darting his eyes at me as if to say that could be us. I ignored him and wrapped my arms around Rory. "You mad at me?" She stiffened and turned to eye me.

"No, I can't be. You are way too … entertained." I chuckled at her repeated response to Spencer and I. Entertained would do for now.

Our last night in New Orleans upon us, we had dinner at some horrible Cajun rip off of a restaurant that Amy swore they had dined at before. Spencer announced suddenly he and I would be spending our last night alone. I didn't argue. The way he was eyeing me over the table said if I did I would be in for it. I was tempted to tempt fate, but decided to play nice instead. I would gladly give him my last night in New Orleans.

I gave Rory a sheepish look and she leaned over the table and whispered to me, "It's okay, Nadine. Only people who wanted to see you miserable would stop you from going with him tonight. Let me be the friend who loved you enough to see you happy." She finished her sentence and gave Jack the stink eye and he immediately quit protesting. I handed her fifty bucks on the sly. I knew she couldn't have much left and wanted her to have a good night. I also wanted to reward her for keeping Jack in check.

Spencer kissed my cheek as he helped me up from my table. "Come on, Nadine." What I heard sounded more like come on beautiful.

"Have fun," Ellie chimed in, giving me a wink and a smile.

I loved these people. I never wanted this trip to end and we were leaving for Pensacola tomorrow. I felt—no, I knew—Spencer was feeling the same dread looming over him as he kept me close. He grabbed my hand as we waved goodbye to the crew and they waved us off in return. He ran me out into the street and kissed me under the hovering street light, lingering sweetly. His kiss only stopped when he recognized music and took my hand to walk toward it. His distraction was a group of guys singing a capella a few yards away from us. He grabbed my hand, swinging me underneath his arm in a twirl, pulled me back to him and began moving back and forth, our chests touching as he wrapped his fingers sweetly around my hand and began dancing slowly. The guys raised their singing voices an octave louder until their song was finished. Spencer stuck some money into a hat one of the singers held out as we passed by, thanking them.

We strolled the streets feeling both elated and melancholy. Spencer would stop every so often to kiss me, brushing my hair away from my face. We crept up and down the streets, hands locked, completely ignoring the parade of people partying. I was about to point out a black cat on the other side of the street to amuse myself at Spencer's expense when he yanked my hand and led me inside a bar. I had no time to recuperate as

I was pulled on to the dance floor as he whispered, "La Vie en Rose," and wrapped his arms around me. It took me a few minutes to register we were in a jazz bar filled with geriatric couples. I immediately pulled away from him to head for the door but was stopped by his firm grip on me.

"Stay," he said as he nodded and smiled at an older couple who was admiring us as they danced expertly across the floor. I looked into his eyes and was immediately lost—black liquid again and with the look I could never place. I wrapped myself around him, loving the scent of him, the feel of his arms. Spencer was all I could see, feel, touch, and I felt the familiar stir he brought on as I buried my head in his shoulder.

"I think I love this song," I whispered, still a little embarrassed to be surrounded by strangers staring at us and smiling. I smiled back at an old couple who had to have been in their nineties. Spencer kissed my cheek and still moving me perfectly in time with the song, he looked into my eyes.

"What is that look, Spencer?"

"Look?"

"Don't play dumb. What is that?"

"It's you, Nadine. It's exactly what I am seeing. It's you."

"Me?"

"God, can't you tell?" He shook his head in disbelief.

"I like the way I look on you." He smiled and dipped his head to sweep his lips over my shoulder. He then turned us so smoothly he made it look like I knew what I was doing. I couldn't keep my next question to myself.

"Do you see the same when I look at you?"

"Of course. I am amazing." He chuckled as I rolled my eyes.

"Just dance, counselor."

He wrapped his arms tighter around me and I laid my head on his chest. I met the eyes of the woman next to me doing the same. Her small smile seemed encouraging. I gave her a small smile back and tilted my head to peer up at Spencer. The intensity of his eyes when they met mine caused me to part my lips slightly. He covered my lips with his so gently, I moaned when he took them away quickly. I had just experienced the most romantic moment of my life. I let it happen. I had let all of this happen. I was dating. I was painfully aware it was temporary. My heart squeezed as a reminder that the clock was ticking on this whole thing.

"What?" Spencer asked, seeing my wheels turning. "Stop over thinking everything." I gave him a small smile and chose to make a joke to lighten my mood.

"Max … I'm … feeling," I said in the best Grinch voice I had while wrinkling my nose with disgust. We both cracked up laughing and he kissed me again as we twirled around the dance floor. I was saddened when the song ended.

It felt like we were racing to close the gap, to slide under the garage door before it closed. We made memory after memory up and down the streets of New Orleans. We walked and talked all night. I thought I would be disappointed not to have Spencer on me, inside me, but it was something else that kept us together that night. It was much stronger, much more than just the never ending need to touch each other.

"Spencer, can I ask you a question?" I said as I grabbed his hand and saw a smile on his lips. We were strolling through some iffy streets further away from The Quarter and I was tempted to tell him we should go back. He seemed unafraid, so I went with it.

"You know you can."

"Amy told me about your … history with women. She said you were … like me. I just wanted to know why."

"Men are naturally promiscuous. I guess woman are, too, just not brave enough to do what you do." He winked at me. "And yes, I guess I was very much like you in that way."

"Oh." I felt the gnawing in my gut that there was more, but was thankful when he didn't make me guess.

He stopped in the middle of yet another deserted New Orleans street and gave me a worried look. "A girl named Allison. That's why."

"So you were hurt?"

"Yes, like you were," he said with emphasis.

"I wasn't hurt." This is going to hurt. You are going to hurt, Spencer. But I kept that observation to myself.

"You were hurt at the time. Nadine, why are you so afraid to show the emotional side of yourself? No one should ever punish you for that, ever, especially not you. Give yourself a break."

I saw the shadow in the corner of my eye and moved quickly. I turned my back to Spencer. With him now behind me, I confronted our intruder.

"What do you want?"

"Whoa, chérie," the guy said in a slur with an accent that in no way entertained he was Creole or a native of New Orleans. "Just coming through to give a greeting."

"We don't want a fucking greeting," I said in the most venomous voice I could muster. Spencer, who was just now coming around, quickly put me behind him and confronted him head on.

"Just fuck off, man," Spencer said heatedly.

I knew this could turn out very badly considering we were unarmed. I couldn't see the man clearly. I surveyed him from head to toe and all I could make out from the street light was that his nose had a bump on it like it had been previously broken, and he was missing teeth, lots of them. His head was covered in a sweatshirt hood and he was sweating profusely. I was burning up in shorts so I immediately drew drugs as a conclusion. There was no reasoning with drugs, ever, but I had to try.

"Nice shoes. Limited edition, right?" I said, rounding Spencer and coming closer to the guy than I should.

"Nadine, what the fuck?" I heard Spencer immediately protest and take a step toward me. I stopped him with a firm wave of my hand.

"Limited, yeah."

He lifted his head up and I could clearly see the outline of his face. He had a scar stretching from his temple to his lip. Easily identifiable and he definitely didn't care now if we saw him. That was a bad sign.

"Looks like they could use some new laces," I said, my voice wavering just enough to let him know he scared me. Shit.

"Yep, I could use a lot of things," he said sloppily. He was definitely drunk. There was no way he was taking us both in a fight, but the confidence he was letting off led me to believe he was packing more than a nice pair of shoes.

"Let me buy you a pair of new laces." I walked up to Spencer, reached into his back pocket and took out his wallet. Spencer eyed me and shook his head vehemently.

I opened the wallet fully so the man terrorizing us could see that I was giving him everything inside and held up the folded offering to him while handing Spencer his wallet back.

"No fucking way, Nadine. No way." I glared at Spencer for two seconds then turned back around.

"Thanks, Miss Nadine?" He fully smiled at me and grabbed the cash as he walked past us. "I would love a new pair." He eyed us speculatively as if he was weighing what more he could get away with.

"I sure hope that's enough, Mr.?"

"Brown, James Brown." If I wasn't so terrified I would have burst out laughing. I felt Spencer pull me back to him protectively and nodded my head at Mr. Brown's hand full of cash.

"Well, Mr. Brown, we both hope that will be enough." I said the last words with so much emphasis there was no questioning my stance. Unless he intended to use the gun he was hiding, he was in for a fight. He tilted his head at me and smiled a toothless grin.

"It's 'nuff. Now hear me, chérie, you two best be getting back up the street. I have some friends all over who need new laces." Wow, he liked me. Thank God for that. Spencer and I quickly made our way back to the more cluttered area of The Quarter. I knew Spencer was livid.

"I will give you every dime of the few hundred back, Spencer."

He paused in the street a few blocks from our hotel. "You think I'm pissed about the money? No, I'm not. I'm wondering how I will ever get the use of my balls back. I should have taken him down. That was totally emasculating, woman!"

I burst out laughing and he grabbed my shoulders.

"Why did you do that? I could have handled that."

"He would have killed us without batting a lash. I don't think I like James Brown."

"That's not funny," he said seriously, scorning me but breaking out into a nervous smile of his own.

"It's kind of funny," I said smiling, still full of adrenaline. "Besides, you going all commando would have gotten us killed."

"I wouldn't have given him all my money."

"Then neither one of us would be having this conversation right now."

"How are you so damn sure?" he asked, tilting his head, doing his best to figure it out.

"He had a gun. Your balls had no chance, I promise. Don't be mad."

"I'm not really. I'm…" He shook his head again grinning at me.

"What?" I said grinning back.

"Glad you're okay. That we're okay. It's the best two hundred dollars I've ever spent."

"Good." I saw the sun begin to peak behind him. We were out of time. He noticed my gaze behind him and my face fall and turned and saw it too. He shook his head and looked back at me. "Me too."

We walked into our room exhausted as the sun came up. I ran to the bathroom to brush my teeth and freshen up. I was praying he wasn't too tired and was thankful he wasn't in bed yet. I pulled off my shirt and sat on the edge to find him staring at me in the dresser mirror. The look he gave me was heated, very similar to the one he gave me when he had me on that dresser gasping his name.

"It's not so bad is it, Nadine?"

"What?" I said breathlessly. I felt my sex twitch and was amazed at how quickly my body responded to him. My nipples were drawn tight, ready for him.

He turned around to face me as a small smile graced his lips. He knew exactly what he was doing. "Being courted. Well, aside from the near death experience."

"Is that what that was?" I said in my best southern accent, keeping his eyes on me as I stripped my clothing off piece by piece.

"Yes, and now finally as repayment you should do as you are told." He jumped on the bed as my body racked with laughter and his hands tortured me, making me jump and beg him to stop.

"So if another man decides to court me in the future, I'm to do what I'm told?" I said, still laying the southern on thick. His face hardened and he looked at me with his jaw set.

"I don't want to think about anyone else touching you, ever." He shook his head as if to rid himself of the thought. "I'm not a man who needs to be told what I want, Nadine. I just know. I have always known since I was young." He reached up and lifted me further up the bed, cradling my head and adjusting us so he was between my legs. I let go of a sharp breath as he got closer to me and felt his sex so close to mine.

"And what I want is every inch of you covered in me. I want you to remember me."

"Then touch me," I said with pleading eyes. His hands caressed me endlessly. I was mesmerized by his touch alone. He didn't kiss me, he simply followed his hand with his eyes as he traced my skin with his fingers. He finally made his way down low and when I gasped as his fingers entered me, his beautiful eyes finally met mine.

"You will remember me."

TWO AMAZING AND easily earned orgasms later and a plea for food and with no sleep, we ended up going for beignets at the famous Café Du Monde. It was torture waiting in a ridiculously long line for our fried donuts with powdered sugar, but we ate so many of them that when we returned to the hotel we settled into a deep sleep. Our peaceful slumber was interrupted a few hours later by the crew. We had to pack, it was time to go.

They all piled out of the room, giving us our space, making sure we stayed awake and packing. Spencer closed the door on Rory who was giving me a huge smile and I gave her one back. I looked to Spencer and wondered if he could see what I felt. He walked over to me and kissed me, turning me away from him and brushing his lips from my neck to my ear.

"Don't. Don't, it's not over yet. Don't." He turned me to face him and I felt the sinking in my chest.

"This is why I don't do this," I whispered to him, touching my chest then his and back again.

"Right now I don't blame you," he said apologetically. "If I make love to you, will you forgive me?"

"I already won't forgive you," I said, sighing my submission as he pushed me back on the bed. He caressed me with his mouth starting at my ankle, kissing his way up my calf and thighs, placing a small kiss on top of my sex, and trailing his way up to my mouth. When he reached my lips he hovered and I brought my hands around his face, which was now covered in a stubble shadow.

"Spencer…" I felt the lump in my throat.

"Me too," he said, surrounding me in a complete cloud. When we finally let go, we packed quickly, not having any idea how long we stayed in our room. They greeted us happily, as if they hadn't seen us in years.

It had all been a mix of time from the beginning of our trip to New Orleans with the group to the fog I was under where only he and I had spent time here. Spencer was right, he had shown me two totally different worlds and I was already mourning the loss of one of them.

"You two look absolutely miserable," Rory said as Spencer put our luggage in the back of the SUV.

"No... We're good," I said, fake smiling at Spencer who refused to return mine. He was feeling the same way I was. "We had a blast. Hell, we even met James Brown."

Spencer burst out laughing and I gave him a wink. The rest of them looked between the both of us puzzled. He smiled at the ground as he closed the trunk.

New Orleans

CHAPTER *Eighteen*

W E MADE IT back to Pensacola in record time. Or maybe it only felt like that because Spencer and I were completely passed out. I caught him laughing at me between our ins and outs of getting comfortable sleeping. I caught him catching the drool coming out of my mouth. I swatted at him angrily as I settled back to sleep, not giving a damn how I looked. He kissed me sweetly as he lay down on the seat, curling me into his arms until our breathing matched. When we arrived in Pensacola, I stretched and gave Rory a smile.

"Tonight's it, babe. Make it count."

"Yeah, yeah, your happiness is getting irritating," she muttered dryly.

"I thought you weren't going to be that friend."

"I lied," she said, swatting my ass and grabbing her bags.

I had no idea what to do at that point. Do we say goodbye from here and go to our rooms? I grabbed my bag from the man who held it and heard him whisper, "Not yet."

I looked into the sad brown eyes and nodded. I was on the verge of tears. This was ridiculous. I had to stop this now.

"Maybe it is time, Spencer. Maybe it should be."

I saw him calculate what was going on in my head and he shook his adamantly. "No. No way, Nadine." I didn't want to argue.

We all went to our hotels and Rory and I took turns taking a much needed shower. I stood under the water, my body sore in places I never knew existed until this weekend. I smiled at the same time my eyes burned. Spencer had completely ruined me. Rory insisted I meet up with them for the farewell dinner, but I couldn't do it. I promised I would catch up, just not now.

I left the room in case Spencer decided to look for me. I just needed a little time to get my head together and my new emotions in check. It was too painful. We were all leaving tomorrow and I was never, or would ever, be one for goodbyes. Not the kind I had to give Spencer. I knew seeing him again was inevitable, but I needed to think, without his all-consuming personality around me. He was like a force of nature, a damn wrecking ball. I laughed to myself as I walked the beach. I must have walked for miles and miles letting the waves soothe me. This is how I survived, this right here. This is what I needed. This is how I dealt with the world—alone.

And it was now completely unappealing.

I wrapped my arms around my shoulders as my dress blew in the breeze. I spotted a large covered lifeguard stand in the distance and made my way toward it. I climbed to the top, watching the last of the sun go down and the movement on the beach. I saw couple after couple walk by holding hands. Most of them didn't say a word. They were in sync with the beach and with each other. It made me long for the same. My eyes drifted to the man walking by, he looked furious, he looked like… "Spencer?"

"DAMN YOU! SERIOUSLY, Nadine?"

"What? I just wanted to be alone for a little while. I told Rory I would catch up with you guys," I shouted down to him as he climbed the white wooden tower and stood in front of me, frustration rolling off of him.

"You can be alone when you get home. We had one more day now and you have cut hours into it. I had a surprise for you … asshat."

I burst out laughing at his ridiculous name calling and he joined me. "Asshat?"

"Seemed nicer than anything else I was thinking," he mused, sitting down next to me.

"Well, I'm ready now. What's my surprise?"

"A sunset cruise," he bit out, still upset, waving his hand to indicate just how dark it was and that we missed it. I laughed again at his amusing aggravation with me and tilted my head so it was resting on his shoulder.

"Awwww, you made me a present and I ruined it. I am an asshat," I said as we shared a smile at my new Adam Sandler movie reference and the way I had twisted it. Only Spencer would get that.

"So are you done sulking? Can we go have some fun? I haven't eaten yet, can I interest you in some crab legs?" He smiled again, another joke at my expense. We were becoming familiar enough to poke at each other and it hurt like hell. I didn't know how to explain to him that being close to him was tearing me apart. I also didn't want to over dramatize the situation.

I took his hand and let him lead me out onto the cool sand. We didn't say a word like the couples before us and it made me smile.

WE HAD OUR last dinner ocean front on a candle lit patio. We were the only two out dining so late. I could tell it was close to time for the restaurant to close by the way the waiter was so attentive and the lightning fast time of our food arrival. Spencer didn't seem to care, though I felt terrible. We shared two bottles of wine, laughing about our Orleans trip and the crazy and amazing parts of all of it. We had a few comfortable silences followed by some intense eye lock. I was breathless by the time we got the check and I could see the need in him building as well. I closed my eyes at the wave of uneasiness settling over me.

"What do you want to do now? Anything you want, Nadine." His voice was hopeful, reassuring.

"You and me back in New Orleans."

He gave me a sad smile. "I can't do that."

"It was too hot there anyway," I said, dropping my eyes to my lap.

He stood and I looked up just as he grabbed my hand, lifting me out of my chair. He put his hands on either side of my face. "But I want to. Do you believe me?"

I nodded and took a deep breath to keep the emotion away from me. I didn't want to ruin what time we had left. I smiled for him, even though I knew he could read me. When the waiter returned, he set down a piece of chocolate cake with a single lit birthday candle.

"Your present was the cruise, but you screwed that up. Happy Birthday." Spencer grinned at me. I looked at him as he still held my face in his hands. "Make a wish."

He kissed my lips, let go of my face and I sat back down in my seat and closed my eyes. I wished for a Groundhog day. I couldn't think past this time in Pensacola with Spencer. I didn't want tomorrow. I wanted to repeat this day forever, or even the day before, or even the day we fought in the street. I would take any one of those days over tomorrow. I wished for a Groundhog week instead and then blew out my candle. When I opened them I smiled and thanked him. He shook his head as if it was nothing and wrapped his fingers around my waist, walking me out.

We walked for a while longer on the beach and I asked Spencer what his specialty was in law. He admitted to me he was a divorce attorney and he hated it.

"It's horrible, Nadine. You see all of these couples fighting to the death over nothing but money and assets. Married for years and years, not worried about their children's best interest. They want revenge, to take everything from the other, leaving them with nothing. They are never interested in anything but their own agenda. I feel so bad for the kids. It completely ruined the idea of marriage for me. That's why I didn't argue with you when you told me how you felt about it. I couldn't agree more."

I thought about his words and nodded my head in agreement. Well at least I didn't have to worry about finding out about a Mrs. Diamond in the future. Why was I twisting this info for my benefit? I looked at Spencer again. I knew he was talking directly to me, but thoughts of the week kept circling in my head. I smiled at him, though what he was telling me was in no way comical. I just loved looking at him, talking to him, being his friend. My chest ached as he caught me staring at him again. He gave me an odd look but finished what he was telling me.

"...anyway, I hate it, but I love the courtroom. So maybe I'll find another specialty. What about you? What will you do when you get home?"

"Not be a lawyer."

"Funny. Why do you hate lawyers so much?"

"I don't hate you." He stopped walking and pulled me to him, his arms held me so close. When his lips met mine our kiss was never ending.

He made love to me for hours when we reached the hotel room. His lovemaking was desperate and hungry, as was mine. He sat in the bed with me wrapped around him, our limbs glistening. I fastened my arms around his neck, easing myself on and off of him achingly slow, our breathing hitched as we kept our eyes locked.

When we were again dressed, he grabbed my hand and pulled the comforter from the bed. He sat us back on the beach, my back to him as he cradled me. He surprised me with a playlist made just for me on his MP3 player, and as I listened to what he was telling me, I felt my chest go completely raw. When the song *Drive* by Ziggy Marley came on, I finally let the tears fall at will. We talked into the late hours of morning and only found sleep when we could no longer keep our eyes open. Our time was up.

CHAPTER Nineteen

I WOKE FIRST TO a cloudy sky with the sun peeking through. I saw fins in the distance on the calm water and smiled at the rainbow in a semi-circle just above the horizon. It was perfect. The sand was soft and silky and cool to the touch, the water a perfect light green. I watched Spencer sleep. His face completely at ease, his sleep was peaceful. I let my eyes wonder back to the water.

I briefly ditched Spencer as I ran inside the hotel to grab my suit. I walked back out to find him still sleeping. Making my way into the water, I took note of how warm it was and how it felt against my skin. I felt the first wave crash into me with its strength and went down fast, underestimating it. I got up quickly, choking on water, and as the next wave hit me I went down again. I saw a storm brewing in the distance and realized why the water had gone from calm to carrying me to my ass. I was almost furious at that point and challenged the next wave, which abruptly took me down. I decided to give in, laughing as I went. I have no idea how long I was out in the sea fighting the waves. I turned to look for Spencer and saw him walking toward me. I ran out of the sea and tackled him on the sand.

"Morning," I said cheerfully.

"Morning," he said, wrapping his arms around me.

"Did you sleep well, counselor?"

"Just fine until I realized you weren't next to me," he said quietly.

"Well hell, we had fun, right? I mean we had a good time. Let's not dwell on it," I said, turning my face away to hide my torment. I had made the decision to act as casual as possible today to keep myself from falling apart. He caught on quickly.

"Best time of my life." He grabbed my face with one hand and dragged his thumb across my lip. I felt it start to tremble slightly.

"Hey, you want to go swimming?" I said cheerfully, failing to convince either of us that my mood was genuine.

"I have to go pack," Spencer said, getting up. I stood up with him as he gathered the blanket.

"I do, too. I'll call you before we leave?"

"Yeah," he said as I eyed him closely. He was shutting down. I didn't blame him. I was as well, it was too painful.

"An hour," I said, dashing off to my room where Rory was still snoring loudly. I brewed a pot of coffee and drank as much as I could. I had packed last night before I took a walk on the beach and ran into Spencer, so I was stuck in the room listening to Rory snore.

The front desk called with the time for checkout and Rory hesitantly got up and into the shower. Even she was in a shit mood. Dread, we were all dreading our return home, back to reality, back to responsibility, back to life. I called their hotel and got Ellie and told her Rory and I would be over to their hotel shortly to say our goodbyes.

When we arrived Amy and Jack were zipping up their suitcases. It was getting more and more official and even more painful. Rory leaped over the bed to bear hug Jack and Amy. They wrapped their arms around her, whispering to her. Rory pulled away with tears in her eyes and hugged Ellie for a solid minute. It seemed Rory had fallen in love herself. I had spent all my time with the man who was standing too far away from me, observing the touching spectacle right along with me.

Rory hugged Spencer next, whispering to him, making him chuckle. I felt the lump in my throat form and quickly pushed it down.

"Bye," I heard Rory rasp as tears streamed down her cheeks and she made a beeline for the door.

"I'll meet you at the car," I called after her.

"Okay my turn, but I don't think I'm going to top that." I walked over and gave Jack and Amy each a one handed hug and they squeezed the life out me in return. I pulled back to give Amy a wink. "Keep it up."

"You know I will." She winked back. Jack looked between us, clueless.

I turned to Ellie next who seemed to be a total mess of emotions. I pulled her to the side of the room. "Ellie, If I tell you what I want to right now, I will cry. Haven't you had enough?" We both chuckled with tears in our eyes and she gave me a long hug.

"Thank you, Ellie," I whispered as Spencer grabbed my hand and we left the room. I didn't ask him where he was taking me and it didn't take long for us to get to the same exact spot at the beach we had just left an hour before.

We stood side by side staring at the water as the thunder rolled in and rain drops began to trickle down. He finally looked at me and gave me a small smile.

"So we can do the phone calls, emails—"

"Stop. I don't want a fucking email, Spencer. We agreed all or nothing."

"Sorry, you're right. I know your right." I stood there as he avoided looking at me. "Well, I better go. I don't want to hear Amy's mouth the whole damn way back to Philly." He turned and gave me a soft kiss and headed for his hotel.

I felt the bullet that had just landed in my chest spread through my veins like acid. It was worse than any sickness I had ever felt. I watched him walk away and the burn in my throat almost kept me from asking.

"So you really don't care if we ever see each other again?" God, did I just say that and sound so damn desperate while I asked? And he had to have heard the crack in my voice. I put both hands on my chest to cover the invisible bullet and tried my best to breathe. He stopped walking right away and stood perfectly still for several moments. He slowly turned to face me. His eyes were filled with apprehension and unshed tears.

"I'm not the guy who gets you, Nadine." His voice was shaking like mine. I looked up to see his face twisted. "I'm not the one. As much as I want to be, I am not the guy who gets you." I shook my head in disbelief as he continued. "The guy who gets you will see you like I do, but he will claim you right away. Watch for him. He won't hesitate. He will shelter you and love you and make you feel protected. He will be hard to handle and sometimes you will want to walk away, but he will be worth it because he will treat you like you are worth it. He will tell you how brilliant and beautiful you are all the time. He will touch you like I did." I heard his voice crack again and saw his face strain to keep him from cracking further.

"So this isn't love?" I croaked, begging him to say something, to give me any sign that I wasn't alone. I didn't know if it was love, but I felt like a piece of me was being torn away and all he had to do was stop it.

"I don't know. For me maybe, for you I think it's trust."

"Trust?" I doubled over and put my hands on my knees. Trust can't hurt this much.

"I don't know why I feel this way." I looked up as more tears poured from my eyes. Spencer was in front of me now, his eyes stormy and full of the same agony I felt.

"I have no idea what happened between us, Nadine. We could live a thousand times and I guarantee it will never happen again. But it was real, Nadine. I felt it, too, but it's fleeting. We have to go back home. I can't leave my dad and you really don't want to leave your family, either." He nodded toward Rory who was watching us carefully from the car. "Even the weather is telling us it's over," he said as a raindrop hit his hand as he held it up.

"I don't know if I should be mad, or sad, or kiss you or what the fuck to do. I don't even know what I want from you," I whispered, clutching his t-shirt.

"More time, it's what we both want."

"So this is how we leave it?"

"Yes and no." He grabbed my face and pulled me to him, searching my eyes. "It was real, don't ever doubt that. And don't ever doubt a word I said, either. I will remember this until the day I die, so will you. I know you will. You can't forget me." He grinned and I laughed through my tears.

He wrapped his arms around me, whispering his next words. "Kiss me goodbye, Nadine, and go hit all your levels. Go take over and do all the shit you were meant to. Just know it's okay to trust and get hurt, or you aren't living at all." I nodded my head and pulled back as he lifted his hands to my shoulders.

"I'll do that," I paused, finding the strength to get myself together, "As long as you promise me you will let go at some point, so you can do the same."

"I will."

"Okay." He kissed me the way he did the night we met, seven days ago, a night that seemed a lifetime ago. It was over. Before I could let him get away I had just one more thing to say.

"You win. You won." I saw shock and awe on his face and the look only he could give me. I wasn't afraid to say anything to him—this stranger who knew me better than anyone in the world now owned a piece of me.

Love, lust, infatuation, whatever the hell it was, it was amazing and I was grateful for every single minute. "You totally won, Spencer, and I'm so damn glad you did," I said whole heartedly as I fought to keep control. I had made this harder for us both.

The Grinch of love… God, I was so full of shit. And he knew it the whole time. He knew it.

"You won the second I laid eyes on you, Nadine." He smiled as he wiped the evidence of his victory away from my face. "Grinch." He chuckled as if he knew what I was thinking.

This was it, we couldn't wait any longer. I didn't feel ridiculous at all for wanting to hold him close to me. It felt like a cruel punishment giving him back to the world—a punishment that left me bleeding and aching without end, no relief in sight, just loss… The loss of him.

"Spencer," I heard my voice lift in a cry as I said his name. I gave him one more slow kiss and I couldn't take it anymore. I turned from him and began to walk, trying not to look back. If I did it would kill me.

Rory was waving me to the car and noticed my face. I turned away from her and back to Spencer, barely catching sight of him as he disappeared rounding his hotel. I looked back at the ocean and saw a small ray of sunshine peek through the clouds. I let the feeling of complete loss wash over me. I sat on the sand letting the reality hit me. I would never see him again. I reveled in the fact that I could feel what I did while it tore my heart apart. If I ever wanted anything in my life close to what I had with Spencer, I had a decision to make. I had to leave her here.

I felt the protest start inside me. A Jonathan landed just inches away from my feet and seemed to cheer me on as I stood and started to shove her away from me. My mind pictured her face filled with rage as I pushed her out. She clung to me for dear life and I closed my eyes and pictured Spencer's smile. It was enough to make her leave. She stood before me screaming, but I couldn't hear a word she was saying. I felt Jonathan eye me with approval before he flew away. I addressed her now, her face filled with rage, still screaming at me to let her back in, but she never belonged with me in the first place.

This whore wasn't me and would never be me. And now, for whatever reason, she had ended up as a contrived part of who I was. I used the rest of my imagination to mentally set her on fire and watched the flames engulf her as she begged and pleaded with me to let her back in. I turned on my heel and left her there, no longer a prisoner to her urging. I smiled as the rays disappeared and the rain started to fall more heavily.

I HAD WIPED a majority of my tears away but they just kept coming. I just liberated myself from my biggest burden and still my heart felt heavy.

Rory, alarmed and waiting for me, was quick to question me. "Holy shit, what's wrong.?

I smiled at the cloud covered ocean, my heart ripped to shreds and looked at her with my tear filled gaze.

"He won." I chuckled. I shook my head at my out of place laughter as Rory started the car.

"I knew he was good for you."

"Oh yeah?" I croaked, crying even more tears for the death and awakening of my heart.

"He told me the very first night that you were going to be good for each other."

I kept quiet for most of the trip home, silently wiping my tears away. I found it fitting that it rained the whole time. I felt Rory pat my thigh every once in a while. I didn't know why I wanted this man in my life, but I sure as hell didn't want to never see him again. Life would get in the way, we both knew it.

It was real, for both of us, but it was also fleeting like Spencer said it was. I had to put it in the right perspective and eventually I would... Eventually.

Summer Fling

CHAPTER Twenty

3 months later

Nadine

I HEARD HER BITCHING as she opened the door. "Damn you, Nadine!"

I couldn't help the pain in my chest. The pressure was unbearable. New Orleans was gone. GONE! She opened the door and paled from looking at me.

"What? What?"

"I want to see it," I said, my voice a near shriek.

"See … it. Oh, I've been meaning to talk to you about that."

I rushed inside and turned her TV on. What I was seeing was unreal. New Orleans was under water, people were dead, dying, crying, begging for help. It was fucked, totally fucked.

"Look, I know I said I didn't want to see, but it's been three months and look, Rory, it's GONE!"

"Nadine… look—"

"Put it on, Rory!"

I had to see Spencer's face, to know our magic place still existed. She plugged it into her laptop, streaming it to the TV and handed me the remote. I saw the huge cloud covering New Orleans as the terror of what was happening swept through me, so many lives were ruined, so many people helpless. I saw the huge cloud disappear as the video from our trip started. The hurricane that was covering Louisiana was replaced by me running toward the blue waves of Pensacola. I was fully clothed and looked like a total idiot running into the water. I felt the gnawing set in, ready to see Spencer's face. All I had was this damn video. I didn't see Spencer anywhere.

"Rory, where the hell is he?" I saw Amy and Jack, a ton of footage of me dancing on the bar, taking shots, laughing with Ellie and then nothing... It was all Ellie, Jack, Amy and Rory.

"Where is he?"

"He's not on there."

"What? No, that's impossible. How, Rory?"

"When I recorded, which wasn't much, this is all I took. If I had known that it would be this important I would have tried harder..."

"RORY, TELL ME HOW HE IS NOT ON HERE!"

"You guys always took off. When I remembered to record either you weren't there or you were doing something so crazy I kept the camera on you. I didn't know you would want him … like you do. I didn't realize."

Her words fell on deaf ears. This couldn't be happening. I had counted on being able to see him, to watch this and to feel better. Our week together haunted me. I missed him. It was all I had. I'd held onto it and now it was gone, just like our magical place. Tears formed in my eyes for the first time since we returned to Oklahoma. I had stayed strong, no calls, no emails. We had agreed it would only make it harder on us both. This gutted me, the last piece of what we had was gone. I searched the video through and through, but never got a glimpse of Spencer. I couldn't believe it, there was not one shot of him. Not one. I felt my heart shred and let the tears come as I looked at Rory, who looked at me just as helpless.

I put the remote down when the screen went black. I looked at Rory whose face said it all. She was sorry. I refused to hurt her over this. It wasn't her fault, but I couldn't talk now. I stood up and turned on my heel, heading towards my apartment. Even if our time together meant more to me, even if his words were meaningless and I was just some girl he spent a week with on a summer trip, I constantly craved the Spencer I had.

"Wait!" I heard Rory yell and turned around to see the screen. It was a shot of me in my bikini getting brutally beaten by the waves.

"So what?" I said, uninterested.

"I didn't take this, Nadine."

"What?"

"I didn't take this."

"Oh my God, turn it up." As soon as she did I heard his voice. "Rewind it!"

We saw the screen go back to black and both sat down. Rory grabbed my hand. It was pathetic really, but I had nothing. It had never occurred to me that it would even matter. It tortured me with how much it did.

The screen filled up with me again. I was standing in the direct path of some pretty massive waves, fighting them. I remembered it was our last day there, our morning together. I heard the words, "You are so beautiful," as they hit me like an arrow to the chest. I didn't imagine anything. Spencer was real. All of our time together was real, it had all happened. I knew in that moment without a doubt I was in love with him. The hum drum of my life had dulled the memory so quickly and the sound of his voice brought me back to life. His words were followed by his laughter of me getting knocked down repeatedly by wave after wave. I looked at Rory who was now crying with me. The screen went dark again. I had thirty seconds of my diamond in the sand on tape and it was just his voice. Still, I was grateful. It took what felt like a decade to swallow the emotion in my throat and finally speak to Rory who was playing with a string on her couch pillow.

"Make me a copy?"

"Of course I will, Nadine." She followed me to her door. "It was really so cool to watch the two of you."

"He was cool," I said, amazed at my fixation on a man I had spent a week with.

It was time to compartmentalize and move on. But as she switched back to the TV and I saw the horror of on the screen, I realized that bitch Katrina had evened the score for all the women I had hurt. She had, in a sense, taken my only man away from me. "Touché," I whispered to the large cloud covering Louisiana on the screen as I made my way back to my apartment.

I went back to my room and opened my laptop. I wanted desperately to talk to Spencer. I struggled with the words to say and felt I had already put myself so far out there at our goodbye. It wasn't enough. I needed him to know how I felt—how much I longed for him, how he crept into all my thoughts, how he had changed me. I looked up his email address and sat staring at the screen. I wanted him to know how I felt without making a fool of myself. After hours of staring at the screen I finally decided to send him something I knew only he would understand. I titled the subject SOS and attached a music file of Blink 182's *I Miss You* and hit send.

He never replied.

Spencer

I WAS STILL listening to her SOS when the cab slowed to a stop at her apartment building. That email was all I needed. I had spent two months in denial and the last lashing out. I hated it that she had to make the first move. That was my job. She missed me. I couldn't wait to see her face. I wondered if she would be just as happy to see me. Would she think I was crazy for coming to her? Hell no, I got her message loud and clear. The words of her song to me echoed in my ears. She missed me. I was a part of her. I was the voice inside her head. I loved her mind. I loved her song choice and I loved that she needed me because I was fucking failing so badly in Philadelphia.

I hadn't kept my word to her.

I had gone back to picking up after my father. I had gone home to the same bad habits, the same meaningless shit, with no life of my own. I dropped everything, and I mean everything, when I got that email. I had an interview with one of the top law firms in Philadelphia and blew it. I had looked up her home address but was unable to get her cell number. I prayed I was in the right place. I was in her world, her life was here. I looked around and heard the cabbie clear his throat. I have no idea how much money I gave him, I was too distracted.

Three months. I had missed her, ached for her. I hit repeat again, letting the song fill my senses. It gave me courage to walk the stairs. I made it up, found her number and knocked on the door while I waited with my heart banging in my chest. She would smile. I loved her smile.

I imagined an immediate scenario of having her undressed, beneath me, saying my name in that breathless whisper. NO SPENCER, don't go there. Oh, but that body was made for me. I would tell her I was sorry, beg her to forgive me for letting her go and spend the night making it up to her. I knocked again, took my headphones off and put my ear to the door. It was Friday night. I might be stuck waiting for her. Fine, she was worth it.

I sat on the steps, the song still reminding me of why I was there. It fueled me. I believed her. I felt the same. I wanted nothing more than to resume what we had. I wanted her. I would wait. I'd had more than one opportunity to fuck her out of my mind and couldn't do it. That was a first for me. I was tempted, but it wouldn't have worked. I replayed Nadine's words as she finally opened up to me just as it was over. *"So this isn't love?"* I saw her face as she stood on that beach, her tears clearly embarrassing her. She was more vulnerable than I imagined possible and in that moment I knew. She wasn't hiding from me anymore.

I just left her there. I wanted to show her the upside to what she was missing and in the end I had ruined my own chances of wanting anyone else. I just left her there, crying. I shook my head and stuck my headphones in my backpack. Hours of waiting turned into more hours. I was tired, hungry. She wasn't coming home tonight and if that was the case who in the hell was she with?

It began to rain heavily. More rain bands from that fucking nightmare Katrina. I couldn't believe I had just been there a few short months ago when I saw the screen filled with people, homeless, crying, desolate, and terrified. It was so fucked up. I wondered what Nadine thought of it. I wondered how she had reacted. I knew she had fallen in love with that city. I wondered if it hurt her the way it hurt me. When the hell did everything become so complicated? Before that trip, it was clear I needed a break, but not for one minute did I think I would be analyzing ever single step I would make. *Damn this woman!* Where are you, Nadine? I gave up a few hours before dawn. I would get a few hours of sleep and try and surprise her again.

AT MIDNIGHT THE next night the rain was still coming down heavily and I was totally fucking miserable. This was a mistake, it had to be. Nothing had gone according to plan. I had been sitting here for eight hours. I stood slowly, sore and tired and hungry. I saw a bar on the corner. Maybe I would get lucky and see Rory. Rory! Fuck, I forgot she lived across the hall.

I hit both apartment doors close to Nadine and got the wrong person on the first and banged on the second. No answer. Maybe they were together. My hopes raised slightly at the thought they were. I hit the stairs, barely escaping being soaked as I reached the bar. It was a decent place, sports themed and big TVs. I wished I had taken up residence there earlier. At least then I wouldn't be soaking fucking wet.

I took a seat at the bar and ordered a draft. I spent the better part of an hour looking out the window watching her complex, cursing the fact that we never exchanged numbers.

"You waiting on Nadine?" I snapped my head to attention and saw the bartender smiling at me knowingly.

"Do I know you?"

"No, man, you just have that familiar look."

"What the hell is that supposed to mean?" I snapped, eyeing him suspiciously.

"Nothing, man. So obviously you are waiting on her."

"She doesn't know I'm here," I said, watching him closely. I was seconds from taking the fucking smug look off of his face.

"She never knows when they come back," he said shaking his head.

Fuck. This is her meeting spot for her invites. I felt sick. What the hell was I doing?

"Don't fall for it, Spencer. I'm not an innocent woman. You couldn't live with the things I've done." I remembered her words to me and wiped my face in frustration.

"It's cool, man, I get it," he said, pouring me a tall shot of whiskey. He left the bottle and gave me a knowing nod. I sucked it down with relief and poured another quickly, still staring at her door.

I looked like some stupid chump who had it bad for her or just another one of her conquests looking for another taste. I wasn't about to justify my shit to some asshole who knew nothing. I hated his image of her. He wasn't important. She was. I felt my phone vibrate and quickly answered.

"Hello." I heard the desperation in my own voice and quickly poured another shot.

"Why the hell weren't you answering your phone? We have tickets tonight!" It was Jack. Shit.

"Jack look—"

"I'm at your place. Open the door."

"I'm not there." I heard a string of curses and smiled. He was only mildly mad now. Games were his chance to be free of obligation. Amy condoned his little escapes with me. Little did he know I had robbed him completely of his escape tonight.

"I'm in Oklahoma."

"What did you just say?" he roared, another string of curses coming out. I smiled again. Jack was never one to hold back, but this time I wasn't going to let him lay into me.

"Come off it, Jack. This was a little more important. I know I'm your only friend and I feel bad for you. If you weren't such an asshole you would have another friend to take to the game."

"Oh, that's bullshit and you know it." I knew him well enough to know his wheels were spinning, he was just about to—"Nadine! You with her man?"

"No, she's not here."

"Well, then do you mind telling me why the hell you're in Oklahoma?"

I poured another shot and as I glanced at her door. I felt the weight of his words. "I'm not sure, myself."

"I know why," he chuckled as if he was onto me.

"That's not it and you know it, Jack," I snapped.

"I know, I know. Look, I'm going to go deep with you for a second, and I swear if you ever repeat this I will ruin your life."

"What's that, Jack? I already know about your undescended testicle."

I laughed as he cursed my good name. The warmth of the whiskey started to spread through me. I pushed the bottle away motioning for a beer.

"I know you, Spencer. You can't fool me. You haven't been the same since we left Florida. My wife is throwing up more than the crazy bitch in *The Exorcist*. I haven't had sex in a month. I hate New Orleans."

"Jack, she's pregnant and you've never been happier."

"Fine, but I am serious about you. The thing is, I liked her for you."

"Wow, that is deep."

"Shut the hell up, Spencer. I had to get into my car so no one would hear me."

I laughed out loud at his admission and slowed my drinking down. Whether he knew it or not, he had already talked me out of drinking more. I didn't want to be my father. No way in hell was I going that route. I sipped my beer but motioned for my tab. I wasn't going to find Nadine at the bottom of a bottle.

"Okay, you ready?"

"Sure, Jack, spill it."

"My mother made me propose to Amy."

"Come again?"

"My mother made me propose. She knew we were having sex and she was staying at my place and my mother went crazy, calling me night and day. It got to the point that I didn't want to have a damn thing to do with marriage or Amy. But I did it anyway and it was the worst proposal ever. She was so happy to see the ring she didn't realize how bad I had screwed it up. It was the best move I have ever made."

"That's the most fucked up thing I have ever heard. How in the hell is this helpful advice?"

"I guess it's not. Just let me be there when you propose. I'm sure you will do worse."

"I can't believe you are my go to. How in the hell does Amy put up with you?"

"I make up for the undescended testicle. Look, okay, maybe that was a bad way to put it, but Nadine is your Amy, except it's good that you know better. I knew I loved Amy, and I knew that I wanted to be with her, but I had to have my mother show me that I couldn't live without her. I regret it. Sometimes I just want to ask her again so it would be all me, but I would really just feel better if you screwed up yours."

"Jack, I am not going to propose you idiot. I can't even find the woman. I don't even have her phone number and I think she might have gone back to her old ways."

"You don't know that. All I am saying is it's good that you are there and your mother sucks."

"Great, Jack. Thanks for that. Anything else?"

"Yeah, you owe me sixty bucks for the tickets … and I hope you find her, man. I really do."

"That's better." We hung up and I threw some money down, motioning to the bartender that I was leaving. I looked at the clock beside the TV, it was three A.M. She wasn't coming home tonight, either.

The next day I decided to go back and try one more time before I hit the airport. All of the excitement was gone from the previous two days. All I felt was empty. I sat outside her door and called a cab. No sign of her. No noise in the apartment at all. I hadn't missed her coming or going. The bartender confirmed for me I was in the right place. I felt like I had lost my mind.

I pictured her running, reaching for me behind the carriage in New Orleans. Her eyes full of hope as she reached her hand out. She looked perfect to me then, beautiful, innocent, and … happy. She trusted me. I refused to believe she was anyone other than the woman I had been with three months ago. And now I was out of time again with no sign of her.

I had no choice, I had to leave. My father had a nasty spill last night and broke his nose and two teeth on the concrete outside of a bar. I hated him then and I hated my mother more. Jack was right, she does suck.

I saw the cab pull up and slowly walked down as if she would appear and save me from the inevitable. I got in the cab, still staring at her door. This was the exact opposite of how I pictured this going. I felt like a complete idiot. I had lost a huge career opportunity to wait on a woman that I had only known a week.

"Airport," I said as the cab driver drove away. I felt my heart sink further and further down as the cab rolled away. I closed my eyes and she was running toward me, tackling me in the sand, her smile and eyes told me I was the only man in the world. Maybe I was.

"Stop. Please, sir, stop," I said with a plea in my voice. I handed him a twenty and asked him to wait. I ran to the bar and then back to her door. I got back in the cab hopeful. That was twice in twenty-four hours that Jack had been right.

CHAPTER
Twenty-One

2 Years Later

Nadine

"SHUT UP, SPENCER. I hear you for crying out loud." His incessant whining had again robbed me from another peaceful sleep. I had run nearly ten miles the night before and could feel every single limb protest as I got up. "I hear you, Spencer, chill out." I walked into the kitchen and grabbed the bag of food and shook it, but didn't have to wait long for his arrival. "I know, I know, all three hundred pounds of you is starving to death."

I poured Spencer's food into his dish and gave his long smooth back a quick massage, grasping his tail because I knew he hated it. I laughed at my stupid attempt at parenthood with my selfish, fat cat. I had gotten him as a reminder of the original. I shook off thoughts of him as I started stacking box after box in my kitchen. It was moving day for me and I had a new city and a new career to look forward to. I heard a light knock at the door and knew it was my boyfriend Thad and realized I hadn't yet brushed my teeth. I opened it and gave him a smile and ran to my bathroom to remedy my morning breath.

"Hey baby, where are you running off to?"

"Brushing my teeth. Spencer woke me up."

"Well in that case, please proceed." I heard him chuckle and closed the door. He made his way into the bathroom, catching my lips as I finished rinsing my mouth.

"Mmmm, I wish you would have let me stay last night."

"Then I wouldn't have gotten any packing done." I turned to give him my full attention.

"No, you wouldn't have." He brought his face nose to nose with mine and gave me a knowing smile.

"Sure you won't reconsider?"

"No, Thad, I live alone. I care about you, but I can't think about it further than that. I just got the offer I've been waiting for and I just can't pass it up."

"I know, I know."

He wrapped his arms around me and I could feel the tension in his body. Thad was the first long term boyfriend I ever allowed myself to have after several failed attempts at dating. We had been dating almost a year and I had turned him down from moving in with him when I got a transfer to my new job. He kissed the nape of my neck as he stared at me in the mirror. I quickly broke our stare and went to my living room to start with the boxes

"Why do you do that with me?" he asked irritated.

"What?" I asked innocently, knowing he was about to start in on the commitment talk.

"I get close, you run away. When you say you care for me, just how much do you care, Nadine?"

"Thad, I'm stressed out. It's moving day, okay. I'm changing everything," I said walking toward him. "Except for you and I do care." I just wish I didn't feel like something was missing. He was better off not knowing that, so I kept it to myself.

His smile was a good indication I may be off the hook. I smiled back, thankful I had his help today. We stumbled into each other at my cadet graduation party and had been inseparable since. We had grown close, but now that I was moving, I felt our breakup was inevitable. I was more concerned about the fact that it wouldn't devastate me than the actual breakup itself. He insisted he would make it work and drive out to see me as often as possible. I knew it was just a matter of time, but kept my mouth shut.

"Well the moving truck is downstairs, get dressed and I'll get started."

A few minutes later we both heard glass shatter in my bedroom and ran to see what had broken.

"Damn it, cat!" I screamed as I found my clear glass wine bottle filled with Pensacola sand on the ground in pieces. Thad picked up the sticky notes buried in the sand and started reading them off.

"Purple Haze? Weed of death?" I snatched them from his hands and quickly started scooping the sand into a plastic cup I had nearby, saving any that I could.

"Can we at least discuss the beautiful girl with a penis?" He chuckled and I joined him.

"It was a road trip Rory and I took a few years ago. A trip I never wanted to forget. So when I got home, I scribbled down the highlights."

"Body shots?" He raised an inquisitive brow.

"It was years ago. We can do body shots." I gave him my best smile, pleading for him to drop it.

There was another knock on the door and I nodded my head to him to go answer it. It was the movers. I was one step closer. This was it, everything I had worked for. As soon as I was free of Thad's questions, I browsed through my sticky notes and smiled. I spent a few minutes letting myself think about him and then quickly cleaned up the mess, saving the notes and the sand in a shoe box.

The move went so quickly, in a hour the movers were grabbing the couch and the larger furniture. Thad wrinkled his nose at the mess underneath the couch. Old hangers, cat hair, left over cereal crumbs and dirt. He swept it up neatly and said with a laugh, "Yeah, you are a total slob. I may rethink asking you to move in with me."

"Oh, shut up," I said offended, but really wrinkling my nose at what a disgusting human I was. I was a little embarrassed and had to question my own housekeeping abilities. He lifted an unopened envelope that had my name on it and handed it to me as he walked out the door with the last few boxes. I smiled at him, whispering a thank you as I opened the envelope. I was prepared to throw out whatever it was until I inspected it further and went deathly still.

Nadine,
Where were you? I practically slept at your door all weekend.

I knocked on Rory's door when I remembered you telling me you lived across from each other. I waited all weekend for you to come home and I have to leave now or I will miss my flight. I got your SOS email, your song, and I came running. I wanted to tell you in person that you aren't alone and that I miss you too. You are all I think about, all I see when I close my eyes. I went back to life and it really didn't seem like much of one without you in it. I want to be with you, I want to be that guy. I wish I could take back leaving you on that beach. I have never regretted something so much in my life. Am I crazy? Were you just trying to tell me you missed me? I don't know. I keep thinking about your Darkman and it haunts me. I didn't want him catching up with either of us before I got a chance to tell you that I want to be with you, Nadine, whatever it takes. I feel like I am going crazy.

This is so far from over for me. Just tell me if you feel the same. I will come running. I will always come running.

I know this breaks all your rules, so If I don't hear from you, I will know why.

S

"No," I whispered "Oh God, NO!" I felt the bullet lodged in my chest again and felt the loss sweep through me. I calculated in my head how long ago I had sent the song. Exactly two years ago. Where was I? Rory dragged me to Texas OU weekend in Dallas. God, I could kill her. I didn't even like football! Spencer was at my door, at my fucking door and in love with me, he wanted to be with me. I buried my head in my hands. I folded the letter quickly and put it in my pocket and wiped my tears away as Thad ascended the steps. It was easy to figure out why the note was under the couch, it sat two feet directly in front of the door. Too much sleight of hand, Spencer! All this time I had thought he had ignored my email, and now I knew he thought I had ignored his letter. He heard my plea and he came running. I never heard his. He had gone all this time thinking I didn't want him back. I played off my emotion on finding the letter by pretending I was devastated leaving my apartment, leaving Oklahoma. Thad tried his best to comfort me and laughed at my overboard display. I felt the loss of Spencer all over again.

I made the trip with Thad and tried my best to forget about the letter. I called Rory, making sure she would be able to meet me at my new place. She was getting out of nursing school for fall break and texted me back that she would be there. I had to talk to someone. Thank God I had Rory. Thad talked to me the whole way to New Orleans and I didn't hear a word.

I WATCHED THAD set the last of the boxes down and head to the kitchen for some water. He gave me a knowing grin when I began to walk toward him. I wrapped my arms around his waist as he finished draining his cup.

"Thanks, Thad. Really, this was so good of you." I heard my own words falter slightly as I removed my arms from his waist. I couldn't handle the pressure bearing down on my chest. I was raw. I took the top box off a stack, opened it and began to scatter its contents on my new counter. Thad walked up behind me, sliding his arms around me and whispering in my ear.

"Baby, please tell me what's wrong. You didn't listen to a word I said on the drive over."

"Nothing, it's just nerves. I'm just a little disoriented, overwhelmed, I guess." I removed his arms from my waist and continued unpacking, but not really putting anything away. I wasn't being fair to him and I knew it, and the fact that he was turning me to face him let me know he knew it too.

"What's wrong, Nadine?"

I stared into his baby blues and took in his features. I had kept him at arm's length most of our relationship, letting him in here and there. He knew me. He knew my habits, my moods. He was no stranger to me, and yet I never really gave him more than tiny glimpses once in a while. It seemed like enough for him. I realized then and there it wasn't enough for me. He was good for me, he treated me well, there was no question I should have opened myself to him more.

"Who is he?" I saw Thad's patience start to ware as my eyes widened at his question, letting him know he was onto something.

I couldn't do this; I couldn't look at him and tell him he wasn't what

I wanted. But why? I quickly opened another box and began taking the contents out.

"Nadine." Something about the way he said my name struck a nerve and I lunged at him, kissing him feverishly, roaming his body with my hands. He hesitated at first and then quickly reciprocated my kiss. I lifted the hem of my shirt and separated us for only a second to throw it on the floor. I unbuckled his pants and felt him stiff against my fingers, keeping my eyes closed as I let him fully taste my mouth, my neck and roam my chest. He undid the button of my shorts, strumming his fingers on the sensitive skin above my panties. He pulled back and whispered to me, "I love you, Nadine."

My eyes sprang open and I pulled away from him quickly. "No, come on, don't do that to me."

"What?" he asked, his face twisting with hurt and anger, "tell you the truth?"

I lunged at him again, trying my best to keep him distracted. I just needed time to … think. As I kissed Thad I eyed the shoe box sitting on the stack of boxes behind him and pulled my lips away, cursing.

"I can't help you if you won't tell me what's wrong," Thad stated plainly. He was irritated, hurt, aroused, and I was doing all of this to him and for what? Thad was my best friend. He had been with me through good and bad and stayed stoic no matter what I had thrown at him. He was gorgeous and charming and quick witted, and up until today had an insane amount of patience. I looked at him now and saw a man who was beyond his limits. He didn't deserve it and I couldn't do it to him anymore.

"I can't tell you what you want to hear," I whispered to him, not quite meeting his eyes. "Thad, it's just not something I am capable of."

I saw his face fall as he whispered back, "Something you aren't capable of? Or not capable of with me?"

"I don't know." I felt the sting of tears and saw recognition in his face.

"Fuck." He gripped his chest briefly and buckled his pants.

"Thad, you don't understand I am—"

"No, stop, don't say another word. My heart can't take it. I knew when we started dating you didn't belong to me, but I never for one second thought you wouldn't after all this … time."

There it was. The word I hated more than any other. Time.

"I don't even know what I want from you, Spencer."

"What we both want, more time."

It was just a fucking letter. It shouldn't mean anything now, it shouldn't matter so much. Why can't I just forget about it? Forget about him? My chest heaved as I saw Thad's anger subside slightly and his hurt set in.

"Tell me this, Nadine. Where is he?" He had contempt in his voice now and I didn't blame him. I was pissed at me, too.

"Not in the picture, he's not. Thad please don't do this."

"Do what? Protect myself? Someone has to fucking care about me." He shook his head back and forth slowly, his eyes closed painfully shut as if he was fighting his emotion. I let another round of salt make its way down my cheeks. I had just broken his heart. I knew what it felt like. I took a step toward him.

"I'm sorry. It's just today, something … happened and I can't really explain it, but—"

He walked away from me heading toward the door, refusing to listen to me. "Thad don't leave, please. Don't leave like this."

He stood in the doorway and slowly turned to face me. His eyes were glazed and radiated nothing but pain. I gasped slightly and felt myself crumble away piece by piece for him. I vowed then and there not to ever hurt anyone like that again. I led him on and I had just figured it out, and apparently so had he.

"Thad, please don't leave. It was just today. I just felt off. I felt fucked up. Don't leave."

"I can't stay knowing how you really feel." He turned again and walked quickly out the door.

I wanted to go after him. I wanted to tell him I loved him too, anything to make him stay, to take his pain away, hell to take my pain away. But I didn't. I couldn't, because I didn't love him. I had settled with Thad. I closed the door and turned quickly, my hurt turning to anger. I kicked over a stack of boxes and saw the shoe box full of sand hit the floor. I walked quickly into my bedroom and laced my running shoes. I wiped a tear away from each eye and knotted my hair. I was exhausted, but there was no way I could sit in that brand new apartment full of boxes.

CHAPTER
Twenty-Two

Nadine

I HAD TAKEN CONTROL of every single aspect of my life, my career was a priority. It all seemed like a natural progression, especially with Thad. What had I done wrong? I quickly took the steps and fled my apartment building, the sounds of New Orleans filling my senses. I made a quick attempt to stretch and took off at a rough pace. I was thankful the air was getting crisp with fall's descent over the city. It wasn't exactly the city I fell in love with due to the huge amount of construction, but its charms still captured me nonetheless. I felt the buzz surround me with each purposeful stride I made, letting my mind race with thoughts of Thad and how I had hurt us both. I must have looked like a lunatic, crying and running at full speed erratically all over the streets. I took a pause to catch my breath at the edge of a park. I sat there completely confused and amazed at how yesterday, at this time, I had it all figured out. I felt the pressure in my chest and took a deep breath. Okay, so you found a letter from Spencer, no need overreact. Too. Late. For. That.

He wanted to be with me, whatever it took. He missed me. I stifled a sob and quickly resumed my run. Rory would be here soon, all I had to do was just hang on.

I rounded a corner and saw a couple gawking at each other and holding hands. I narrowed my eyes. "On your right, assholes!" They jumped in unison at my remark, looking genuinely offended and confused as I passed quickly. Okay, that was uncalled for.

I had never even considered the melancholy that might accompany me moving to this city. Spencer was always in the back of my mind. I knew that. I put him there. He set the standard for the men I would date. It was purposeful and was meant to help me navigate. Our time here wasn't what had convinced me to move. It was my love for this city. The city had an amazing effect on me, the history, the sights, and not to mention the corruption which was both a blessing and a curse for my new career.

Damn it! If I hadn't of found that letter, I knew I would be none the wiser. Thad and I would be unpacking my apartment, instead I was practically crawling back to it to shower. I washed the day away, still feeling a heavy heart. I began to text Thad a hundred times, but had no right words. I would have to be a big girl and call him. I had to give him some time.

Freshly showered, I tried to get myself a little more excited about my situation and unpacked my entire closet. When I reached the kitchen, I quickly grabbed a broom and dustpan to sweep up the sand, putting it back in the box. I grabbed the closest sticky note and read it.

"Pillow Talk."

I closed my eyes. *"You will remember me, Nadine."*

I put the lid on the box and carried the sticky note with me to my bed, sticking it on my computer monitor. I hadn't let myself so much as think about looking him up after I thought he hadn't answered my SOS. I never let myself entertain thoughts of seeing him ever again, until today. I would just do a simple search, no big deal. I made it five minutes into my search when I found him.

YOU HAVE GOT to be fucking kidding me," Rory said, reading the letter. "Why does this always seem like my fault!"

"Don't worry about that part, Rory. You were just trying to cheer me up with that trip."

"But you hated that weekend, you hate football, and Spencer was at your place!"

"Rory, forget about it. Just tell me what to do."

"Nadine, this letter is two years old, he could be married. Have you looked him up?"

"You know I did. No he isn't married, he doesn't believe in marriage."

"No twenty-five year old man does."

"Rory!"

"Ask them again when they're closing in on thirty."

A wave of panic swept through me.

"Rory, you are not helping," I said, bringing up his law firm portfolio.

"Stalker… Let's see what you got." She read his profile and whistled.

"Yeah, I know. He's one of the best lawyers in Philadelphia. He went to a huge firm. I can't find a picture anywhere on the web."

"You know damn well you could find out everything if you wanted to," Rory piped suggestively.

"No."

"He could be fat." I gave her a menacing look. "Well, damn it, Nadine, you have his number, it's right there on the screen. Call him!"

"What about Thad? I can't just forget about him and—"

"Nadine, I can't believe you haven't spit him out by now. You know better."

"I know," I said as I lowered my head under her stare. We were sitting side by side on my barstools. Rory was just as excited to be back in the city as I was. We agreed to come together after I got my job offer, otherwise I wouldn't have left Oklahoma.

"So when are you coming?" I asked, trying to change the subject.

"Spring semester and I'm here. But listen, I'm not moving in with you."

"Why?"

"I'm too old for that. I'll have a job and my own place when I get here."

"Fine with me. You are a nudist," I teased.

"Okay, I came down here to celebrate, not bellyache over a guy you—"

"This isn't just some guy, Rory. He's my green," I said as serious as I could muster. Rory studied me with a knowing smile.

"Well, then I guess it's time you bet on God, honey."

"What do I do?"

"It will come to you," she said, putting her arm around me. "Now please, take me somewhere, anywhere."

I SAT IN bed that night slightly buzzed and in the same damned position I was in two years ago. Email up and ready to type, but completely
terrified of what I wanted to say. I spent hours typing out an email only
to delete it one after another. In the end, I found a bottle of vodka made
the words flow smoother.

> Spemcer,
> I moved to today and found your letr under my couch. My
> cat Spencer my cat! And broken bottles. I know who james brown
> is. I tried to tell you how I feel in the email with the band. Rorys
> here and yelling but you are my green and I need you to run. So
> run. You said you would run.
> Nadine

I hit send and passed out with a swallow of vodka left.

I woke the next morning to see if I had any emails. I had nothing but
a horrible hangover. I checked my outbox to make sure the email went
through and winced as I began to read my message. I screamed bloody
murder when I realized what I had done. Rory came in with just a G-string
on and I threw a t-shirt at her as I buried my head under the covers. She
threw on the t-shirt and sat next to me.

"Another reason why I won't ever room with you, ever. Blood cur-
dling screams and no respect for sleep. What the hell is wrong?"

"Just look." I pointed in horror to the screen and she turned my laptop to read.

"Oh God, Nadine, a monkey could type a better email." I lifted the
comforter over my head and glared at her.

"Rory, I swear to God, you are going to be the worst nurse on earth!
Please make sure to stay away from the suicidal patients."

"No need to freak, just type another email and tell him you were
drunk."

"Yeah, because he will want to come running then. I can't tell him I was drunk, have you forgotten about his dad? Just forget it, maybe it went to his junk, maybe it went to his secretary. He is a high profile lawyer. I'm sure his emails get filtered."

"Don't give up, Nadine. Come on, you owe it to yourself to try again."

"Let's just unpack." I moaned at the hammer pounding incessantly in my head. I grabbed the vodka bottle and took the last swig. I had blown it. I couldn't think about it, I had to put it in the back of my mind.

Rory's infamous chatter kept me busy most of the day. She turned to me when she opened the shoe box full of sand and sticky notes and I grabbed it from her, quickly covering it up. I ignored my email for a week. When I finally opened it, I was relieved to see I had no messages from Spencer. I was also devastated. I didn't know this man anymore. But in the last forty-eight hours my life had been turned upside down because of his letter. I had to get a grip. I read the letter one last time and threw it in the shoe box with the sand and put it away. It was time to start a new chapter in New Orleans without Spencer in it. It was just time.

CHAPTER
Twenty-Three

Spencer

ANOTHER BORING MEETING. I was beyond sick of this shit. A group of grown men congratulating each other on being rich, it made me sick. I sat at the conference table for yet another meeting on how well the firm was doing and the next set of high pro-file cases we would be taking on. I already knew the Staley case would be mine. I had a ridiculous case load as it was due to the seniors pushing me to make partner. It was a far cry from what I signed up for, but at least I was doing it well.

I scrolled through my phone for email, opening each one. Janey, my receptionist, was on maternity leave and my sub wouldn't be in until noon. Fuck, like I didn't have enough to worry about. I saw a text from my ex, Sarah, telling me I was to meet her at Shoally's at eight. I texted her back letting her know that it wasn't happening. I was done with her. A year of hints that she wanted me to propose was more than enough, besides the fact that I really couldn't stand her after six months.

I scrolled through the emails and opened every one, answering the senior partner when I was called upon with whatever he wanted to hear. I was drowning here, and not because I couldn't cut it, but because I hated it more than family law. I opened the last two emails and paused at the last. The subject was SOS. This had to be a joke. I read the email twice and burst out laughing in front of the entire senior board.

"Mr. Diamond, care to share?"

"No, sir, in fact it's sort of an emergency. I have to run." I tried to keep my laughter inside but was hysterical by the time I reached the door.

"Mr. Diamond?"

"Sir, really, I was asked to run. I must run." I left the meeting, not giving a damn what the consequences were.

I stopped in my office to get a better view of the email. This couldn't be her. I couldn't stop my laughter as I read the email over and over. What in the hell, Nadine? From what I could interpret, she didn't find my letter until yesterday and was really drunk. What the hell happened to this woman? What the hell had happened to me?

I took off my jacket and threw it over my desk chair. I wish it had been months since I had thought about her. The truth was, it was only yesterday. If she never got my letter, that means she thought I never answered her email. Talk about an epic fucking backfire.

I knew nothing about her now, where she lived, who she was. From the email I couldn't be sure that life had treated her well. I searched the web for her and came up with only a Facebook profile that had been closed. I should email her back. I should tell her I got it. I queued up my mail and hit reply. What the hell do I say to that? Run? I knew what she meant, because I knew that I meant I would always come running. She wanted me to come running? She still wanted me? God, and if that was the truth, what the hell exactly would I be running to? This had to be an accident. But a drunken email? I knew this woman. I knew her well enough to know it couldn't be typical. Could it? Jesus, the last thing I needed was another drunk in my life.

I closed my eyes, and for the millionth time thought of her beautiful smile, her body next to mine, telling me about her Darkman. Her laugh, her kiss, her bathed in sunlight in a bikini dodging waves. This woman, who I thought had crushed me, had no idea she had. I remembered her scent, her taste and the last time I made love to her. I felt myself go hard at the thought of being inside of her. If I had the chance, I would do it over and over again. I still missed her.

"Nadine." I smiled and read her email again. What the hell was I supposed to say to her?

"Mr. Diamond your mother is on the phone. She said it's urgent."

"Thanks, Kylie."

"Mom?"

"Spencer." I heard her sobbing on the phone and I knew. I just knew.

I felt my chest tighten because even though I knew the words were coming, I had to brace myself.

"Spencer, he's … gone."

"Mom, I'm on my way."

8 months later

Nadine

I STARED AT the picture Rory sent me from her honeymoon. She looked so cute. Her new husband Doug stood almost seven feet tall and they looked ridiculous and perfect. She met him her first day as a nurse. He was a paramedic and they had literally bumped heads. She refused a date the first time he asked, but when she saw him arrive to work on a Harley and later that day got the ride of her life in the supply closet, she was over the moon. Rory had met and married a man in less than six months. I shook my head in disbelief, but in all honesty, I truly liked Doug. The message under the picture read.

> **Asshat,**
> **Having a blast in Belize. When I get back I am determined to get that stick out of your ass so we can have some fun.**
> **PS. I know the real you, and she dances on bars and sings Blondie, bitch. I have ammo, don't make me use it.**

I shook my head and texted her back.

> **Hey, I'm not the one who took a nosedive into marriage, idiot. You're the one whose fun is over. Good luck with that…**
> **Although, I do love Doug and it's good to have a tall man around for light bulbs and such, so yes, you may keep him. Tequila when you get back, promise.**

The buzz from my desk phone had me jumping out of my skin.

"Detective Rhodes? Line One."

"I'm busy, Jennifer."

"He says it's really important. It's a judge—"

"I don't care." I picked up the phone and slammed it down. Today I would relax. I had spent months building this case and today I was officially done and looking forward to a long break. The problem was I had no Rory to spend it with. I felt a small tug of jealousy but pushed it down. I had begun dating again after I'd separated from Thad, but after a series of strike outs decided to concentrate on my case load. Be happy, Nadine. I sat looking at the file in front of me smiling. This file, this file was flawless. There was no way Edger Reynolds would ever see the light of day again. He was the worst kind of serial rapist and I was the one who was going to put him away for the rest of his disgusting existence.

My supervisor burst through my office door and threw a set of photos on my desk.

"I'm off today, Mark."

"I know, Nadine. Just look at them, that's all I'm asking."

"What am I looking for?"

"Abnormalities at the crime scene."

"Fine, I'll call you if I find something. And just so you know my vacation started two hours ago."

"Thanks, Rhodes."

I picked up the photos and studied them for twenty minutes before I picked up the phone and called him. "Mark, did you notice the chip in the wood panel?"

"Yeah, we saw that. It was obviously hit with the same weapon that the victim was bludgeoned with."

"Yeah, except for the fact that there is a bullet hole in the opposite wall behind it. Have you gotten the blood samples back?"

"Not yet."

"I guarantee you have two blood types come back and the victim was also a shooter and we have a missing gun."

"Thanks, Rhodes."

"Anytime."

"One day you are going to have to explain how you do this shit."

"I would rather just take your job."

"Nice. I'll be happy not to see your ass for a week."

"Likewise, but I'm pretty sure you like my ass." I was smiling now and I knew Mark was too.

Now that I had sweet freedom, I had no idea what to do with it. I looked up tickets to Maui where my Dad was currently residing for the month and decided it would be awesome to spend a little time with him. When I graduated the police academy he stayed in Oklahoma with me for a month, afraid that I wouldn't make it past the first few weeks with a gun. I couldn't help but laugh at his attempts to bribe me out of my career choice. We spent an entire month reconnecting and had made it a point to stay that way. I was just about to call him when the door burst open and two uniformed offers walked in.

"What the fuck?"

"Sorry, detective, you need to come with us now."

"I am also an officer of the law, gentlemen. You will not touch me and no I won't come with you. What the hell is this all about?"

"He said this would be a nightmare," one cop remarked to the other.

"Let's just cuff her."

"Look, dumb and dumber, I will fuck you up if you take a step near me, I swear to God!" My voice got higher as they came closer. I didn't have a chance in hell. I wore a skirt today of all things, that in itself kept me from struggling much. In a matter of minutes I was read my Miranda rights and was being escorted downstairs to a holding cell.

"What in the hell is going on?"

"Obviously you're in some kind of trouble, ma'am."

"So are you, you stupid son of a bitch. I will have BOTH your badges for this!"

They eyed each other with a worried look on their faces and I continued. "Do you know who I am! Who is the new circuit judge?"

They led me into a holding cell and I saw it was completely empty. I also had my badge, gun and phone. "What the hell are you idiots doing? You haven't even removed a thing from me or printed me! Jesus, if this is how you book perps—" I stopped mid-sentence. Something was off, way off. "What the hell is going on here?"

The cops smiled at each other and walked out of earshot.

It's my boss, congratulating me on the case in a sick way. Jesus, Mark, you could have sent lunch. I texted Mark quickly. Maybe I had pissed him off with the job remark.

You are a sick and twisted bastard, Mark. I would really appreciate it if you let me out of here.

A few minutes later I got his reply.

What the hell are you talking about, Rhodes?

You know exactly what the hell I am talking about, sir. I am sitting in a jail cell.

Well at least the world is safe from you for a while.

Very funny, Mark. I am supposed to be celebrating. Can you please get me the hell out of here?
It wasn't me, Rhodes.

Well can you kindly figure out why the hell I am in here?

Already on it, Rhodes. Sit tight.

A thousand different scenarios went through my head. What the hell was going on?

I called for my arresting officers and no one came. This was way more than a simple arrest.

I rolled my eyes and tapped my phone to look up and see who the new circuit judge was. Panic was beginning to set in. I was waiting for the picture to come up on my phone when I heard a door buzz and an officer mutter, "Judge Diamond."

My heart did a free fall as my cell brought up a current picture of the circuit judge. Spencer T. Diamond. The picture alone had my heart racing and I could feel the heat in my cheeks. In the picture he looked the same, more professional, just a little older but still insanely beautiful. I instantly was lost.

I was in a state of complete shock and turned to the man standing on the opposite side of the bars as I shook my head back in forth in disbelief. A flood of recognition of who he was and what he meant to me hit me in the gut. My chest instantly filled with a burning. I had no choice but to shed the tears my eyes were holding and laughed through them. It was the only time I did it, with Spencer. I stood quickly, feeling faint, and walked toward him slowly, taking in all the air I could. He wore a familiar devilish grin and his beautiful brown eyes peered at me, making me way more emotional than I thought possible. I gathered my strength to speak.

"Judge, just what in the hell am I being charged with?"

"Ignoring a circuit judge when he calls you. It's just rude."

Our matching smiles had to look absolutely ridiculous. He looked perfect. He wasn't the beach babe I had rolled around with on the sand. He had very much grown into himself, tall, dark and insanely handsome, more so than ever. His beautiful long lashes feathered against his lids and I ached to trace the scar above his eye. His tailored suit fit him to perfection. He had the air of a distinguished gentlemen, but I knew the stranger he was to me now was the same stranger he was to me then. He was in there and his eyes told me so. I had to look down for an instant to make sure I looked the part for him. When my eyes met his again it was an electric connection. Spencer found me. He came.

"I know what you're thinking," he whispered.

"What am I thinking?"

"That you won."

"You told me I did," I whispered back emphatically.

"I am not the one in jail." Dimples, Jesus take me now.

I immediately saw my future. I thought of all the wildest most random things. Jonathan Seagull came to mind last. He was here. My heart melted as he wrapped his arms around the bars between us.

I put my hands under his and peered into his eyes.

"So how do I get out of here, Judge Diamond?"

"What did I tell you about the man who gets you?"

Lips parted, I tried to take in steady breaths.

"How do you know he didn't get me already?" It felt like a clever line, but everything in my body language had to be telling him otherwise.

I saw a perfect eyebrow raise in response. He had to know through office personnel or otherwise I had been living like a monk. My success case ratio was off the charts. I could interrogate a murder suspect for hours, taunt them, bring them to the point of hurting me physically and getting a confession, but I couldn't look Spencer in the eye for more than a few seconds without losing my composure. I closed my eyes remembering his face as he told me goodbye. I felt that gnawing feeling in my gut that I always did when I thought of him. I opened my eyes and it disappeared. The words came to me quickly.

"You said he would … claim me right away, and he would shelter me and protect me and…" I saw a small smile on his face taunting me, but his eyes were full of the familiar look. I had to check myself before I lost any more of my ability to function.

"Go on." He peered at me again through those amazing eyes and I felt my knees weaken.

"He will be a pain in the ass but he will be worth it." I rolled my eyes at him through the cell.

"And." He moved his hands down to touch mine and I felt my heart fall further… if that was even possible.

"Spencer … how? How did you do this?"

"What else did I say?" he asked, his eyes intent on mine. I felt his kiss in New Orleans, his kiss in the sea. I exhaled a deep breath. "You said he would touch me and look at me the way you do and he would always be invited."

"So am I invited?"

"Jesus, Spencer, you moved here?"

"I also said he would be worth it because you are. You still are." He opened the door and our hug lasted longer than our conversation. I was completely overwhelmed.

"Sorry I'm late. It took me this long to decipher your email." I laughed into his chest through my tears and looked up at him.

"This is so weird," I said bluntly.

"But it's so good, just like it was. I really believed I wasn't that guy. How the hell I expected to move on past you, Nadine, is beyond me." I kept my arms wrapped around him tightly. This whole scenario was just insane, and I had never felt more comfortable in a man's arms.

"So I guess I need to take you on a date?" he said sweetly, lifting my chin to meet his eyes, his smile making me forget the last few years of hardships searching for his equal and coming up completely empty.

"Guess so." The woman in me sighed into him as he held me close and whispered in my ear.

"How about Pensacola?"

First Date with Spencer

CHAPTER
Twenty-Four

Nadine

HOW IN THE hell was I supposed to act when my daydream was sitting right next to me? I surveyed the interior of the car to keep from staring at him and took a deep breath. I finally looked over to Spencer who was smiling at me. I smiled back. I couldn't say a word. I was too terrified to screw it up and then again I was completely baffled that he had done the grand gesture of moving to New Orleans without so much as speaking to me first. But this was Spencer, my green, my ideal, the man who had kept me his with the mere memory of those days spent a few years ago. He set the bar and now I found myself worried he couldn't compete with the memory. I looked at him again as he started the car.

"Just so you know, my move is temporary. I have to be elected to sit as judge and I also signed a three month lease."

He could still read me.

"So you're testing the waters?"

"In the same way you are. Looks like you are looking for the lifeboat right now. It's okay, you know, to feel the way you do."

"Spencer, please don't think I'm not happy."

He stopped from pulling out of my complex, put the car in park and looked at me, really looked at me.

He had followed me home and I had packed a bag quickly. He was really taking me to Pensacola. I asked him to wait because I didn't want Spencer the man coming face to face with Spencer the cat. It wouldn't be good. I called Rory and had to beg her to stop screaming and ask her to watch him when she returned from her honeymoon in two days, leaving him with my neighbor George until then. I had to hang up on her to be able to pack. I had a nervous breakdown in my closet and fifteen minutes later I was handing Spencer my suitcase to add to his trunk. I was amazed that he was so sure I would come. Spencer looked at me now and could tell I was terrified. I had no idea why I couldn't relax.

"Relax," he said, leaning over to brush my hair away from my shoulder. "Tell me what you're thinking."

"You're crazy."

He chuckled and then peered into my eyes. "And your mouth is still a nightmare." He reached over, so close to me I took in a breath thinking he would kiss me. This was the moment I had been waiting for. I let out a heavy breath when he grabbed my seatbelt and wrapped it around me. Disappointment at the loss of a kiss, well that was a good sign.

"Me too," he said reassuringly. A wave of recognition hit me as he put the car into gear and we began our trip.

I couldn't stop eyeing him from the passenger seat. Still in his suit, the view of him was too tempting to pass up. I felt the flutter of my insides go off in random waves with each gesture he made, turning on the radio, setting the air. I quickly realized every time he moved I was bracing myself for his touch. I had been with him less than two hours and already I craved him.

"Tell me how in the hell a two year cop makes detective," he said, eyeing me for a brief second before putting his attention back to the road.

"I noticed things, and they noticed me. It's that simple. I just did what I have always done. I've always known it's what I wanted to do."

"Why didn't you tell me?" he said, a small amount of hurt in his voice.

"I didn't want to say it until I was going to do it. You know me and my crazy idea about levels. I didn't want to put it out there until I really wanted it."

"Put it out into the universe, huh? And you think that's how it happens, you wish for it and it comes to you?"

"You're here aren't you?" His answering smile was brilliant. I was surprised at my own words, but didn't regret them. He grabbed my hand and I couldn't help the small gasp at the electricity of his touch. He slid the pad of his thumb over my hand and I felt my whole body warm.

"Better?" he said, giving me a warm glance. I nodded my head looking out my window, squeezing his hand.

"Why are you so late?" I asked in a whisper.

"The day I got your email, my father died." I quickly turned my attention to him and saw his demeanor was the same, but there was a sadness in his face.

"Spencer, God, I am so sorry. I am so so sorry." He looked at me, a silent thank you in his eyes.

"I knew it would happen. I was expecting it. Didn't make a damn bit of difference. It still hurts like hell."

"I don't know what to say."

"Then sit there, beautiful," he teased, still testing the waters.

"It's okay now, to be nice to me, to say things … like that. I kind of got rid of the chip on my shoulder."

"That's good news. What made you change your mind?"

"I changed my own mind. It happens often." I chuckled and squeezed his hand. "Spencer, really your father, I can't even…" I clutched my heart with my free hand, showing him I knew how hard that loss would affect me. "If you ever want to talk about it, or just whatever, you know."

"Yeah, I will. It's good to see you, stranger," he said as the cabin of the car became smaller and the feeling more intimate. I was relaxed and more than ready to explore the waters with him. In a matter of minutes Spencer had not only smoothed away my worries, but had my heart bouncing in every corner of my chest.

Spencer

SHE WAS JUST as beautiful if not more so than she was at twenty when I left her. It had been years since I'd seen or spoken to her and I knew the minute I saw her in that jail cell I wanted all of her. That fucking brilliant mind of hers was more than enough to start, but I couldn't help the need in me. I had only grabbed her hand and every single fiber of me had come to attention. The chemistry was still there.

She had called me crazy. I chuckled to myself hoping it matched whatever she was saying. She gave me a smile and looked out her window to the darkness. I used the leeway to adjust myself quickly. Damn it, I had waited so long to see her, to touch her. I wasn't about to screw it up with my raging need to ruin her or the chance we had to finally be us.

I couldn't believe I was sitting next to the New Orleans "it" detective. I knew she was more than capable. Whether she knew it or not, she would exceed all her own expectations and then some. I wanted to tell her how much I admired her, how amazing I thought it was that she had accomplished so much in our time apart. I had made a name for myself, but was only mildly proud of my accomplishments until asking for an endorsement to claim the seat as judge. I had tried my best to heed my father's warning to not make my life about my career. Though I didn't know it at the time, it was the most important conversation of my life.

I was putting my father in bed after another one of his endless self-destructive days. He was skin and bones and looked ghostly pale. He reached for the bottle of scotch on his nightstand and when I pulled it away he smirked.

"I am proud of you, Spencer." His voice was distant as if he was talking to me while in a daydream.

He looked nothing like the man who sat me on his lap when I was a boy and patiently waited as I pounded on the keys to find my musical grace. That man was long gone, and what was left was horrifying. He looked far past his fifty-six years and his eyes were bloodshot with a hint of yellow. I could barely stand the sight of him, trying to keep the memory of who he once was fresh in my mind. I felt my chest tighten as he commanded my attention once more.

"Don't make your life all about your career, Spencer. Don't do it. There is nothing more profound, nor will there ever be, than your place in the heart of the woman you love." He took a series of breaths as if to fight off some overwhelming pain.

"My ambition ruined me, son. It ruined me. I had it all. I got greedy and wanted more. I had her love, her loyalty, her respect and I threw it away. I pushed her away to be … more. All I had to do was look at her to know I was enough. It was never my failures in my work that made her look at me that way, it was her disappointment in the way I loved her."

"You should sleep, Dad. I'll check on you in the morning." I turned out his bedside light and he quickly sat up and turned it back on.

"Spencer, listen to me. I may not have your respect anymore but I know that you aren't happy. I know it, son. I just want you to think long and hard about what you are doing. Don't waste any more time running a fool's errand!"

"And just what do you suppose I do, Dad?"

"Do better!"

"Okay, Dad."

"Promise me, Spencer." He didn't wait for a response. He was out.

I studied his frail body as he lay unconscious on his colossal bed. I studied him for a minute longer and whispered, "Why couldn't you do better?"

I looked around the enormous bedroom. It hadn't changed much at all over the years. I felt a chill run through me as I looked back at his place in the bed and the empty spot next to it. I really couldn't blame her anymore. I also knew I could never forgive her.

I grew up in nothing short of a spectacular townhome. I noted the high ceilings, marble floors, and intricately carved wood throughout. It seemed cold to me now, and I knew why. My father had brought the warmth to this home and now he was less than a shell of a man, it had more of a museum feel to it now. Every picture, every piece of furniture screamed 'Don't Touch.' I descended the stairs and traced the banner, following it to the curved end with my fingertips like I did when I was a kid. I stared in the parlor room at the grand piano. I walked over to it to see an absolute mess of completely unreadable sheet music. I felt another stab in my chest as I picked them all up and stacked them neatly, leaving them on the top of the piano. I felt another shiver wash through me as I locked the door when I left. It was the last time I saw my father, and the last time I ever set foot in that cold home.

It took the better part of six months to settle my father's estate and set my mother up comfortably. I wanted no part of my mother's new life. She was now free to live how she pleased, and so was I. I will never regret being near my father or the fact I had ironed out our relationship to the extent that I had, finally started living before he started dying. He understood. He loved me. He never held it against me even though he needed me and at times I wasn't there. It was never my fault. I had to repeat that daily. My grief led me down a dark road, and when I'd had enough I decided to do better, like he asked me to. And by better I meant leaving a job I hated and city I had grown tired of for a complete change. And by better I also meant Nadine who was smiling at me now, waiting on a response. Shit. What did she ask?

"Spencer?"

"Sorry, I was watching the GPS. What was the question?"

"Amy and Jack, how are they? Rory spoke with them for a while after our first trip you know."

"No, I didn't. They didn't mention it." Probably because I had told them I didn't want to know anything at all after I had felt dismissed, after pouring my chest out into a letter to her. I was still kicking myself for that stupid stunt.

"Sooooo?"

"Oh, they're fine. They have a son," I said, taking my hand from hers, and feeling the loss, to adjust the GPS.

"I know. They had him exactly nine months after our trip," she said chuckling.

"What's so funny?" I asked, eyeing her long legs.

"Nothing," she said in a whisper, taking my hand out of my lap, accidentally brushing against me and making my whole body stiffen. She noticed, I had no doubt about it, but she didn't acknowledge it.

"And Ellie?" she asked sweetly. "I did look her up and we spoke a few times. She said she was dating an artist?"

"She married and divorced him. It was an annulment, actually, and I handled it. Poor thing. Luckily he didn't try to take her for anything. He was a true piece of shit, a wolf in sheep's clothing. I actually set her up with the new one. He's a good guy. I think they are doing great. I don't know, it's been a while since I spoke to her."

"I still miss Jack and Amy." I felt the tug in my chest when I heard the small amount of sadness in her voice. She finished with, "They were the best people I had ever met. Still are."

"They're coming to New Orleans in a few months." This made her happy and for that I was grateful. It's all I wanted. This was definitely better. She turned my hand over in her lap and began making circles with her pointer. I felt my heart free fall. This was better than better.

CHAPTER
Twenty-Five

Nadine

A LL I WANTED was his touch, so I touched him as much as possible. It was almost impossible not to crawl into his lap while he was driving. I couldn't bear the thought of this not working out. I was babbling on and on about Rory and work and everything that came to mind. I was still a little on edge, but this time for a different reason.

I wanted him. I needed him to know it. I started making circles in his palm, similar to the ones he had made on my back after we made love the last time. I was consumed by his scent. I glanced at the GPS and was relieved when we only had twenty miles left on our trip. I could comfortably say we were reacquainted. What I didn't know was how long I could keep myself in check. The girl he had known was a self-proclaimed whore. I wasn't her anymore and hadn't been since the day I left her on the beach. I couldn't sleep with him, not yet. I had to let him know I had grown in that way, I had already proven it to myself. I didn't want him to think I was the same girl. I was far from it. Though opening myself to the possibility of love had been a total nightmare, aside from Thad who was unfortunately too nice of a guy, I had realized so much from my few years of dating. I hoped to show him.

"So tell me about them," Spencer said, guarded.

"Them?" I asked, almost sure he was digging around in my mind.

"The men," he said, clipped.

"The men?" I chuckled and saw him give me a stern look. Whoa, he wanted to know if I was still the way I used to be.

"Oh, there have been thousands. I mean I had at least a dozen lined up this week."

"Very funny. Really, I want to know."

"Why? No way, no need, really. Sex has been a mirage for me for a solid eight months. I've grown to be an old cat lady."

"The hell you say?"

"Really, I have a cat … named Spencer."

"You didn't." He chuckled.

"I did. I wanted to re.." Shit. Shit. Shit.

"Remember me?" he said, hopeful.

"Yes, Spencer, I did. I didn't need that sack of fur to do it, either. I dated too and it wasn't fun." I turned in my seat to confront him. "You know you ruined practically all of my dates. And are you aware dragging a girl inside a bar full of geriatrics and dancing with her in the street is highly romantic? After that, dinner and a movie really doesn't cut it. What the hell were you thinking? No one does that shit."

"Thank you," he said chuckling. "And there are romantic men out there, Nadine."

"I've only dated one. Well, Thad was good to me. He was my first boy—" I felt the tension in Spencer surface. "Are you sure you want to hear this?"

"Sure. I dated. I had a girlfriend. Sarah."

"Great," I clipped out.

"No, she wasn't." I smiled to that and we let the subject drop.

"Anyway, you were my real first boyfriend," I said enthusiastically as he parked the car at the hotel.

"I was?"

"Absolutely," I said without hesitation. He seemed touched as he cupped my cheek and I leaned into his hand.

"Before we get checked in do you want to take a walk?" he asked, hopeful.

"Of course." He let go of my cheek and as I rounded the car he pulled me into a long hug.

"God, you feel good." His lips tickled my senses as I squeezed him tight and he brushed his lips over my jaw line and then landed a slow sweet kiss on my mouth.

"Spencer," I felt the familiar pull of him. This was better than my daydreams. He stood holding me with his body at a distance. He put my hands on his shoulders before leaning down to take my heels off, gently removing each one and kissing my ankle sweetly as he gathered the shoes and threw them in his back seat, discarding his own and cuffing his pant sleeves.

It finally hit me that we were back where we started, the beach. I breathed in the air and a wave of excitement raced through me as he grabbed my hand and led me to the patch of sand next to the hotel leading to the sea. We walked over a small sand dune as I noticed the moon in its half-illuminated state. We heard beachgoers in the distance laughing and talking as I drank in the dark night sky and braced myself for the expanse of dark water I had held onto the memory of. I felt the pounding of my heart as the sea came into view and the sound of the waves lulled me into a hypnotic state. I literally gasped with delight at the full feeling in my chest as I gripped Spencer's hand and we made our way to the foam. I stuck my toe in to test the water and when I felt it's coldness I did a small shimmy.

"It's probably going to be a little cold," he said, a worried look on his face. He had been trying so hard. All this effort, all these amazing lengths he had gone to. I had to let him know it hadn't gone unnoticed. I felt a trail of renewal make its way across my heart. I felt alive. I felt amazing. He was amazing and it was finally our time. To be.

"It's perfect, Spencer. This is all so amazing. Thank you. You couldn't have done better."

He turned to me then and brought his lips to mine. "I can always do better for you, Nadine. I will always do better."

WE CHECKED INTO our hotel room and I noticed the presence of two beds in it. He had made a reservation while I had packed at home. He noticed my look of puzzlement.

"I don't expect anything," he said, quickly unloading our luggage and taking a change of clothes to the bathroom.

"You've already seen all of me," I reminded him as he shut the door and I got no response.

I took a fresh dress out of my suitcase and made a quick change, unhooking my bra and sliding on the halter top emerald green sundress. I let my hair down and was grateful it lay perfectly around my shoulders. I spent a few minutes on makeup and was done by the time he walked out dressed casually in jeans and a t-shirt. I hadn't braced myself for the heat in his eyes, but I reveled in it.

He made quick strides to me and took my mouth with a ferocity I can only describe as possessive. He erased every single kiss I had in the last few years, his tongue stroking mine over and over until I was so completely taken by it that I had to grip his shoulders to keep myself standing. I felt the heat in my abdomen and the flutter of my stomach. His kiss was all consuming and I felt completely touched when he pulled away from me.

Neither of us spoke as he dipped in again, stroking my lips with his tongue as I moaned and leaned my body further into him. I lifted my neck as he trailed his kiss from my lips past my chin to my neck. He paused at the nape, nipping, licking and sucking gently, and I knew then I didn't have a chance in hell of stopping him if I didn't break his hold now. He saved me the struggle when he pulled away first and grabbed my hand.

"I'm sorry. I had to. I had to know what it would be like to kiss you again, Nadine."

"Don't," my voice was a high squeak. "Don't apologize, Spencer. I wanted it, too. I want you," I paused, "but I—"

"No, no analyzing. Let's go."

We quickly made our way out of the room and headed to the hotel restaurant. A few drinks in we found our old familiar dance of conversation. We were completely caught up two bottles of wine later and laughing hysterically at nothing at all. It was amazing. It was familiar and new and we were both still chuckling as we made our way back up to the room. It was an awkward silence as we again reached the room. He roamed my face and body and planted a soft kiss on my lips before opening the door. He undressed quickly, leaving himself in boxer briefs, and I took my clothes to the bathroom, feeling foolish for acting like a virgin on prom night.

He wanted me and I clearly wanted him. Everything inside me was telling me to go to him, let him ravage me, get it over with. It was going to happen, there was no doubt. Still I hesitated, putting on a t-shirt and boy cut underwear. I walked out to greet him as he pulled the cork on another bottle of wine. We sat with the sliding glass door open, listening to the ocean waves on the patio and talking until we both drifted off in separate beds.

I woke up before him and watched him sleeping from the opposite bed. It was still surreal he was so close to me. I had spent so many days and nights dreaming of him, missing him, lusting for him. I wanted to kiss his dark lashes and was completely tempted to do so. I thought about undressing and getting in bed with him. I thought about his smile at the restaurant last night and how when I spoke he really listened, unlike the number of dates I had who only pretended to be interested. He opened his eyes slowly and met mine as he gave me a slow, sleepy smile. I was toast.

"Hey you," he whispered, his dimples making my heart pick up pace quickly.

"Hey back," I said, admiring the strength of his frame, my mouth watering at the thought of him inside me. I made the decision then. "I need to run an errand."

"Really? Okay, I'll take you anywhere you want to go."

"I need to do it alone. Can I borrow your car?"

He looked alarmed and quickly sat up. "What is it? What's wrong?"

"Nothing's wrong. I just need to run an errand." I couldn't think of one damn good alibi and I listened to them daily. Damn this man could shake me to the core.

"Okay, I'll wait for you here. Breakfast?"

"It's noon, Spencer."

He looked at the clock shocked. "So it is." He smiled at me and I returned it. I hadn't slept this late in as long as I could remember. I was guessing the same for him. "You are still a lousy lay," he chuckled as he rid the space between us and leaned over and kissed my forehead.

CHAPTER
Twenty-Six

Nadine

WHEN I RETURNED from my running around that included shopping, a quick wax, and pedicure, he took me for a late lunch and we spent the rest of the day at the beach. We braved the waves together one by one and spent a majority of the time teeth chattering. It wasn't the same and it never would be. Those memories we held so dearly were all immaculately kept intact, but we were making new memories and it felt just as good.

We had no one but each other to entertain, we weren't chaperoned. We were free to be Spencer and Nadine and it was in itself the most beautiful day I had ever had. He and I were trying to become an us.

We slow danced at a seedy bar near our hotel. I hoped the look in my eyes matched the one in his. We were desperate for each other's touch. When I'd had enough with the pleasantries of long sinful thought filled kisses and the way his hands gently grazed me in places I knew he was longing to touch, I grabbed his hand and we walked in silence back to the hotel.

I left him standing next to the bed, a longing in his eyes and his curiosity piqued.

"I'll be right back." I turned away from him with a smile on my face. Tonight the only man I have ever really trusted would get all of me.

Spencer

I AM A horrible man. I am so ruined by this woman. I can no longer hear my own thoughts. All I want to do is make love to her. All I can think about is my tongue in her mouth, her gasps being as sweet as I remembered them. The throbbing in my pants is controlling me completely. I took a shot from the mini bar and knew the damn two ounce bottle would probably cost me forty times its worth, but I didn't give a damn. I needed to feel numb, I was in pain. I couldn't stop touching her. She was already flowing through my veins as she had been years earlier, it was like a sickness. I needed to touch her, to see the pools of aqua blue in her eyes while I made her moan and call out to me. I was losing the battle with my body.

I already knew that she would be worth the trip, worth the change. She was everything I thought she would be: strong, brilliant, and even more self-assured, which was new. I didn't need to figure her out, I already knew her. I knew she wouldn't be the exact same person and I was fine with that. I didn't expect her to be so … perfect. I had no idea how I got lucky enough to find her single, but she was. No woman had ever compared to Nadine. She challenged me and I loved it. She called me on my shit, and I craved that now. I could also totally see why a man who wasn't strong enough to deal with a woman like her would have to tap out. She had one hell of a mouth on her and I would never get enough of it. Her whit, her beauty, her career, had to have intimidated the hell out of most men. I chuckled again as I thought of how she might have handled some of those situations. There was no way I was letting her slip away. I was determined my need for her wouldn't ruin this, either. I wouldn't push sex. I would wait as long as she wanted.

The bathroom door opened as I downed another shot. I held my breath as she entered the room wearing nothing but a pink teddy. Pink. Teddy.

"I want you to be my last, Spencer." Her eyes were glossy. I knew she was scared, but I couldn't move. It was one thing to see and want a devastatingly beautiful woman. It was another to have her make it clear to you that she wanted you back.

This woman had just made my life worth living … again.

Nadine

I WAITED FOR his response, feeling elated and terrified. I wanted to make some grand gesture of my own, but more than that I truly meant what I said. I hadn't had a single sentence ready for him, only the idea of him knowing I only wanted his touch, his mouth, his body, him period, to be it for me. I had drawn that conclusion years ago. Now I held my little ball out and had thrown it right at him.

He sat stunned on the edge of his bed and I stayed where I was as well. He closed his eyes briefly and stood up, soaking me in. He took slow, painful steps towards me. Painful because I had to wait for each one of them for him to get to me. He didn't say a word as he scooped me up in his arms and took my mouth with a gentleness that only he had for me. He slid his tongue over mine in a gentle soothing pace, taking his time and completely overwhelming me. I was instantly under his spell and had no recollection of even being placed on the bed.

He was covering me with his kiss from head to toe, every single hair on my head stood at attention. He pulled himself away, peering down at me. The look in his eyes was something I had longed for my whole life. He gave me love, acceptance, praise. I surrendered my heart to him completely.

He took his time tracing his fingertips over the top of my breasts that were spilling out of the top of my teddy. I couldn't hold still. I buried my hands in his hair, moaning his name, begging for release, but knew I was in for much more. He put himself between my legs and thoroughly kissed me until I lost my breath and I began to beg for my desire to be quenched. He ignored my pleas, taking time to run his hands from my ankle to my sex and gently brushing the top with his fingers over my paper thin panties. I knew he could feel my warmth. I knew he needed me, too.

"I have thought of you every single day, Nadine. I thought about your smile the most. I love your smile. I thought about your beautiful body, too, touching you like this." I sucked in a breath as his hand found the fullness of my breast and lifted it out of my teddy. He clamped his mouth over it finally, sucking and biting gently until I was grinding myself into him, lifting my hips, writhing and moaning. He dipped his head to my other breast and took my arousal into his mouth, sucking hard as he started to slide my panties down slowly with one hand, taking down each side with special care.

When he got them to my knees he sat up, eyeing me with pure desire as he slipped them off the rest of the way. He spread my legs gently and slid his hands from both knees to my sex as his mouth met my center. His tongued tasted all of me with such precision I cried out to him seconds later, crashing through a wall, quaking and moaning and begging for more. He took my orgasm into his mouth with greed, making sure he got all of it, and taking me into another wave, then another. When he finally made his way up to my mouth I was begging for him. He caught my mouth again, lowering his briefs and entering me when his tongue met mine.

"I love you, Nadine," he whispered to me as he stroked me over and over. "I love you, and I will never leave you again."

His hands were everywhere, the feeling of him flush against me overwhelmed me and I let go of my cries as he slowly pushed himself inside of me, watching my face as I cried out to him. He lifted my neck to his mouth and gently pushed himself further inside as I pushed out breath with my release. He let himself go with the next thrust, intensifying my orgasm, and we both lay gasping and stroking each other, kissing again and again with a fever so intense we were making love again in minutes. I lost myself to him that night and took the deepest part of him into me.

Never and forever are both infinite words; alternate in meaning and both just as meaningful. We all say them, and we all feel passionately about them at the time they cross our lips. I was never going to love a man, never going to trust, never going to be the woman in love with her heart held in the hands of a man she trusted. I was sure when I said the word *never* I was referring to *me*. I felt a wave of pure relief wash over me as Spencer turned my never into forever.

Epilogue

Nadine

"DETECTIVE RHODES, ONE more word out of you and I will find you in contempt!"

"Sir, clearly you are overlooking the obvious."

"You presume to tell me how to run my courtroom!"

"No, sir, but—"

"Counsel and detective Rhodes, in my chambers now." Spencer threw down the gavel and I felt panic take over as I shuffled to the left of the witness stand and into the room adjacent, hearing the prosecution and defense counsel snickering in unison about the trouble I was in. I knew I had just pushed too hard, still I was furious.

"Gentlemen, are we in need of Ms. Rhodes' presence during these proceedings?" Spencer asked without looking at any of us, standing on the other side of his desk next to his chair.

Both of them had just made themselves comfortable for the show and they looked at each other, both answering with a resounding no. I stood next to the window with my head turned and my arms crossed, feeling like a child at the principal's office. Almost all the evidence had been deemed inadmissible due to shady and sloppy police work. I would make sure the entire CSI team was fired. That is, if I still had my job at the end of the day.

"Thank you, counsel, you are dismissed," he said curtly with a nod of his head toward the door.

They both scrambled to their feet sensing his fury, and I didn't blame them. I was pretty terrified myself. Then I remembered his lips on my

195

body the night before. The way he smiled at me this morning. The way he looked at me when I got out of the shower. My man, my beautiful man was … pissed. He glared at me for several moments and didn't utter a single word.

"Spenc—"

"That's judge Diamond, detective Rhodes, and don't ever forget that again."

"Sir, yes, sir," I challenged. "Look, sir, judge Diamond—"

"Four hundred dollar fine, you want to make it five?"

"Spencer!"

"That's six, want to make it seven?"

"You can't be serious."

"Oh, I am, detective Rhodes. You worked this case and I commend you for the detective you are, but when it's put into process, I owe the tax payers and my position to do my damn job, understood?"

"I can't believe you are—"

"Eight hundred dollars, you were completely out of line. You have absolutely no more right to speak in that courtroom than a common citizen. I let you in as a courtesy, but never again. Your job is to collect evidence and let the counsel and I do our jobs. And please tell me in what universe is what you just did acceptable?"

I shut up and I shut up fast. I had never seen him so angry. This was the first case he had taken that I had worked and I was already screwing it up. But it was completely unjust. He was ruthless with me right now and I knew why. I still let my fury boil over in my stance and my glare. The crazy part was I was completely turned on. I watched his chest heave as he sat in his oversized chair, his knees drawn up to the edge of the seat. He was not enjoying this, he was truly angry. It had been a year since our trip to Pensacola and we had never had a personal argument this intense. I was blown away with him, truly impressed and completely and utterly turned on. And pissed he had complete authority over me at this point.

"Is there something you want to say, detective?"

"Will I be fined?" I asked sarcastically, glaring at him.

"Yes, let's make it an even thousand." He glared back. "Make no mistake, I don't ever want to see you in my courtroom again, or I will fine you. " He rose out of his seat so quickly I jumped back on the defensive. He walked around his desk, moving closer to me standing at the window.

"I don't think you quite get it. Maybe I should throw in some time."

"Spencer, damn it, you know we have company coming!"

"Well, detective, I see you need a little bit of a learning curve considering you just again addressed me incorrectly. I'll give you plenty of time to think about this." He opened the door. "Murray, take detective Rhodes to holding for no less than four hours. She's fined one thousand dollars for contempt and do not let her out until exactly four hours is served."

I gasped in utter disbelief as I let a string of curses go while I was held by the elbow by Murray. I looked back at Spencer and saw him glare at me before slamming his door. Shit. Shit, shit, shit, shit.

FOUR HOURS LATER and one neck breaking ride to the store and home to prepare for the night and I was still beyond furious. I couldn't stop thinking about the way he had handled me with such viciousness. Asshole!

I began cracking eggs. I was making homemade beignets, and a breakfast fit for a king. It was not the meal I had hoped to make, but it would have to do because my evil judge boyfriend from hell had robbed me and thrown me in jail. I cracked another egg furiously and put it into the bowl. Son of a bitch. Son of a bitch. I had matured. I had grown as a woman. Yes, my outburst in his courtroom was 'completely unprofessional and ridiculous' as Mark had put it. I knew it had set me back. I knew it was going to take time to make things right. I never expected Spencer to react so violently. The more I thought about it, the madder I got. Okay, so I deserved it. Still this was my best friend, my lover, my green. Fuck green, all I was seeing was red.

"How many eggs are you going to put in that?" I jumped at the sound of Spencer's voice. Without thinking, I saw the egg flying through the air hitting him directly in the chest. Good, I ruined his shirt. I bought him that shirt. Shit it was my favorite shirt. His expression was priceless. He was utterly shocked. Idiot. I threw another and another, egging my bastard of a boyfriend as he rushed toward me, pinning me to the wall with an egg still in my hand.

"Nadine, I'm sorry but you deserved it."

"Spencer, I carry a gun for a living every day, you are aware of that, right?"

He chuckled as I barely struggled against him. I wanted to hear his excuse. I was sure I could take his ass down if I wanted to. I couldn't keep the anger inside.

"Wow, this is new," he said amused, noting the fury in my face. "Fuck, you're hot when you're really mad." I bumped his thigh with my leg and he flinched forward, letting my arm have just enough leeway to crash the last egg into the side of his head. I watched his face contort into anger as he pinned me again. This time I wasn't getting out of it.

"I love you, but I may have to kill you if you don't stop."

"Son of a bitch, you dealt with me like I was just some … nobody!"

"I dealt with you like you were a cop trying to tell me how to do my job!"

"So what! I'm sure it happens all the time. We were alone, and you still wanted to make an example out of me! Spencer, how could you do that to me?"

"It's work, Nadine, and I know you are smart enough to figure out why and that I will do it again. I know you know better. You know you are in the wrong."

"Oh, you go to hell!"

I felt more laughter before he kissed me roughly. I caught his lip and bit it hard. I felt my wrist numbing as he kept me pinned. He bit my lip back and I cried out as he clamped his mouth around my neck and moved his knee to separate my legs. I moaned and he immediately let go of my wrists. I pushed his chest and he pushed me back gently, but hard enough to land me flat against the wall. He ripped my blouse open and buttons flew everywhere around us. I moaned again as he buried his head between my breasts, biting and sucking without mercy. I had never been so turned on in my life. He undid my jeans and roughly ripped them off. My panties disintegrated in seconds.

"You want to be fucked?" he whispered harshly. I nodded, spreading wide for him as he scooped me up and wrapped my legs around him and plunged himself in so deeply I almost came then and there.

"Oh fuck," I moaned in unison with him as he pounded into me. I came apart around him, furiously pounding his shoulders with my fists as he continued his relentless assault.

He paused for only seconds as he brought me to the counter and laid my body down over the mess of flour for the beignets. I brought up my hands to stroke his hair and realized I was covering him in the white powder. I didn't have time to think about it. His body wouldn't let mine relax. He drove into me, his anger and mine meeting perfectly as we slung heated words at each other. With one hand on my breast and the other on my waist, his eyes were beginning to soften as his pace slowed and I was crying out his name again.

"I'm sorry," I said catching his gaze and holding it. He pulled me to him and I couldn't help the tear or two I let fall between us as he stopped completely, pulled out of me, carried me to our bed, and nested between my thighs.

"I didn't mean to make you cry. Was I too rough?" I shook my head no furiously. I loved it rough. He knew that.

"Take me," I begged, urging him on. He pushed himself in while finding the sore spot of my lip, soothing it by sucking it gently. A few minutes later he emptied his last drop into me and his head was in my neck as he kissed the divot in my throat. He lifted up to look at me, still upset he may have hurt me.

"I love you, Spencer, do you know that?"

I saw his eyes glaze over slightly and his smile was filled with relief.

"I love you," I whispered again as his forehead touched mine.

"Helloooo! Guys where are you?"

I saw Spencer's eyes widen as he replied, "Jack!" We scrambled in our closet and pulled on two of the worst mismatched outfits imaginable. We quickly headed into the living room where Jack and Amy stood completely open mouthed, until the hysterical laughter started. Spencer and I leaned into the two of them for a hug and were stopped by Jack's outstretched palm.

"I think we can wait until you two get cleaned up," he said, stepping forward and fishing an egg shell out of Spencer's hair. "I'm not going to ask what happened here because I'm pretty sure I don't want to know." He looked at the kitchen counter full of beignet flour and clearly sexual activity mixed in it. "And we will be dining out."

Spencer burst out laughing as I stood still in shock. I quickly got Amy and their sleeping son, Jack Jr., into the guest room while Spencer and Jack shared a beer and I cleaned the mess in the kitchen. There was egg everywhere and it was a cesspool of bacteria. We were going to have to move and Spencer had just moved in.

"Come on, baby, you've done a good enough job. I'll get it later. Let's go get cleaned up."

"No, I've got it."

"No, come on. I'm sure they want to eat dinner."

I looked up at Jack who was smiling at me with his eyebrow raised. It struck me then just how much my world had changed since I met these people years ago on a beach in Florida. I had taken a trip on a whim. How my life had changed because of the man standing in front of me holding out his hand to take me to the shower with him. I loved him, I lived with him, we had just started our life together, and he was mine. All mine.

I couldn't help the feeling of elation in my chest. He loved me then, when I thought I was incapable of feeling this way, the way he would love me tomorrow. I was sure of it. I was sure that the best decision I had ever made was giving my heart, my trust, all of me, to Spencer completely. I repeated my words in front of Jack.

"I love you, Spencer." I saw his chest rise with emotion, and regretted I hadn't said the words before today. He knew but he deserved to hear them. He pulled me to him and kissed my forehead, peering down at me. "I love you, Nadine."

"Marry me," I said louder than I had meant to. Jack spit his beer out all over us. We collectively glared in his direction. Spencer brought his shocked face back to mine.

"Nadine," he said completely taken with my question.

"Marry me. Make me happy … and miserable. I'll even call you sir at work and make you dinner at night, like a real wife. We are all we have, beside our friends. We are it. Let's do right by ourselves, by us. Marry me."

He took a step back and looked at Jack.

"Well you heard the girl. She'll even make you dinner," he chuckled.

"You said never," he whispered, finding my eyes again.

"So you're saying never?" I asked, my eyes filling, the emotion in me stronger than ever. I was willing to fight for it, but I was humiliated at the same time.

"I'm going to shower," I said, handing him my rag.

"That's the worst proposal I have ever heard," Jack said, downing the rest of his beer. Spencer glared at Jack and he cowered away, hands up.

"I can do better," I said to a still shocked Spencer who was shaking his head back and forth.

"You don't have to, Nadine. Wait."

"I'm sorry I did that to you," I said, confused and unwilling to drag it out. I had just made a total fool of myself.

I sat under the hot water humiliated. I heard the shower door open but refused to open my eyes. Spencer grabbed my hand and slipped a ring on my finger.

"Emasculating. I mean, Jesus, how the hell am I going to stick around if you won't let me do my job day or night?"

I opened my eyes, quickly looking down at the ring, shaking my head in disbelief.

"I was going to do it when I was sure you wouldn't run for the hills," he chuckled. "I bought it last week," he whispered, watching me shudder with sobs. I completely lost it when he went down on one knee. "I've been thinking about what I would say and how I would do this, and I think I came up with something pretty damn clever, so if you don't mind, let me do it my way?"

I nodded my head up and down, laughing through my tears.

"I love you, and I'm not scared to take a chance with you because I am not a man who makes the same mistake twice. I let you slip away when I was unsure about everything, even the idea of marriage. But this I do know, I won't let you go, Nadine. I won't let you go one more day of your life not knowing that you belong to me, that I belong to you, that no matter what happens, I'll be here. This is how I am so sure I can ask you now to be my wife. This is how I am so sure that I will do everything in my power to make sure you want to stay, because I won't ever let you go. I can't. Marry me, and I will prove every day that this is the truth." I waited for him to finish and saw the sincerity in his face. He was mine as much as I was his.

"I liked mine better," I said, getting on my knees with him.

"Your mouth, that mouth," he whispered, pulling me to him, shaking his head.

"This mouth says yes," I whispered back, holding him to me.

WE MET RORY and her husband and had a long laughter-filled dinner followed by a few short beers and called it a night. It was a million years away from our first trip to The Quarter. We walked the streets that night as a foursome with a mini Jack. We stayed away from the crowded bars and kept the night young when we found our way home. It was a different world and I was fine with it because I had the same family. I had the same sense of belonging. I had a future that, for the first time, had a small degree of certainty and I wasn't afraid. I studied my future as we lay facing each other on our pillows and laughed at his ridiculous new errands for Darkman. He would be busy for a while.

Never Me

To listen to the Never Me Playlist as well as Spencer's Playlist for Nadine follow authorkatestewart on Spotify
Never Me Playlist
Spencer's Playlist for Nadine

ABOUT THE Author

USA Today bestselling author and Texas native, Kate Stewart, lives in North Carolina with her husband, Nick. Nestled within the Blue Ridge Mountains, Kate pens messy, sexy, angst-filled contemporary romance, as well as romantic comedy and erotic suspense.

Kate's title, *Drive*, was named one of the best romances of 2017 by The New York Daily News and Huffington Post. *Drive* was also a finalist in the Goodreads Choice awards for best contemporary romance of 2017. The Ravenhood Trilogy, consisting of *Flock, Exodus,* and *The Finish Line*, has become an international bestseller and reader favorite. Her holiday release, *The Plight Before Christmas*, ranked #6 on Amazon's Top 100. Kate's works have been featured in *USA TODAY, BuzzFeed, The New York Daily News, Huffington Post* and translated into a dozen languages.

Kate is a lover of all things '80s and '90s, especially John Hughes films and rap. She dabbles a little in photography, can knit a simple stitch scarf for necessity, and on occasion, does very well at whiskey.

Other titles available now by Kate

Romantic Suspense

The Ravenhood Series
Flock
Exodus
The Finish Line

Lust & Lies Series
Sexual Awakenings
Excess
Predator and Prey
The Lust & Lies Box set: Sexual Awakenings, Excess, Predator and Prey

Contemporary Romance

In Reading Order

Room 212
Never Me (Companion to Room 212 and The Reluctant Romantic Series)
The Reluctant Romantics Series
The Fall
The Mind
The Heart
The Reluctant Romantics Box Set: The Fall, The Heart, The Mind
Loving the White Liar

The Bittersweet Symphony
Drive
Reverse

The Real
Someone Else's Ocean
Heartbreak Warfare
Method

Romantic Dramedy

Balls in Play Series
Anything but Minor
Major Love
Sweeping the Series Novella
Balls in play Box Set: Anything but Minor, Major Love, Sweeping the Series, The Golden Sombrero

The Underdogs Series
The Guy on the Right
The Guy on the Left
The Guy in the Middle
The Underdogs Box Set: The Guy on The Right, The Guy on the Left, The Guy in the Middle

The Plight Before Christmas

Let's stay in touch!

Facebook
www.facebook.com/authorkatestewart

Newsletter
www.katestewartwrites.com/contact-me.html

Twitter
twitter.com/authorklstewart

Instagram
www.instagram.com/authorkatestewart/?hl=en

Book Group
www.facebook.com/groups/793483714004942

Spotify
open.spotify.com/user/authorkatestewart

Sign up for the newsletter now and get a free eBook from Kate's Library!

Newsletter signup
www.katestewartwrites.com/contact-me.html

THANK

FOR MY HEAVENLY father God who helps me to take notice of my blessings every day. I have never, ever regretted betting on the green.

To all the bloggers who have supported me and continue to take the time to do what you do because it's what you love. My hat is off to you. I am in awe.

Erica Fischer-Thank you for knowing me so well, and telling me I am ugly when I cry and holding my hand through the rough stuff. You never give up on me, so I don't either.

Lisa Rutledge, Cezanne Dilbert and Giulie Kiessling- you are the greatest virtual friends a girl could ever meet.

Sarah-Jane Bookham-I love thee!!!, Tabatha Washington, Jessica Berthelot, Stacy Hahn, Cheryl Dent, Sharon Dunn, Akeisha -Unique-Rain, Donna Mackenzie and all my Asskickers, wow. Wow, WOW!! You guys are truly amazing. I can't believe how lucky I am every day to have an amazing group of women who support me and my novels with such enthusiasm. I am shaking my head as I type this because it's still unbelievable.

Abbie Moore- My first #1 fan, because of the blessing of your friendship I have done nothing but grow as an author. Thank you for forming my street team, for being so insistent that I deserve it, for believing in me, and for making me laugh so hard I choke. I stand firm you should have been a comedian.

Jessica Ramirez-Wow, you really surprised me by being a true friend on some dark days. I thought about you when writing Ellie for the book, so I sure hope you like her. Thanks for putting up with my crazy, and for your support and your awesome friendship.

Thanks to my Charleston Girls -Dawn, Allyson, Caryn, Maria, Teresa, Joan, Mandy, Amanda, Nichole, and Jill. I am a better friend because you set the standard.

Thanks to my amazing and supportive family. I still laugh every time my brothers call me to congratulate me on writing a smut book, but it means the world to me. To my amazing step mother Alta and my father Bob, thank you, thank you, thank you!! I am beyond lucky to have the parents I have, and I know it. To my mother who rests in heaven, Nancy (fancy pants), you are always with me. And to my beautiful sisters Kristan and Angie, I hope you see our relationship throughout my books. It's the only way to document our insanity without naming names. I love you both madly.

To Nick-My partner, my best friend, my nightmare on legs, I love you. No one will ever know me or love me better than you do, and I am so thankful for that. Thank you for teaching me what real love is.

Printed in Great Britain
by Amazon

59419457R00126